Eileen knew she should not be focusing on Simon's charming smile.

"I've always heard one should be cautious when dealing with a woman who insists on having the last word." Simon shook his head with an exaggeratedly solemn expression that was belied by the twinkle in his eyes.

"As you should be. Most women with that trait tend to have a quick mind and a sharp wit."

He chuckled. "I'll keep that in mind." And with a wave, he turned and sauntered away.

Had they actually been flirting? Eileen shook her head to clear it. Time to concentrate her efforts on something productive, like the mending that sat in her sewing basket.

Strange, though, how difficult it had become to complete even the simplest of tasks. Surely it was due to nothing more than the presence of so many houseguests.

As she accidentally jabbed the needle into her thumb, she acknowledged that perhaps there just might be something more specific tugging at her focus.

Books by Winnie Griggs

Love Inspired Historical

The Hand-Me-Down Family
The Christmas Journey
The Proper Wife
Second Chance Family
A Baby Between Them
*Handpicked Husband
*The Bride Next Door
*A Family for Christmas
*Lone Star Heiress
*Her Holiday Family

Love Inspired

The Heart's Song

*Texas Grooms

WINNIE GRIGGS

is a city girl born and raised in southeast Louisiana's Cajun Country, who grew up to marry a country boy from the hills of northwest Louisiana. Though her Prince Charming (who often wears the guise of a cattle rancher) is more comfortable riding a tractor than a white steed, the two of them have been living their own happily-ever-after for thirty-plus years. During that time they raised four proud-to-call-them-mine children and a too-numerous-to-count assortment of dogs, cats, fish, hamsters, turtles and 4-H sheep.

Winnie retired from her "day job," and now, in addition to her reading and writing, happily spends her time doing the things she loves best—spending time with her family, cooking and exploring flea markets.

Readers can contact Winnie at P.O. Box 14, Plain Dealing, LA 71064, or email her at winnie@winniegriggs.com.

Her Holiday Family

WINNIE GRIGGS

⟨H⟩ **HARLEQUIN**® LOVE INSPIRED® HISTORICAL

Recycling programs
for this product may
not exist in your area.

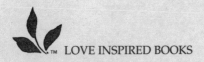 LOVE INSPIRED BOOKS

ISBN-13: 978-0-373-28286-9

Her Holiday Family

If anyone among you thinks he is religious, and does not bridle his tongue but deceives his own heart, this one's religion is useless. Pure and undefiled religion before God our Father is this: to visit orphans and widows in their trouble, and to keep oneself unspotted from the world.

—*James* 1:26–27

To my marvelous Starbucks writing buddies,
Connie and Amy, who helped me smooth over
rough spots and figure out what direction
to take my characters when I lost my way.
And to my wonderful editor, Melissa Endlich,
who always helps me tweak my stories and nudges me
to take my writing to the next level.

Chapter One

Turnabout, Texas
November 1896

Simon stood at the front of the church with hat in hand, trying very hard not to look as rattled as he felt. Ten orphan kids—TEN!—all looking to him to turn this disaster around and set their world to rights again. What in blue blazes did a bachelor like him know about taking care of kids, especially so many of them?

When he'd agreed to this venture he sure hadn't counted on ending up as the sole caretaker of these kids. But they *were* his responsibility now, and he'd have to see it through.

Sending up a silent "Lord help me" prayer, Simon made himself smile in what he hoped was a relaxed, neighborly fashion as he watched the members of the small-town congregation file into the hastily called emergency meeting. He and the kids were strangers here—didn't know a soul—and he had no idea what to expect from these people. If they didn't help him, he wasn't sure what in the world he was going to do.

The children stood lined up in front of him, and they

edged closer together as the church began to fill. Some of them held hands, as if trying to draw strength from each other. He could do with a bit of that himself, but unfortunately he was on his own—just like always.

Fern, a much-too-serious thirteen-year-old, was looking out for the youngest, as usual. Three-year-old Molly and four-year-old Joey stood on either side of her, holding on to her hand. He quickly checked over the rest of them, feeling a little kick of relief at the way they held themselves. He knew they were worried and scared, but not one of them uttered a word, and all the tears had been dried before they left the confusion of the train depot. Miss Fredrick had taught them well.

He glanced over their heads, studying these strangers who held his and the children's fate in their hands—at least for the next few days. He disliked the idea of begging for handouts, but for the sake of his charges he would swallow his pride.

If there was ever a time he needed help, it was now. Hopefully there was a motherly sort out there who would know what to do and would be willing to take care of his charges.

At least he wasn't facing these folks entirely alone. The town's minister, Reverend Harper, stood at his side with his wife and daughter nearby. Thank goodness someone had had the presence of mind to call the clergyman in when they'd arrived. The reverend had assured him that the folks in his congregation were generous, warmhearted people who would help in any way they could.

As the people settled into the pews, he noted their expressions were a mix of curiosity and sympathy. Most offered encouraging smiles to the children. How many had already learned of their situation?

When it appeared the last person had taken a seat,

Reverend Harper stepped forward. "Thank you all for responding to the bells and joining us here on such short notice." He motioned toward Simon. "This gentleman is Mr. Simon Tucker and he'd like to introduce these fine children to you."

Ready or not, he was up. How best to personalize these children for the congregation? Considering he'd only gotten to know them himself over this past week or so, it wouldn't be easy.

He laid his hand lightly on Fern's shoulder. "This young lady is Fern. She's thirteen and the oldest of the children. She's very responsible and is always looking out for the younger ones."

He moved his hand to the shoulder of the boy on her right. "This little man here is Joey. Joey is four and loves animals." Joey had told him more than once that Miss Fredrick had promised him he could have a dog when they reached Hatcherville, and it was as if she'd promised him the moon.

Simon shifted to the child on Fern's left. "And this little sweet pea is Molly. She's three and the youngest of our group." Molly slipped her thumb in her mouth, and Simon couldn't find it in his heart to blame her.

Next he moved on to the children he had the closest ties to. "These two are Audrey and Albert. They're seven years old and twins." They were also his niece and nephew.

He quickly went down the row, introducing the rest of the children—Rose, Lily, Tessa, Harry and Russell—trying to mention something positive about each of them. His gut told him it was important that these folks feel sympathy for the children.

When he was done, Reverend Harper spoke up again. "Thank you, Mr. Tucker." He signaled his wife and daughter. "Now, while we grown-ups talk, Mrs. Harper and Constance will escort the children over to Daisy's Restaurant, where Abigail is planning to serve them up a nice hot meal."

Several of the children looked to Simon for reassurance. It once again drove home how dependent they now were on him. Scary thought. But he smiled and nodded.

Mrs. Harper took Lily's hand while her daughter Constance took the hands of the twins. Together the whole lot of them filed out.

Simon resisted the urge to rake his hand through his hair. He needed to make a proper impression on these people.

When the little troupe had made their exit, Reverend Harper spoke up again, placing a hand on Simon's shoulder. "Mr. Tucker finds himself in need of our assistance, and I've assured him that the people of Turnabout are up to the challenge. As some of you may already know, there was an emergency on the train when it pulled into town this morning that required Dr. Pratt's services. It turned out to be very serious indeed. I'll let Mr. Tucker tell you more about what's happening."

Simon nodded to the clergyman. "Thank you, Reverend Harper." Then he turned to the people seated in the pews. "The lady who is now in Dr. Pratt's care, Miss Georgina Fredrick, is the guardian of the children you just met. I was escorting her and the children to a new home that's waiting for them in Hatcherville. But just before we pulled into the station here, she had an attack of some sort. Your Dr. Pratt tells me she suffered a stroke. And her outlook isn't good."

He was encouraged by the sympathetic looks focused his way. But would it translate to action? "First, let me tell you a little about this dear lady. Miss Fredrick is a warm, generous and caring person. For the past nine years she's opened her home to children who had nowhere else to go. Over that time, all of those children you just met have been left in her care and have found not only a safe home but have formed a family bond as strong as any blood kin." His admiration for the woman knew no bounds. To his way of thinking there was no higher calling than to care for children.

He let his gaze roam across the people seated before him, briefly holding a gaze here and there before moving on. "Recently Miss Fredrick decided that her existing home in St. Louis could no longer accommodate her stretched-to-its-limits household. So I helped her find a new place. That's where we were headed. I'm here because she asked me to provide an escort for her and the children, and to help them get settled in."

He slid the brim of his hat through his fingers. "We obviously can't move on until she's recovered enough to travel." *Please God, see that she* does *recover.* "So what I'm asking you folks for is a place for me and the kids to stay while we await that outcome." Had he said too much? Not enough? He prayed he'd touched their hearts in some way. Simon drew back his shoulders. "I figure you all might have some questions for me before you respond, so feel free to fire away."

A plump woman in the second row stood. "May I ask what your actual relationship is to Miss Fredrick and these children?"

"My sister Sally was Miss Fredrick's housekeeper for a number of years and helped her care for the children." He felt his chest constrict as he remembered his feisty younger sister. "Sally passed away three months ago, and Miss Fredrick continued to give her two children a home when I could not." He would be forever grateful to the woman for taking in Audrey and Albert—goodness knows she was able to give them a better home than he ever could.

A tall bearded man near the back of the church stood. "Have these children been given a Christian upbringing?"

"Absolutely. Miss Fredrick sees that they attend church services regularly and reading from the Bible is part of their daily routine." He gave what he hoped was a reassuring smile. "And just so you know, they've also been taught proper manners and behavior."

Apparently satisfied, the man sat back down. After a short silence, Reverend Harper stepped forward. "If there are no other questions for Mr. Tucker, we need to discuss his request for temporary lodgings for himself and the children. Is there anyone willing to step up and answer this call?"

To Simon's relief, a number of hands went up. At least he'd be able to lay *that* worry aside.

"I can take three or four of them in."

"I can take two."

"I can take one."

"I can take three."

As the offers came in Simon's optimism faded. He held up his hand to halt the offers. "That's mighty generous of you folks, but I'm afraid there's been a little misunderstanding. I need to keep them all together right now." The idea of splitting them up brought back unpleasant memories of how he and his sisters had been farmed out all those years ago. But it was more than that. "It's not that I don't appreciate your very kind offers, but since these children are in my sole care right now, I need to be able to keep an eye on all of them. And separating them when they're already feeling so anxious about their foster mother is just going to upset them more."

That announcement was greeted with an uncomfortable silence. What was he going to do if they couldn't make this work? He'd promised he wouldn't separate them—he personally knew how wrenching that could be. Even if they all had to sleep on pallets on the floor, it would be preferable to scattering them, especially now when they needed each other.

He tried again. "It's not as if they each need their own room. They're used to sharing tight quarters."

Reverend Harper cleared his throat. "I think we all understand and sympathize with your reasoning, Mr. Tucker, but what you're asking is a mighty tall order to fill. There are eleven of you, after all."

The reverend said that as if Simon weren't already painfully aware of the situation.

But before he could respond, the man continued. "You may have to accept the need to separate them for a few days. We can likely find accommodations for two large groups, but there's not many households large enough to accept eleven guests for an overnight—"

He paused as if he'd just had an idea, and Simon immediately felt his hope rise. Had the man come up with a solution? Simon was ready to grasp at any straw.

Reverend Harper had looked to the pews on the right-hand side of the church as if seeking someone out. "Unless… Ah, there you are, Mrs. Pierce. Perhaps you would allow us to impose on *your* generosity?"

Simon followed the minister's gaze, trying to figure out who he was looking at. Then a slender, blonde woman, dressed in the purple and gray of half mourning, stood. There was something arresting about her. She was taller than the average woman and held herself with an elegant grace, but it was more than that. Aloof, cool, distant—she seemed not so much a part of this gathering as a disinterested observer. Her face seemed expressionless, but her thickly lashed brown eyes seemed to miss nothing.

And yet he sensed something vulnerable about her, a just-below-the-surface fragility that tugged at him.

While her expression gave nothing away, he had the distinct impression this ice queen was not going to go along with the reverend's verbal arm-twisting happily.

Which didn't bode well for just how "motherly" she would be toward the children.

As all eyes in the church turned her way expectantly, Eileen Pierce hid her surprise, maintaining the composed, disinterested pose that was second nature to her.

She had just been thinking how shocked her neighbors, who had ignored or outright snubbed her for the past two years, would be if she volunteered her home. The idea had amused her, almost to the point that she'd been tempted to do it just to see the scandalized looks on their faces.

Almost. Because she hadn't had any real intention of doing so.

God had seen fit not to give her any children of her own, and she'd come to accept that there was a reason for that—she wasn't the kind of woman who was cut out to be a mother. She wouldn't know what to do with one child, much less ten.

But she wasn't truly surprised that Reverend Harper had turned to her, even though she was persona non grata in Turnabout. After all, she owned the largest house in town, one that could easily accommodate these stranded visitors. But as satisfying as it would be to dispense a bit of noblesse oblige, it wasn't worth the risk. Opening her doors to so many outsiders would mean exposing how far she'd actually fallen from her days as the wife of the town's wealthiest and most prominent businessman.

For just a moment, however, she was disconcerted by the way Mr. Tucker looked at her, as if she were his lifeline. She could feel the impact of his intently focused blue eyes from all the way across the room. It had been some time since she'd felt herself the object of such interest. She finally recognized the emotion—he *needed* her. She couldn't remember a time when anyone truly needed her. And she wasn't certain how she felt about it now.

Eileen gave her head a mental shake, refocusing on the current situation. She couldn't let herself be distracted by such frivolous emotions. Or by a winning smile from a man with intriguing blue eyes and hair the color of rich, loamy soil.

Still trying to figure out how to extricate herself, she gave a nonanswer. "I assume by that question you are asking me to open my home to the entire group."

Before Reverend Harper or the stranger could speak up, Eunice Ortolon, the town's most notorious busybody, stood. "Excuse me, Reverend, but while Mrs. Pierce's home is large enough, surely that shouldn't be the only consideration." The woman drew her shoulders back. "While I understand Mr. Tucker not wanting to separate the children, perhaps it would be best to house them in two or three homes with families that are more—" she cut a quick look Eileen's way "—let us say, accustomed to dealing with children."

Eileen stiffened. Eunice might as well have used the word *suitable*—it was so obviously there in her tone.

Ivy Parker, the only other person sharing Eileen's pew, and the closest thing she had to a friend here, stood up immediately. "As a former boarder of Eileen's, I can attest to the fact that her home would be the perfect place to house these children—her home is both roomy and welcoming." She gave Eileen an encouraging smile. "That is, if she feels so led to make the offer."

Eileen appreciated that Ivy had come to her defense, but now was not the time for everyone to suddenly approve of her. Unfortunately she could see several folks giving her tentative smiles of encouragement.

The urge to give in to her frustration was strong, and Eileen maintained her impassive expression by sheer force of will. She wanted so much to be accepted by the community again, but this was not the way.

Of course there were still those, like Mrs. Ortolon, who looked either hesitant or disapproving.

How in the world could she extricate herself without sounding selfish and uncaring?

And why was she so oddly reluctant to disappoint Mr. Tucker?

Chapter Two

Eileen decided to buy herself some time with a question. "How long do you suppose you and the children would need a place to stay, Mr. Tucker?"

He didn't seem to take offense at her question. "I wish I could tell you, ma'am, but to be honest, I can't really say. We're completely dependent on when Miss Fredrick recovers enough to travel again. And Dr. Pratt couldn't give me any indication of when that might be."

It was the answer she'd expected. "You have my sympathies, sir. But you must understand, boarding so many individuals for an extended length of time is quite a challenge, regardless of the size of one's home. Especially on such short notice."

"As I said," Mrs. Ortolon declared in a self-righteous tone, "the children will be better off if we send them to smaller but more suitable homes."

The words and the tone they were delivered in got Eileen's back up again, though she refused to show it. It was the stab of disappointment and frustration that she saw in Mr. Tucker's eyes, however, that prodded her next words. "I didn't say I *wouldn't* invite them in, Eunice, merely that it would be a challenge."

"You *do* have the space to house us all, though?" Mr. Tucker pressed.

At her nod, he continued. "I wouldn't ask this if it wasn't important, ma'am. The children need the comfort of each other's company right now. I'd be mighty grateful to you if you could see your way to providing that for them. If you'd find it in your heart to provide them with a place to stay, I promise to do my best to keep them out of your way. I assure you they are well behaved." Then he flashed her a disarmingly self-deprecating smile. "Or as well behaved as kids their age can be expected to be."

She nodded again, entranced by the friendly warmth of his manner. "Of course."

"Does that mean you'll do it?" His expression held a guarded hopefulness that she couldn't bear to disappoint.

"I suppose I will."

No sooner had she uttered the words than she came to her senses. Why had she said that? This was a disaster. There was no way she could keep her state of affairs hidden in the face of such an invasion.

But before she could find a way to take it back, she found herself being thanked and applauded by various members of the congregation.

Ivy stood. "Since you're providing the housing, I believe I speak for all the members of the Ladies Auxiliary in saying we will do our part to help in other ways." She looked around the church, where she received a number of nods, then back at Eileen. "We can provide meals and anything else you might need to help accommodate your new guests."

Eileen wasn't particularly pleased by the offer. After all, she was *not* a charity case to be accepting handouts. If she was going to do this, then she would do it in a manner befitting her position. "I appreciate the offer but there is no need." She kept her tone polite. It would stretch the limits of her pantry if the group stayed with her more than three or four days, but she would manage somehow. Better to go hungry later than have folks think she was unable to provide for her guests.

Ivy gave her an uncomfortably perceptive look, then spoke again. "It's very commendable of you to do this, Eileen," she said in a gentle tone, "but you're already opening your home to our visitors. Surely you won't rob the rest of us of the joy that comes with sharing our blessings."

Bless Ivy for coming up with the perfect way to help her save face. "Of course not." Eileen waved a hand in gracious surrender. "Since you feel so strongly about this, I will defer to the Ladies Auxiliary to provide the meals."

"Excellent." Reverend Harper beamed approval at his flock, then turned back to Eileen. "Mrs. Pierce, your generosity does you great credit."

His words made her feel like a fraud, so she held her tongue.

But the reverend seemed not to expect a response. Instead he clapped Mr. Tucker on the back. "I told you these people would rise to the occasion."

"Thank you folks." Mr. Tucker executed a short bow in her direction. "And you especially, Mrs. Pierce." He left the preacher's side and approached her with a broad smile on his face.

Ivy stepped out of their shared pew to allow him to step in.

"You have no idea what a wonderful thing you've done for the children," he said, stepping past Ivy.

Goodness, was the man planning to join her in the pew? She should have followed Ivy into the aisle.

Keeping her features carefully schooled, Eileen nodded. The whole congregation was watching them and the pew suddenly seemed crowded. The impact of his warm smile and deep blue eyes was even more arresting up close. And he was a good half foot taller than her.

It didn't help her equanimity that her feelings of being a fraud had deepened. "There is no need for thank-yous," she said stiffly. "One does what one can to help those in need."

There was a flicker of something she couldn't quite read in his eyes, then his smile returned. "Nevertheless, you have my gratitude. I don't have much money to offer you, but I'm a handyman and cabinetmaker by trade. I'd certainly be willing to repay you by taking care of any repairs or other work around your place that needs attending to."

There were certainly a number of things that could use a handyman's touch around her place. Eileen allowed a small smile to escape her lips. "Thank you, Mr. Tucker. We shall see." Then she took a mental step back again. "I will, of course, need time to get everything prepared for your stay."

He spread his hands. "Understood. Will a couple of hours be sufficient?"

She'd like to have more time, but she supposed she couldn't ask him to keep ten children standing around indefinitely. And besides, more time would not make her sold-off furnishings magically reappear. "I shall see that it is."

His smile grew warmer. "Again, thank you. And please don't go to a lot of trouble. All we really need is a place for everyone to sleep."

If he only knew—she was going to have trouble providing very much more than the bare necessities.

"I don't want you to feel like you're in this alone." Ivy's

words brought her back to the here and now. "Tell us what you think you'll need, besides help with the meals."

Eileen considered that a moment. She supposed she shouldn't let the children suffer for her pride. "Some extra bedding would be helpful."

"Of course. I'll work with the Ladies Auxiliary to round some up for you."

Eve Dawson approached them with a smile for Mr. Tucker. "After the children finish their meals at the restaurant, bring them down to the sweet shop and I'll treat them to some candy."

Mr. Tucker turned his smile her way, and Eileen felt an unaccountable stab of jealousy that it wasn't still directed at her.

"That's going to really perk up their spirits," he said. "Thank you."

Eileen took herself in hand. That little prickle of jealousy was a clear indication she'd let her guard down much too far. That wouldn't do at all.

The meeting broke up, and folks were chatting in clusters or slowly filing out. He had his back to her now, releasing her from the strain of keeping her expression neutral under his gaze. Instead she had a view of the back of his head. His hair was worn shorter than what was usual for the men around here. But she decided it suited him.

Then she straightened. What in the world was she doing thinking of such things, especially about a stranger? Just because the man had looked kindly at her was no reason to get moon-eyed over him.

Mr. Tucker's hand was being shaken and encouraging words said to him, giving Eileen time to gather her wits. A quick glance toward the front of the church revealed several members of the Ladies Auxiliary were already gathering.

She mentally winced. At one time she'd been head of the Ladies Auxiliary and now, despite the face-saving efforts of Ivy, guests in her home had become the object of their charitable efforts, and by extension, she had, as well. What a long way she'd fallen since her husband's ignominious death two years ago. If her mother were still alive today she would be mortified, but probably not surprised, by her daughter's loss of status in the community.

Time to get some air. "If you will excuse me, I should return home and prepare the house to receive guests."

Mr. Tucker stepped out into the aisle to let her pass. "Please allow me to escort you home."

She again felt that tingle at his friendly, dare she say approving, smile. And again she strove to ignore it. "Thank you, but it's only a few blocks away and I'm sure you want to get back to the children."

But Mr. Tucker didn't take her hint. He raised a brow with a teasing look. "I insist. The kids are in good hands for the moment. Besides, not only will this allow me the pleasure of your company, but accompanying you will let me know where your place is so I can escort the children there when it's time."

Before she could protest again, he turned serious. "And there are probably a few things we should talk about before I bring the children around."

There was no polite way to refuse such a request. "In that case, I accept." Again she'd acted against her better judgment.

She would definitely have to watch her step with this one.

Simon allowed his soon-to-be-hostess to precede him from the church building. She had returned to the cool, aloof individual she'd been when she first stood up in the meeting. Usually he had no use for pretentiousness and haughty airs. He'd seen too much of that in the home of his Uncle Corbitt, the man who'd taken him in when his folks died.

But for a few minutes he'd seen behind the mask she wore to a warmer, more vibrant woman. And that intrigued him, made him think that perhaps she was a person worth getting to know better. And she had, after all, opened her home to him and the kids. He could forgive her a lot for that.

But which one was the real Mrs. Pierce—the ice queen or the vulnerable, warmhearted lady? It would be interesting to find out.

He'd sensed some uneasy undercurrents between this woman and the rest of the townsfolk, and that, too, intrigued him. Not that the situation was any of his business. Besides, he preferred to form his own opinions about folks rather than pay attention to hearsay and gossip.

And the fact that she wasn't exactly enthusiastic about having them as guests—that just made it doubly generous of her to have done so as far as he was concerned.

As for that standoffishness she wore like armor—he was just going to have to go into this arrangement knowing he couldn't count on the kids to get any warm motherly attention from her. But perhaps there was a housekeeper or someone else in her household who could supply that. And if not, then at least they would all be together.

Still, there was something about Mrs. Pierce that made him want to look deeper, to find out what was at the heart of this woman.

Then Simon took himself to task. What *really* mattered right now was how much help she'd be with the kids.

"You said we had something to discuss?"

Her dry words and tone brought him back to the present. Truth to tell, he hadn't had anything specific in mind when he said that—it had just been a way of getting around her protests. But there *were* a few things he was curious about. "Do you live alone?"

"I have one boarder, Miss Dovie Jacobs."

Boarder—not family. Interesting. "Is Miss Jacobs likely to be bothered when we all descend on your home this afternoon?"

"I don't believe so. Miss Jacobs is a very motherly sort of woman. In fact, she is much like your Miss Fredrick, though on a smaller scale. She once took in and raised an orphaned child. If I'm wrong, however, she can always retreat to her own room."

"That's a relief—that our presence won't bother her, I mean." At least there'd be one person in the house who knew how to deal with children. Assuming she was willing to lend a hand.

If this Miss Jacobs was the only other person in her household, however, that would mean…"Forgive the personal question, but you were addressed as *Mrs.* Pierce. Is there no Mr. Pierce?"

"My husband has been deceased a little over two years now."

There was no change in her expression and she didn't expand. "My condolences."

"Thank you."

Again there was no emotion. Mrs. Pierce was obviously a very private person. Which made him all the more curious to learn more about her. And was it wrong that he was just the tiniest bit pleased that she was single?

Before he could ask about household staff, she halted next to a small wrought iron gate and waved a hand toward the place the gate guarded. "This is my home," she said simply.

He studied the three-story house with interest. He could see why Reverend Harper had thought this would be the answer to his need. Not only was the structure impressively grand, it was also set on a large piece of property with plenty of room for rambunctious kids to run around. It was also one of the few brick buildings he'd seen in this town. From the front porch that was supported by imposing columns, to the rounded, turretlike section that jutted from the right side of the structure, to the dormered roofline edged in stately woodwork, this place spoke of wealth and elegance, much as the woman herself did.

It seemed a waste that Mrs. Pierce and her boarder were the only residents—the place practically cried out for a large family to inhabit it.

A closer look at the structure, however, showed that it wasn't quite as well maintained as it seemed at first glance. Some of the woodwork was in need of painting and at least a few of the shingles on the roof were loose. The yard needed raking and trimming. And that was just what he could see from here. One thing was certain; he'd definitely be able to make himself useful while he was here.

A profusion of well-manicured plants fronted the structure—the garden hadn't suffered from the same neglect as the house. A woman with a pair of garden shears in her gloved hands knelt among the plants lining the front walk.

A gardener perhaps? It stood to reason that a woman such as Mrs. Pierce, with an impressive house like this one, would have servants.

The woman stood as soon as she saw them, and Simon was surprised by how tiny she was. She couldn't be any taller than four foot six or seven. And she looked old enough to be his companion's mother.

"Well, hello." The woman tugged off her gardening gloves, her eyes alight with friendly curiosity.

Mrs. Pierce gestured toward the smiling gardener. "Miss Jacobs, this is Mr. Simon Tucker. Mr. Tucker, this is Miss Dovie Jacobs, the boarder I mentioned."

He touched the brim of his hat. "Pleased to meet you, ma'am."

She acknowledged his greeting with a friendly nod. "Did you two just come from the town meeting?" She absently brushed the leaves and dirt from her skirt. "I'll admit I've been nigh on bursting with curiosity."

Simon wondered why she hadn't gone to the meeting herself. But it wouldn't be polite to ask. "We did," he said as he opened the gate. "And it so happens *I* was the subject. I find myself stranded here in town with ten children and their guardian who has taken seriously ill." He nodded deferentially to his companion. "Mrs. Pierce has generously agreed to open her home to us while we await the outcome of our friend's illness." He gave her what he hoped was a winning smile. "I hope that won't inconvenience you any."

"Not at all. And I'm sure enough sorry about your friend. I'll pray she recovers quickly."

Then she turned to Mrs. Pierce and gave her an approving smile. "Good for you. I've thought this place was crying out for a big family ever since I moved in. And ten children, bless my soul—that will certainly keep us on our toes."

From Miss Jacobs's tone, the two women's relationship seemed more friendly than the businesslike face Mrs. Pierce had put on it. Good to know that the tension he'd sensed at the meeting didn't extend to her household.

Miss Jacobs turned back to him. "You can count on me to help with the little ones in any way that I can."

He was glad to hear it. He could already sense she would be one who balanced doting and discipline the way Miss Fredrick had seemed to. "Thank you, ma'am. From what I've seen of them on this trip, these are a mostly well-behaved lot, but they *are* children."

"Don't you worry none, young man, between me and Eileen here we'll manage nicely."

Mrs. Pierce didn't respond to that. Instead she gave him a puzzled look. "So you don't know these children well?"

He shook his head. "Up until a short time ago, I knew Miss Fredrick and her charges mainly through my sister's letters. I popped in and out over the years to visit Sally and her children, of course, but that was all." He straightened. "Make no mistake, though, these children *are* my responsibility until I get them to where they're going."

"Of course." One delicate brow rose a fraction of an inch. "Was there anything else we needed to discuss right now?"

"No ma'am, unless you have questions for me."

She gave him a "you're dismissed" look. "I thank you for walking me home, but if you will excuse me, there are many preparations to be made."

Simon touched the brim of his hat again. "Then I'll be on my way. Thank you again for your hospitality, and I'll bring the kids over in a couple of hours."

Then he paused. "Can you direct me to the restaurant?"

With a nod, she turned to face the way they'd come. "Go back as far as Second Street, then turn right. The restaurant will be a block and a half on your left." She faced him again and the movement brought them unexpectedly closer together.

Her eyes widened and for a moment her aloof exterior cracked the tiniest bit. Her breathing seemed to hitch for just a heartbeat and her fingertips fluttered to her throat as if seeking a pulse there. Oh, yes, beneath that ice-queen exterior, an ember glowed. An ember he'd like to see burn brighter.

She recovered quickly, though, dropping her hand and schooling her expression. "The sign in front of the building reads Daisy's Restaurant," she said coolly. "You can't miss it."

With a thank-you for Mrs. Pierce and a tip of his hat for Miss Jacobs, Simon took his leave.

Meeting Miss Jacobs had relieved at least one of his concerns. The woman seemed willing and able to provide whatever mothering the children would need these next few days.

But his wayward mind was more interested in Mrs. Pierce than her boarder. That little close encounter they'd just had had obviously rattled her. And he wouldn't deny he'd felt something, as well. It was nothing more than mere curiosity, though—he couldn't let it be anything more. He had no time in his life right now for anything but meeting the kids' needs. Still, there was nothing to say he couldn't enjoy getting to know his hostess better while he was stuck here.

Would she be able to maintain that ice-queen demeanor once the children invaded her home? Or would that other, less confident but much more interesting Mrs. Pierce show through?

Well, if anything could strip the standoffish tendencies from a person, it was dealing with a houseful of kids. And he was rather pleased he'd be around to watch it happen.

Chapter Three

Eileen watched Mr. Tucker walk away, studying the casual confidence of his demeanor, still confused by her own reaction to him. There was nothing sophisticated or polished about the man. He'd called himself a handyman and cabinetmaker, which to her translated into a common laborer with some carpentry skills. His hands had been callused and even had a couple of rough-looking scars.

Not at all the kind of man she should be attracted to.

So what was it about him that drew her? There was the confidence in his bearing and his earnestness. And then there was his warm smile that reached all the way to his cornflower eyes that just drew a person in.

"That Mr. Tucker seems like a nice young man."

Eileen started, as if she'd been caught mooning over some imaginary beau. She turned and stepped through the gate, ignoring Dovie's knowing smile. "I suppose."

She returned to a businesslike manner, dismissing her wayward and totally inappropriate thoughts. Better to focus on the trouble that was about to descend on her. Ten children—what had she been thinking? She had no idea how to deal with children of any age, much less a horde of them.

But she *could* handle this. After all, she had been trained to be ready to rise to any sort of social emergency with grace and confidence. How much worse could this be than handling household servants or an unruly party guest or even a last-minute menu disaster? As for the matter of her financial straits being discovered, she'd have to put a good face on that as best she could. Surely it was only a matter of remaining unruffled and not allowing her guests to get overly familiar.

She turned to Dovie with returning confidence. "As the person in town with the biggest home, I felt it was my duty to offer shelter to these poor stranded children." Not entirely true—she hadn't volunteered so much as been cornered, but in the end she *had* agreed to help.

Dovie eyed her approvingly. "Opening your home to them was a generous, Christian gesture, especially being as you're such a private kind of person. And don't you worry, like I told that young man, I'll pitch in and help where I can."

Thank goodness Dovie liked to keep busy. This new situation would certainly afford her boarder plenty of opportunities for that. "I appreciate your offer." She unbent slightly. "I'll admit, I don't have experience dealing with children." No, that was one lady-of-the-manor skill she had never been taught.

"Don't you worry about that none. The only thing you have to know is that what children need most is love, patience and discipline. And of course a grounding in the Good Book. Give them that and the rest will work itself out."

Eileen didn't have a response for that, so she moved on to something else. "The members of the Ladies Auxiliary have agreed to help with the meals."

Dovie fell into step with her as they moved to the

house. "It's always good when a whole community comes together to help those in need." She gave Eileen a sideways look. "So when are the children supposed to get here?"

"In about two hours."

"Then we'd best get to work."

Eileen took a deep breath. Since her husband's death, she'd found herself overwhelmed by the debt he'd left behind. She'd been reduced to selling many of her prized furnishings, as furtively as possible, of course, and had had to do some creative rearranging of the remaining pieces to try to cover it up.

The result was that many of the unused rooms were stripped to the bare essentials and had been closed off from view, even from her boarder. Not that she had many visitors these days.

But now she was going to be forced to open those rooms up for her guests' use and there would be no hiding anything. It would be best to prepare Dovie for the reality she would soon see. "You should know that the furnishings are rather sparse in most of the extra rooms."

Dovie seemed to see nothing wrong with that. "As long as your guests have a bed to rest in, I don't imagine they'll be doing any complaining."

"There are six girls and four boys to accommodate besides Mr. Tucker." It was just hitting her that the man who'd thrown her so off balance today would be residing here, as well. She would really have to keep her guard up for the next few days. But, strangely, she was more energized than irritated by the challenge.

Not that Mr. Tucker was of any more import than the children. "There are five extra bedchambers on the second floor and four on the third." She frowned. "But I don't think it necessary to give each child his or her own room."

"Oh, my, no. In fact, they'll probably be happier if they

have someone to share with. Why don't we put the girls in three of the second-floor rooms and Mr. Tucker and the boys in three of the rooms on the third?"

Eileen nodded, relieved that Dovie agreed. That would mean fewer rooms to prepare and fewer bed linens to deal with. "That sounds like an acceptable approach."

The two women had barely started when the doorbell sounded. Eileen left Dovie to finish opening the windows and stripping the beds while she went to see who was at the door. Surely Mr. Tucker hadn't returned already?

When she opened the door, however, it was Ivy Parker, and right behind her was her husband, Mitch, and a couple of young boys. All four of them were loaded down with armfuls of linens.

"Hello," Ivy said cheerily. "Where would you like us to set these?"

Eileen stepped aside. "Please come in." She waved to the open doorway on the left. "You can set it all on the table in the dining room."

As they trooped into her home, Ivy chattered away. "The members of the Ladies Auxiliary all contributed something. You'll find sheets and coverlets enough for eight beds. If you need more, let us know. We also figured you'd need some extra towels so we brought a stack of those, as well."

Extra towels—of course. She should have thought of that. What else hadn't she taken into consideration? And the thought of ten children needing baths was enough to send a shiver up her spine.

But it would never do to show a lack of confidence—she was the lady of the house. It was her duty to make all of her guests feel at home. "Thank you. I'm sure we will be able to put all of this to good use."

Once everything was safely deposited on the table, Ivy

shooed her husband and the youths away, then turned to Eileen. "Now, what can I do to help you get ready for the invasion?"

"That's really not necessary. Dovie is assisting and between the two of us—"

Ivy interrupted with a wave of her hand. "Fiddlesticks. I don't mind a bit, and it'll give me a chance to visit with Nana Dovie."

Ivy had been orphaned as an infant and Dovie had been the one to raise her. They were very much like mother and daughter even though there was no blood tie between them. Eileen supposed, more than anyone else in town, these two women could truly relate to these children and their situation.

Without waiting for a response, Ivy headed for the stairs. "By the way, Reggie volunteered to take care of the evening meal for you all today so there's no need to worry about that."

Regina Barr was Eileen's nearest neighbor and the current head of the Ladies Auxiliary.

Ivy looked back over her shoulder without slowing. "And there's a list forming of volunteers to handle the meals for the next several days."

At least that was one worry off her shoulders. The food she'd put up from her garden this past summer and what she had left to harvest from her fall planting was supposed to take her through the winter. She could ill afford to feed an army of children solely from her own stores for more than a few days without adversely affecting her future menus.

With a start she realized Ivy was already headed up the stairs. Since Ivy had boarded here for a while before she married the schoolteacher, she knew where everything was.

Managing to catch up to her without breaking into a hoydenish rush, Eileen decided it would do no good to argue—she'd learned Ivy usually went her own way.

Ivy rolled up her sleeves and set to work as soon as she reached the second floor. As far as Eileen could tell, her former boarder seemed to see nothing amiss with the stark furnishings and lack of fancy drapes and coverlets in the spare bedchambers. She supposed, if anyone in town had to see her true state of affairs, then Ivy and Dovie would be the most sympathetic to her situation. Neither had known her before her fall from grace or had witnessed the lavish way she'd conducted her life back then. For that matter, nor did any of the visitors who would be here for the next few days. So there were no unflattering comparisons for them to make, no unpleasant history for them to remember.

As for Mr. Tucker, the admiration she'd seen in his eyes had been very disconcerting. No one had looked at her like that in a very long time. And she was honest enough to admit, just for a moment, she'd wanted to bask in it.

Perhaps it was worth all this bother just for that small, precious gift.

She just had to make certain she didn't get used to it.

Because it wasn't likely to come from anyone else anytime soon.

When Simon checked in at the restaurant to see how the kids were faring, the women there assured him they had everything under control. He'd been surprised to see that one end of the restaurant housed a library. He hadn't expected such niceties in this small-town community.

The reverend's daughter, who looked to be about sixteen or seventeen, was reading a book to several of the younger children, while some of the older ones were browsing the shelves and thumbing through books on their own. Mrs. Harper pulled him aside to assure him they would keep an eye on the children for as long as he needed them to.

Satisfied they were in good hands, Simon headed to Dr. Pratt's clinic to check on Miss Fredrick.

He was thankful they'd landed in the midst of such good people. On his own he'd have been totally inadequate to the task of looking after the children. After all, what did a thirty-year-old bachelor like him know about taking care of kids, especially little girls. And while Mrs. Pierce might not be the maternal type, her boarder, Miss Jacobs, would know how to deal with the needs of the children. Surely between the three of them, they could manage whatever was required over the next few days.

And hopefully they wouldn't be here in Turnabout longer than that. He had to keep believing Miss Fredrick would recover soon and they could be on their way once more. Surely God wouldn't allow for any other outcome.

That thought made him wince. He of all people should know that bad things *did* happen to good people, even innocent children, and God alone knew the reasons.

Unbidden, his thoughts turned to when he was nine years old and his own parents had died. He and his sisters had been farmed out to different relatives and rarely got to see each other again. In fact, his youngest sister, Imogene, had passed away the following year without him even knowing until the funeral was over and done with.

Just one more sign of what Uncle Corbitt's opinion of "that side of the family" had been.

Simon determinedly pushed those thoughts away and entered the doctor's office trying to maintain a hopeful outlook. "How's Miss Fredrick doing?"

The somberness in the spare, white-haired doctor's

demeanor wasn't encouraging. "I wish I had better news for you, but she's not showing any signs of improvement."

"But she *is* going to get better, isn't she?" He couldn't quite mask the hint of desperation in his voice.

The doctor came around his desk and leaned back against it as he faced Simon sympathetically. "I'm afraid you need to face facts. There's a very real possibility she might never regain consciousness. If there's anyone to be notified, I would do it now."

Simon raked his hand through his hair, not wanting to accept what the doctor was saying. "She has a brother— his name is Wilbur I believe—but they had a falling-out. Other than the children, she doesn't have anyone else that I'm aware of."

"Notify her brother." The doctor's tone was firm. "I find most people put their differences aside at a time like this."

"Of course. But it *is* possible she'll recover, isn't it?"

The doctor looked at him with sympathy. "Anything is possible, son. But it's very much in God's hands now."

Before Simon could respond, one of the side doors opened and a woman dressed in black with a crisp white bibbed apron stepped out. The doctor straightened. "Mr. Tucker, allow me to introduce my niece, Verity Leggett."

Simon tipped his hat. "Pleased to meet you, ma'am."

"She and her daughter have recently moved in with us," the doctor continued. "Verity is helping here at the clinic. Between her, my wife and me, someone will be with Miss Fredrick at all times."

"Thank you. I appreciate all you're doing for Miss Fredrick." He scrubbed his jaw, trying to collect his thoughts. "The kids have been asking after her. Would it be okay if they came around to see her?"

The doctor hesitated before replying. "As long as they

are prepared for what they will see. Unless something changes, she'll be unconscious and unable to move or speak."

"Mr. Tucker." Mrs. Leggett's tone was sympathetic but firm. "I hope you don't mind my interference, but as a mother myself, I feel it would be unwise to bring the children here just yet. It would only serve to upset them further."

Simon nodded. "I appreciate your advice, ma'am."

He thanked them both again, then asked the whereabouts of the telegraph office and took his leave.

What was he going to do if Miss Fredrick didn't make it? More to the point, what would become of the children? He'd given Miss Fredrick his word that he'd do everything in his power to get them all safely to their new home. But what was the use of getting them to Hatcherville if Miss Fredrick wasn't there to look out for them? He certainly couldn't step into that role himself, not alone at any rate. He'd take in his niece and nephew, Audrey and Albert, if there was no other choice but to separate the children. But he'd scour heaven and earth to keep them all together if he could.

Almighty God, please let this dear woman live. She's doing Your work here and it doesn't seem right to not let her finish it, especially now when she is in reach of her dream of giving these kids a new and better life. They need her—they have nowhere else to go, no one else to look out for them.

And I certainly didn't sign on to become their full-time guardian. You, who know all things, know that I wouldn't be the kind of caretaker they need—they need a mother's touch.

Simon rubbed the back of his neck, remembering his own mother, aching a little that she'd been taken from him so young. Uncle Corbitt's housekeeper had been a poor substitute. He didn't intend to let that happen to these children.

Exactly two hours from the time he'd left the church, Simon led a parade of children to the front gate of Mrs. Pierce's home. He was doing his best to keep up a cheerful facade, trying to paint this as an adventure, a temporary stopover on their journey to their new home, rather than a tragedy.

They'd just come from the sweet shop, which was located in the same space as a toy store, so the children had been chattering happily when they set out. But now they had quieted, and he sensed nervousness and some anxiety in the group.

Understandable. He'd tried to give them a hopeful report on Miss Fredrick's condition, but he hadn't wanted to lie, so he was sure the older ones, at least, had read between the lines. And now they were approaching a strange place, owned by a person they'd never met, to reside there for an unspecified amount of time. It would be a nerveracking situation for many adults to walk into—how much more so for children?

"It's a castle." Molly's eyes were wide as she stared at Mrs. Pierce's home. "Just like in a fairy tale. Does a queen live here?"

Simon smiled down at her. "Not a queen, but a couple of very nice ladies."

Molly stuck her thumb back in her mouth, appearing unconvinced.

With a mental sigh, Simon climbed the wide stone steps onto the porch and twisted the ornate brass doorbell. The ring echoed from inside the house. Then the silence stretched out for what seemed forever. Behind him the children shuffled restlessly. And he had a sudden stab of fear that Mrs. Pierce might have changed her mind. After all, it had been obvious she wasn't thrilled with the idea of housing them.

He was just contemplating whether or not to give the bell another twist, when the door finally opened.

Chapter Four

Simon was almost embarrassed by the wave of relief that flooded through him. He hoped he did a good job of hiding it. Then he saw who'd opened the door and had to hide his reaction all over again.

Why was Mrs. Pierce answering her own door? Didn't she have a housekeeper? Surely the elegant widow didn't care for this huge house herself? Perhaps her servant was otherwise occupied at the moment.

Mrs. Pierce stepped aside to let them enter. "Forgive me for keeping you waiting. Miss Jacobs and I were just finishing preparing the rooms for you."

Again, no mention of a servant. It was beginning to look as if there truly were no servants after all. If that was true, then he was doubly in her debt for agreeing to take them in. And it made him rethink a few things about her, as well.

As he ushered his charges inside, Miss Jacobs bustled down the hall toward them. "Hello, Mr. Tucker. And here are the children. Welcome, welcome. I've been looking forward to meeting you ever since I heard you were coming."

Simon wondered how two such different women could

get along under the same roof. Miss Jacobs seemed as approachable as Mrs. Pierce was aloof.

As the last of the children entered, he stepped forward to make the introductions. "Kids, this is Mrs. Pierce, the nice lady who has opened her home to us. And this is her friend, Miss Jacobs, who also lives here."

They all nodded and there were a few mumbled hellos. Simon quickly went down the line, introducing the children one by one.

When he was done, Mrs. Pierce gave them a reserved smile. "I'm pleased to meet you all. Welcome to my home."

"Are you a queen?" Molly asked.

To give her credit, their hostess didn't so much as bat an eyelash. "No, I'm not," was her only response.

Joey, apparently emboldened by Molly's question, turned to Miss Jacobs. "Why are you so short?" he asked.

"Joey!" Simon was caught off guard by the boy's artlessly uttered and much-too-personal question. Would Miss Jacobs be insulted?

But the woman merely smiled at the young boy. "I reckon God made me this way because He knew how much I love being around young'uns. It makes me feel closer to kids than to grown-ups."

Miss Jacobs shifted her gaze to include all the children in her next comment. "And I'd be right grateful if you children would call me Nana Dovie while you're here. It's what my own daughter calls me."

Yep, these were definitely two very different women.

Joey wasn't done with his questions, though. He turned to Mrs. Pierce. "Do you have a dog?"

This time the widow frowned slightly. "I do not." There was definitely a tone of "and I don't want one" in her voice. And there was also no offer to let the kids call her by an endearing name.

"When we get to Hatcherville," the boy said proudly, "Gee-Gee says I can get a dog."

"Gee-Gee?" Mrs. Pierce cast him a questioning glance.

"It's what the children call Miss Fredrick," Simon explained. "Her first name is Georgina."

Mrs. Pierce nodded, then turned to Joey. "I'm sure that will be very nice." Then she turned back to Simon. "The rooms are ready for you and your charges. I hope the children won't mind doubling up."

"They're used to sharing," Simon assured her. "Their former home wasn't nearly as grand as this one and they had much tighter sleeping arrangements." He'd seen their bedrooms, crowded with bunk beds like a cramped dormitory. It was one of the reasons Miss Fredrick planned this move. "Do you have a specific way you'd like to assign the rooms or are you leaving it up to us?"

"I have put you and the boys in three rooms on the third floor," the widow responded. "The girls will be in three rooms on the second floor with me and Miss Jacobs."

He nodded. "An excellent arrangement. If you'll show us the way, we'll get everyone settled in." He paused. "By the way, I asked the young man over at the train depot to have our bags delivered here so they should be arriving soon." Most of the kids' belongings, along with all the household items, had been sent on ahead to Hatcherville, but luckily Miss Fredrick had seen that they each had a change of clothing packed for the trip. At least clothing wouldn't be a problem for the next few days.

He wished the same were true about everything else to do with this setback.

Eileen led the way up the stairs, trying her best to remain composed. Seeing all those children up close was

more than a little overwhelming. The questions the two
youngest had asked had bordered on impertinence. They
were little more than toddlers, of course, but her mother
and instructors had always insisted one was never too
young to learn good manners.

She certainly hoped Mr. Tucker had told the truth when
he said they were well behaved. Of course, the conditional
that he'd tagged on about their age hadn't inspired her
with much confidence.

These visitors seemed impressed with her home, but
they were about to see how starkly furnished their rooms
were. What would they think? Of course, one could hardly
expect children to be discriminating in such matters. But
Mr. Tucker was a different matter. And she found his
opinion did matter.

When they reached the second floor, she turned to
Dovie. "Would you please help the girls get settled in
while I show Mr. Tucker and the boys to the third floor?"

"Of course." Dovie smiled at the girls. "I'll let you all
decide how you want to pair up and then we'll pick out
rooms for everyone."

Eileen led the way up the stairs to the third floor. A
part of her envied Dovie's easy manner with the children.
It might not be dignified, but the children seemed better able to relate to her. Then she mentally took herself
to task. As her mother had often drilled into her, Pay-
lors *always* maintained their dignity and composure, no
matter what.

As they stepped onto the landing she felt the need to
apologize. "These rooms haven't seen any use in the past
two years. Miss Jacobs and I aired them out but they may
still be a bit musty."

"I'm sure it'll be just fine." Mr. Tucker looked around

and she watched him closely for signs of judgment. To her relief, he seemed to see nothing amiss.

"Do you have a preference for who gets which room?" he asked.

Good—they were going to keep things businesslike. "The three on this end have been made ready—you may assign them however you wish."

With a nod he turned to the boys. "Harry and Russ, you two take the far room. Albert, you and Joey can have the middle one. And I'll take the one nearest the stairs."

The doorbell sounded and Mr. Tucker turned back to her with a smile. "That's probably our bags." He waved to the two older boys. "Harry, Russell, come help me get everything carted upstairs."

"We're coming, too," the one he'd called Albert said.

"Yeah, we're coming, too," Joey said with a great deal of bravado.

To Eileen's surprise, Mr. Tucker merely grinned at this bit of assertiveness. "All right, men, the more hands, the lighter the load I always say."

By the time they made it to the first floor, Dovie had already opened the door to their caller. As Mr. Tucker had predicted, it was Lionel from the train depot.

As soon as Lionel saw Mr. Tucker over Dovie's shoulder he straightened. "I brought your things, Mr. Tucker, just like asked. It's all on the wagon—I'll get it unloaded in a snap." He reached into his pocket. "And I brought this telegram that came for you, too."

Eileen stiffened slightly. Mr. Tucker was already getting telegrams here? It certainly hadn't taken him long to make himself at home.

She watched as he sent the four boys to help Lionel unload the cart, and then unfolded the piece of paper.

Whatever the news, he didn't appear to like it. Had he received more bad news on top of today's events?

Simon stared at the very terse telegram he'd received in response to the one he'd sent Miss Fredrick's brother.

KEEP ME APPRISED
W. FREDRICK

Apparently Wilbur Fredrick didn't intend to rush to his sister's bedside. Simon didn't understand that—he would have given anything to have had that opportunity with Imogene, to have been able to have a few last words with her before she passed on.

He refolded the paper and shoved it into his pocket. Perhaps this was his fault. Maybe he hadn't made it clear just how serious Miss Fredrick's condition was. Should he send another telegram?

He glanced up and caught Mrs. Pierce watching him, a hint of sympathy in her expression. But she immediately turned away, her demeanor once more aloof, and he wondered if he'd merely imagined it.

Lionel and the boys deposited the first load of baggage just then and went back for more. Before he could join them, the girls were trooping downstairs to investigate what was going on. So Simon pushed aside thoughts of Wilbur Fredrick, and Mrs. Pierce's show of concern, to ponder at a quieter time.

He joined the "menfolk" unloading the wagon and they managed to get the remaining items in one more load.

Once everything was deposited in the entry hall, he dismissed Lionel with a coin and his thanks. When he turned back, the children were already digging into the pile with noisy enthusiasm as well as a bit of good-natured shoving, each looking for their own items. Mrs. Pierce cringed and drew back into herself. Was it the noise level or the overall chaos that bothered her more?

Then she straightened. "Children, please." Her voice, while not loud or strident, carried the ring of authority, and the children closest to her paused in their scrambling to look her way.

"Quiet, please." This time her voice carried to the rest of the children, and everyone turned to stare at her in surprise.

"There is no need for this unruly behavior. You are all old enough to know how to conduct yourselves in a more orderly fashion."

Simon frowned. This might be her home, but she couldn't expect the children to act like miniature versions of herself. "Mrs. Pierce, I believe what you are seeing is enthusiasm rather than unruly behavior."

"One can be excited and show decorum at the same time." She turned to the children. "Now, starting with the oldest and the youngest, step forward and find your things. Then take them up to your room."

Fern stepped forward stiffly. "Yes, ma'am." She held out a hand. "Come on, Molly, I'll help you find your things."

To Simon's surprise, the children followed her instructions, and two by two, with one of the older children helping one of the younger ones, they each collected their things and headed up the stairs. There was no more horseplay and very little chatter, and the task was accomplished in short order.

Okay, so maybe her way was effective, but it certainly hadn't done anything to make the children feel more at ease here.

He glanced Miss Jacobs's way. She was observing in

silence. Did she agree with Mrs. Pierce's approach? Or was she just hesitant to disagree with the woman who was, after all, her landlady?

When the last of the children had headed upstairs, Mrs. Pierce turned to him. Was that a glint of triumph peeking out from her serene expression?

"I realize this is your home," he said before she could comment, "but I would appreciate it if you would give the children a bit of latitude. They've been through quite a bit."

She appeared unmoved. "They have my sympathy, of course, and I understand they are anxious. But I believe maintaining discipline is for their good as well as that of those around them. It gives them a sense of order that can be a comfort when the rest of their world appears to be falling apart around them."

Did she truly believe that? "They also need the chance to work off some of their pent-up energy."

"Within the proper parameters." Then she waved a hand. "Are these last few bags yours?"

He swallowed his response and accepted her change of subject. "That brown duffel is mine and the trunk contains my tools. The smaller trunk belongs to Miss Fredrick." He furrowed his brow thoughtfully. "It seems pointless to cart the heavy tool trunk up two flights of stairs, especially since I'll need most of the tools down here if I'm going to do some work on your place while I'm here. Is there somewhere down here where I could store it?"

She hesitated a long moment—so long that he thought about withdrawing his request.

But then she drew her shoulders back and nodded. "Of course. Follow me."

He couldn't quite pinpoint what it was, but something in her demeanor made him wonder if there was more going through her mind than simply finding him some storage space.

Without a word, she led him down the hall and around a corner. They went down another shorter hallway until she finally stopped in front of a closed door. Taking a deep breath, she threw the door open and indicated he should precede her inside.

He stepped into a darkened room that, from the musty smell, hadn't seen use in some time. It had a definite masculine feel to it and was dominated by a massive desk.

She crossed the room and pulled open the curtains, letting in some much-needed light. It was only then that he noticed that the *only* piece of furniture in the room was that desk, which he could now see was finely crafted and graced with some fine parquetry work.

The walls were bare, although there were indications that several large paintings had hung in here at one time. The built-in bookcases that flanked the fireplace were also empty. And there was a thin layer of dust over everything. But the paneling and richly carved woodwork spoke of bygone elegance.

"This was my husband's study," she said, "but as you can see, it is no longer in use." She folded her hands lightly in front of her, and he thought he detected a slight tremble, though it might have been only his imagination. "You may store your things in here for as long as you are in residence."

It seemed a bit grand to be used as a storage room, but it wasn't his place to question her choice. "Thank you. I'll get one of the boys to help me carry the trunk in here later." He could also store Miss Fredrick's things here.

She looked around. "I apologize for the state you find it in."

Other than a bit of a musty feel, he didn't see anything

that required an apology. "No need. And I certainly don't expect you to go to any trouble on my account."

She nodded and continued to stare at the room as if picturing it differently. Was she remembering her husband seated in here? Did she still mourn him? The temptation to move to her side to comfort her was strong. He'd actually taken a step forward when she suddenly straightened.

"If that is all," she said, "I have a few matters to attend to."

Not sure if he was more relieved or bothered that she'd unknowingly forestalled his impulse, he gave a short bow. "Of course. I'll get the last of the baggage cleared from your entryway." As they shut the door behind them, he added. "I'll encourage the children to either nap or entertain themselves quietly in their rooms for the next hour so you shouldn't be interrupted by any of them."

She gave another of her regal nods and they retraced their steps in silence. When they arrived back at the foot of the stairway she excused herself and headed into the parlor. Was she still thinking of her deceased husband?

Simon watched her go—elegant posture, graceful movements, unhurried pace. He should have told Molly that yes indeed, a queen *did* live in this palace-of-a-home.

But he had the feeling that Eileen Pierce was a very sad and lonely ruler of her faltering domain. The question was, did she realize it, and if so, did she want to change things?

Chapter Five

Eileen sat in the parlor, working on a bit of embroidery. Stepping into Thomas's study had conjured up memories not only of her husband but also of all her past sins. How could she have been so blissfully blind to what she'd been doing to him, of how much her extravagances had cost him, not just in money, but in his integrity and sense of honor? He had paid with his life. Her justly deserved penance was to have been brought low.

The house had grown quiet at last—there'd been no sounds from upstairs for the past ten minutes and even Mr. Tucker and Dovie had disappeared into their own rooms.

So far, things appeared to be working out moderately well. It had been hectic for a while but the children had responded appropriately to her authority. Now that she'd set the proper tone, perhaps the worst was behind them. As long as Dovie and Mr. Tucker took most of the responsibility for actually dealing with the children, and she was left to just play hostess, she was certain they could get through these next few days just fine.

She stilled. What was that noise? Had Mr. Tucker decided to come back down? This unexpected zing of anticipation she felt whenever he was near, or she even believed he was approaching, was new to her. And it was affecting her ability to maintain her impassive facade.

Then she heard the sound again and she realized it had to be one of the children. Ignoring the little stab of disappointment, she set her sewing aside. She couldn't have the children roaming around her home unattended. Then again, what if the child needed something? Would she be up to handling whatever it was on her own?

But she was the lady of the house and she had responsibilities to her guests. Rising, Eileen moved into the hall and stopped when she saw the youngest child—Molly, was it?—coming down the stairs. The little girl was dragging her doll forlornly behind her and had her right hand on the banister.

As soon as she saw Eileen, she stilled.

Eileen stared at her uncertainly. "Shouldn't you be taking a nap?" she asked.

Molly pulled her doll forward and hugged it tightly. "Gee-Gee always rocks me before I go to sleep."

Why did the child think it important to tell her this?

"But Gee-Gee is sick," the little girl added in a mournful tone.

Eileen felt her heart soften. "That's right. And I'm certain, when she gets better, Gee-Gee will be happy to rock you again."

The little girl studied her with disconcerting intensity. "Will *you* rock me?"

Eileen was both touched and thrown off-kilter by the child's request. What did she know about such motherly activities? But something inside her ached to try. Then common sense reasserted itself. "I'm sorry, but I don't have a rocking chair," she told the child. "Why don't you just go on back up to your room and lie down. I'm sure—"

"I want to be rocked." The little girl's mouth was now set in a stubborn line.

Eileen looked around. Where were Dovie and Mr. Tucker? They were so much better equipped than she to handle an obstinate child. "I told you, I don't have a rocking chair. But—"

"I want to be rocked." There was almost a wail in Molly's voice this time and she rubbed her eyes with her fist.

Gracious, was she about to *cry?* That just would not do. Then Eileen remembered the porch swing. It wasn't a rocking chair but it might serve to calm her down.

"All right," she said quickly. "I think I have a suitable compromise."

The little girl's expression changed from pouty displeasure to uncertainty. "What's a com-prize?"

"Com*pro*mise," Eileen corrected. "It means I don't have a rocker but I have something I think will work just as well." She nodded toward the front door. "But we'll have to go outside."

"Okay." Molly, now all smiles, came down the last three stairs and held out her hand.

Surprised by the trusting gesture, Eileen hesitated for just a moment, then accepted the girl's small, pudgy hand into her own. Together they exited the house and Eileen led her to the porch swing.

When Molly saw it, she giggled in delight. "A big rocker swing. I like your com-prize."

"Compromise," Eileen corrected again, but more gently this time. She sat down on the swing and the little girl scrambled up into her lap.

As Eileen set the swing gently into motion, Molly snuggled down more comfortably in her lap, leaned her head against Eileen's chest and stuck her thumb in her mouth again. A happy sigh escaped her as she cuddled her rag doll.

Placing her arms around the child, Eileen felt something deep inside her stir to life.

"This is my fault. I shouldn't have fallen asleep." Fern's eyes were wide, her tone bordering on hysteria.

"You were tired." Simon kept his tone matter-of-fact, trying to keep her from panicking. "And I'm sure Molly hasn't gone far."

"That Mrs. Pierce lady scared her. I don't think she even wants us here." Fern was obviously looking for someone to blame. "Maybe we should find someplace else to stay."

He was surprised by how strongly the urge to defend Mrs. Pierce kicked in. "Fern, this is Mrs. Pierce's home, which means she's allowed to make the rules. She's just not accustomed to being around children, especially as large a group as we have. Give her time to get used to you all and she'll come around. Besides there *is* no other place, unless you want everyone to be split up."

Simon ushered the agitated girl out of the bedchamber and toward the stairs. He'd checked in on all the kids a few moments ago, just to assure himself they were settling in okay, when he'd discovered Molly's bed was empty.

He'd crossed the room to see if Molly was hiding somewhere. Unfortunately Fern, who was the toddler's roommate, had awakened. And now she was blaming herself. Truth was, Simon knew this was his fault. He should have made certain they all knew to stay in their rooms until the clock chimed the hour.

"Maybe we should just call out for her," Fern suggested. "Sometimes she likes to hide."

Simon shook his head. "Not yet. I don't want to wake

the others and get them worried unless we need to. I'm sure she hasn't gone far. Let's just look around a bit first."

He and Fern checked the corners and niches on the second floor then headed downstairs. "Can you think of something she likes to do or someplace she likes to go that would give us a clue where to look?" Simon asked. Regrettably, he didn't know enough about Molly or any of these kids to figure it out for himself.

"She might try to find the kitchen if she was thirsty." Fern's tone was doubtful.

"All right. You check the kitchen—down that way I believe—and I'll see if Mrs. Pierce is still in the parlor to find out if she's seen her."

Fern nodded and took off at a sprint.

He'd already turned in the opposite direction, How would the widow feel about the interruption? Would she help in the search or lecture them on discipline? Not that he minded squaring off with her under less troubling circumstances—getting a rise out of her was actually quite entertaining.

When he looked in the parlor he found it disappointingly empty. He even checked behind the sofa and softly called Molly's name to make sure the little girl wasn't hiding.

When he stepped back out in the hallway he noticed the front door was slightly ajar. Molly was too small, of course, to open the heavy wooden door. But if someone else had left it open…

He quickly crossed to the entryway, pushed open the screen door and stepped out on the porch. He could see the front gate was closed, which eased one worry at least. Perhaps she—

A movement he'd caught from the corner of his eye grabbed his attention.

There, on a porch swing that he hadn't even noticed when they arrived earlier, sat Mrs. Pierce with a sleeping Molly cuddled on her lap. And the widow had the sweetest, gentlest smile on her face, for all the world as if Molly were her own beloved child. The soft expression transformed her, turned her from an ice queen to an achingly sweet image of maternal devotion.

Then Fern came up behind him and he heard her quick intake of breath. Before he could stop her, the girl gave vent to her feelings.

"What are you doing with Molly?" There was outrage and accusation in the girl's tone.

Mrs. Pierce stiffened and the softness disappeared from her expression. In its place a cooler, more impersonal facade settled in. Simon felt a physical sense of loss at the transformation.

"The child insisted on being rocked." Her tone was dispassionate. "It was this or let her wake the house with her crying."

"You should have called me." Fern marched forward. "I know how to take care of her."

Simon knew Fern was still rattled by Molly's unexpected disappearance, but rudeness was never a proper response. "Apologize for taking that tone with Mrs. Pierce," he said quietly but firmly.

Fern threw him a defiant look, but he kept his gaze locked to hers and his expression firm. After a moment she turned back to Mrs. Pierce. "I'm sorry." But her tone was anything but contrite. She stiffly bent down to take Molly from Mrs. Pierce's arms.

"As you wish." Mrs. Pierce smoothed her skirt across her now-empty lap, then stood. "If you'll excuse me, I'll return to my needlework."

Simon wanted to let her know that he appreciated her

tenderness with the toddler, that Fern hadn't really meant what she'd said. But the kids had to be his first concern right now. So he settled for giving her a quick thank-you.

She acknowledged it with a frosty nod, barely pausing as she stepped past him into the house. The ice queen had returned with a vengeance.

He turned back to Fern, careful to keep his irritation out of his voice. "Where do you think you're going?"

"I'm going to put Molly to bed." That touch of defiance had returned.

He stepped in front of her. "Give her to me." When she balked, he gave an exasperated shake of his head. "She's too heavy for you to carry up the stairs. Once I've got her in bed, you can tuck her in and fuss over her all you want."

With a reluctant nod, Fern handed a still-slumbering Molly over. The three-year-old was definitely a sound sleeper. Simon crossed the foyer to the staircase, noting that Mrs. Pierce had returned to the parlor and had her head bent over her sewing. She was as composed as if nothing had just happened. If Fern's tone had upset her there was no sign of it.

Simon quickly carried the little girl up the stairs and placed her in her bed. Then he left Fern to tend to her while he headed back downstairs to see the widow.

He had some fence-mending to do on Fern's behalf.

Chapter Six

Eileen stabbed the needle through the fabric, trying to keep her hands from trembling.

She had gotten used to being something of a social outcast in Turnabout these past two years. But to have that same distrust and dislike focused on her from the eyes of this newcomer, a child no less, was altogether unnerving. It had stung more than she cared to admit.

And all the more so because she'd let her guard down with Molly. She would need to remember these people were just temporary guests in her home. Getting attached to any of them was not to be allowed.

As for Mr. Tucker, she hadn't been able to tell what he thought. He'd wrested an apology from Fern, but other than that, he'd shown no sign of what he was thinking.

She tried to tell herself it didn't matter, but knew that to be a lie.

She looked up when she heard a tap at the parlor door frame. Mr. Tucker stood there watching her. Had he just walked up or had he been there awhile? It bothered her that he might have been watching her without her realizing it.

"May I come in for a moment?" he asked.

Was he here to take her to task as Fern had? Well, she was prepared now; she would not be caught unawares a second time.

Placing her sewing in her lap, Eileen nodded permission.

He smiled diffidently as he moved farther into the room. "I wanted to apologize on Fern's behalf. I'm sorry if she seemed rude—she was just worried about Molly."

Some of her tension eased at his obvious sincerity. But it seemed to her that Fern should do her own apologizing. "I was not harming the child." Had she managed to keep the hurt from her voice?

"Of course not. In fact, I appreciate the attention you were giving her. Molly seemed quite comfortable there with you."

And she had been surprisingly comfortable holding the child. It was the first time she'd been in that position, and it had left her aching more than ever from the knowledge that she would never have a child of her own. "Molly was insistent that she be rocked before she could sleep— humoring her was a simple enough thing. As for Fern, she should know better than to take such a tone with an adult. It appears your Miss Fredrick was not big on teaching the children manners."

"It's been a rough day for them, and they're only children." He'd frowned at her words, but his tone remained calm. "One can't expect them to react with the control of an adult."

"I disagree." Her teachers had gone to great lengths to school her on the correct behavior for a young lady of breeding. It was only when she had proven that she could conduct herself with proper decorum that she had been allowed to dine with adults or join them in the parlor, and then only on special occasions.

"Still and all," he said, interrupting her thoughts, "it was very good of you to comfort Molly."

Eileen deliberately pushed away thoughts of the little girl's snuggling presence in her lap. She might not have the makings of a good mother, but that didn't mean she didn't have maternal longings. "One does what is needed."

To her relief, the doorbell sounded, putting an end to their current discussion. She rose from her seat, setting the sewing aside. "If you'll excuse me, I need to see who is at the door. And I'm sure you have matters of your own to see to, as well."

He stepped back as she exited the parlor, but rather than following her pointed hint, he trailed along behind her. Was he just curious? Or was he expecting someone?

When she opened the door, Regina Barr and her housekeeper, Mrs. Peavy, stood there holding cloth-covered baskets. It seemed the Ladies Auxiliary had put their promises into action.

She greeted them, then stepped aside. "Please come in."

"The Ladies Auxiliary worked out a schedule for meals and I made sure we were first up," Regina said with a smile. "I wanted to get this food to you early so it would be ready whenever the children got hungry."

"Thank you, that was most considerate." What time did the children normally eat? She supposed it would be up to her to set the schedule now.

Mr. Tucker stepped forward. "Good afternoon, ladies." He reached for the baskets. "Let me help you with those."

"Oh, hello. I'm Reggie Barr, one of Eileen's neighbors." Regina waved to her companion. "And this is my friend, Mrs. Peavy."

Mr. Tucker gave a short bow, then reached for her basket, but she resisted with a smile. "These aren't heavy."

She waved a hand toward the open door. "But if you'll help my son Jack with the rest, I'd be most obliged."

Eileen glanced outside to see Jack standing at the foot of the porch with a small wagon containing two large hampers.

As Mr. Tucker stepped outside, Eileen turned to the women. "You can set your baskets down on the dining room table."

But Regina shook her head. "Nonsense, we can carry these to the kitchen for you."

Mr. Tucker returned with the two hampers, and Jack was right behind him with a smaller basket. Eileen didn't have any choice but to lead the small procession to the kitchen. At least that room was not expected to be lavishly furnished, so perhaps they'd see nothing amiss.

As they walked, Regina described the contents of the baskets. "We have a sliced ham, some squash, butter beans, fresh-baked bread and two pecan pies." She grinned. "I figured with ten kids and three adults to feed, you'd be needing a goodly quantity."

"That will make a fine meal," Eileen said. Actually, it sounded a veritable feast. She couldn't remember the last time she'd had ham.

"Tomorrow," Regina continued, "Hortense Peters promises to deliver a basket of fresh eggs in the morning along with a generous length of summer sausage. And Eunice is going to bring over a roast with some vegetables that should be enough to take care of your noon and evening meals."

Eileen nodded. Eunice Ortolon might be a gossipy busybody but there was no denying she was a great cook. "I'm certain the children will be quite grateful for your generosity." It seemed as long as the children were under her roof she would be eating well. An unexpected benefit.

Mr. Tucker set his things down, brushing closely past her. Had he done that on purpose?

He made a short bow in Regina's direction. "Absolutely, ma'am. I can't begin to tell you how grateful we are to have fallen among such kind and generous folk."

Regina smiled, obviously not immune to the warmth of his tone, either. Then she turned to include Eileen in her comments. "And don't you worry. We have folks lined up to take care of your meals for as many days as you need us to."

Eileen was getting hungry just smelling the tempting aromas coming from the hampers. She hadn't eaten such fine fare in some time—meat was a rare treat indeed.

Regina sent a subtle signal to Mrs. Peavy, and the older woman made her exit, taking Jack with her. Then she turned to Mr. Tucker. "Thank you so much for your assistance getting these inside. I'll just help Eileen get everything put away before I go."

This time Mr. Tucker took the not-very-subtle hint. "If you'll excuse me, then, I'll leave you ladies to it. I think I'll check in on Molly to make sure she stays put this time." He gave Regina another of those warm smiles. "Thanks again for the food, ma'am."

Once he'd gone, Eileen turned to Regina. "It's really not necessary for you to stay and help me. You've done enough already." She really wasn't comfortable having people poking around in her cupboards and closets.

Regina opened one of the hampers. "I don't mind. And there's something else I wanted to say."

Eileen steeled herself. Was Regina, like Miss Ortolon, concerned with her suitability to house young children? Was this to be some sort of advice or condition set down for her?

But there was no hint of censure in Regina's expression. "Daisy and I discussed how children can be hard on dishes, and it didn't seem right that you should bear the brunt of that. So she sent over some of the plates from her restaurant that have seen a bit too much wear and that she was ready to take out of service. I hope you don't mind. They have some small chips and cracks but are still serviceable."

Regina seemed to sense her hesitation. "If you'd rather not use them, that's okay, too. But Daisy wanted me to assure you that either way she doesn't need them back— she was ready to replace them anyway."

Had these women suspected her true circumstances and decided to offer her charity? That was a lowering thought, but Eileen couldn't afford to turn down the offer. She hadn't given much thought to place settings, but she'd be hard-pressed to set a table for the ten children, much less the full complement of thirteen now residing here.

First towels, now dishes. Was she forgetting anything else?

At least Regina had worded the offer in a way that left Eileen with some of her dignity intact. She nodded matter-of-factly. "I had not considered the added wear and tear these children could have on my things. I will have to thank Daisy when next I see her."

Regina touched her arm lightly. "I know you were put on the spot earlier. And given all that's occurred the past couple of years, it was mighty generous of you to open your home to these folks. If you need any help at all in the coming days, you know where I live. Don't hesitate to fetch me."

Eileen was surprised by the genuine warmness of the gesture. Was this the start of a thawing of the community toward her? Or would the friendly overtures disappear as soon as her houseguests departed?

* * *

Once Regina took her leave, Eileen made quick work of unloading the various baskets and hampers. Dovie joined her just as she emptied the last one.

"Goodness, but isn't this all a welcome sight. I don't mind saying I'm not a bit sorry we won't need to rustle up supper from scratch for all these folks."

Eileen folded her hands in front of her. "I'll admit I don't know how much children eat, but there seems to be enough here to feed us all."

Dovie peered inside the various bowls and pots. "I agree—this should be more than enough. There might even be some ham left over to serve with breakfast in the morning. I'll get the stove stoked. We can set these things on the warming rack so it'll all be heated through when we're ready for it."

Eileen glanced up toward the ceiling. "How much longer do you think the children will nap?"

"I imagine some of them are awake already, if they slept at all. It's been an emotional day for them and different children will react differently to that."

Emotional—Eileen didn't like the sounds of that. Orderly and obedient—that's how children should behave.

But Dovie was still speaking. "As to your question, Mr. Tucker instructed them to stay in their rooms for at least an hour." She grinned. "I imagine it was as much to give you a reprieve as to let the children rest."

Eileen relaxed, pleased that he might have indeed been thinking of her feelings. And it seemed there was an expectation that the children were at least able to quietly amuse themselves. Good. "That being the case, I don't suppose they'll have the energy for much activity the rest of the day."

Dovie shook her head sympathetically. "You really don't know much about children, do you, dear?"

Eileen didn't like the condescending tone. "I remember my own childhood quite well."

The older woman gave her a long, considering look, and it was all Eileen could do not to fidget under that gaze.

"Don't you remember how hard it was to sit still for long periods?" Dovie finally asked. "You can't expect them to stay in their rooms all afternoon. An hour or two, yes, but no more. Children need activity to keep them from getting restless."

Eileen disagreed. It was merely a matter of training and discipline. Most of her childhood, at least that part after her father's death when she was five, had been spent with boarding school teachers in quiet, educational pursuits. Those teachers had believed in the adage that children should be seen and not heard, and they had vigorously drilled their students on matters of etiquette, deportment and other matters of social acceptance.

But if indeed these children had *not* been trained properly, she would have to find other solutions. If she hadn't had to sell her pianoforte or stereopticon she could have entertained them in a decorous, proper style. She'd also sold most of her books and her husband's finely carved chess set. There was nothing even remotely appropriate for entertaining company of any age left in her home.

Dovie startled her by patting her hand. "Don't worry," the woman said. "Children are easily entertained. Just leave it to me."

"And so I shall. In the meantime, I should take care of organizing our meal."

Just as Dovie had predicted, thirty minutes later there were sounds of stirring from the upstairs rooms. When

Eileen stepped into the hallway a few minutes later, she saw Dovie leading the entire group of children into the parlor. Curious as to what the woman was planning, Eileen followed, as well.

Dovie knelt down next to the low table in front of the sofa and signaled the children to gather around. "I want to show you a game my mother used to play with me." She untied the cloth and spread it open with all the flair of a pirate revealing his treasure. The children all pressed closer to get better looks.

Eileen couldn't resist taking a step forward herself. Peering over the children's heads, she identified a thimble, coin, needle, spoon, button, pumpkin seed, pecan, twig, two rocks, a hairpin, hat pin, chalk, a bit of ribbon, a candle stub, a feather and a spool.

"Now, I want everyone to study all these items very closely," Dovie said solemnly. "In a moment you're going to turn around, and I'll mix them up and take one away. Then we'll see who can be first to figure out what's missing."

The children immediately leaned in closer to study the contents intently.

Eileen was amazed. Dovie had managed to capture their attention with very little effort. And with such a simple device.

"It looks like she's in her element, doesn't it?"

Eileen turned to find Mr. Tucker at her side, his gaze on Dovie and the children.

"Very much so," she agreed.

He turned to her. "If you don't mind, perhaps we can step into the hall to talk for a moment?"

"Of course." What did he want to discuss? Had she done something he didn't approve of?

"I want you to know that I meant what I said about taking care of any maintenance or repair work that needs tending to while I'm here."

Some of her tension eased as she settled back into her lady-of-the-manor role. "As it happens, there are a few things that could use some attention."

"Good. If you'll let me know what you think are the most pressing tasks, I'll start figuring out how to best tackle them."

Eileen didn't have to think about it. "The gutters require a good cleaning and there are a few loose rails on the back porch."

He nodded. "That shouldn't be a problem. Is there anything else?"

Surprised he hadn't balked, even a little, she added another item to the list. "Since we'll need to do more cooking than usual and heat more wash water and more rooms, there's the matter of firewood."

"Of course. I've split many a cord in my day."

"You may need to gather the wood as well as split it."

"Understood. Why don't you show me the porch rails you're concerned about now so I have a better idea of what's needed?"

Relieved that he didn't seem overly concerned by her requests, she nodded. "Of course. This way."

As she led the way to the back of the house and out the kitchen door, she was very aware of him walking beside her. What was wrong with her today? She'd never let herself be distracted by such feelings before. Nor even admitted that she had them.

They stepped out onto the back porch, and she immediately put some distance between them. Moving to the far end of the porch, she pointed out the loose railings.

"These three spindles and a couple of the ones lining the steps, as well."

Mr. Tucker followed her and examined the rails in question more closely. "I'll need to replace at least one of these, maybe more, but it shouldn't be difficult to do. And I might as well check all the other spindles while I'm at it."

It would be such a relief to have those things taken care of. Perhaps he could even get a little ahead on the firewood so she wouldn't have to buy so much when winter set in.

He stepped down onto the lawn and looked up at the roofline, rubbing his chin. "I have my own tools with me, of course. But I'm going to need a ladder for getting up to those gutters." He glanced her way. "And an ax for chopping firewood."

She waved a hand toward a structure at the far end of her property. "I believe you'll find what you need in the carriage house. Feel free to look around in there and make use of whatever you need." The carriage had been one of the first things she'd sold off. The only thing she used the structure for these days was as a storage shed and a place to keep her gardening implements.

"I'll check it out first thing in the morning." He took a long, slow look around her property. "I could get the boys to rake up these leaves for you, too, if you'd like."

"That would be appreciated." She was beginning to feel as if she were taking advantage of him. She hadn't expected him to work for his keep.

"Good. It'll give them something to focus on besides Miss Fredrick's situation."

She wondered what he was really thinking about the state of her home and property. It had to be painfully obvious to him that she hadn't been able to take care of the place as she ought for some time now.

But his next comment indicated nothing of the sort. "It appears you have quite a garden," he said.

She felt her cheeks warm in pleasure. "It's done well this year. There's not much left to it right now, but I should still be able to harvest a few things from my fall planting until first frost."

"You take care of it yourself?"

Was that surprise in his expression? She tilted her chin up. "I do. Though Dovie helps." Truth to tell, she actually enjoyed working her garden. What had been a pleasant hobby in the past had turned into a means of survival. Many was the day the only thing she ate for her meals was what she'd harvested from her garden. And she'd learned to preserve what she didn't need for her immediate sustenance so that she could stretch her bounty even further. It was surprising, the sense of accomplishment she felt at having vegetables she'd grown and harvested herself in her pantry.

He nodded. "Miss Jacobs seems like a fine person. And I can tell she knows how to deal with children."

Unlike her—was that what he was thinking? And was he assuming Dovie did most of the gardening, as well?

She turned and moved back toward the door, feeling suddenly rattled by all these unaccustomed thoughts. Time to take control of the conversation again. "Speaking of the children, perhaps we can discuss what sort of routine they are accustomed to. And then determine what routine will work best while they are here."

She felt better already. Routines and discipline, that was what provided order and structure, the two things that were essential to a smoothly run household. And it was becoming obvious to her that these children could benefit from some training in that department.

She had a feeling, though, that she and Mr. Tucker would not see eye to eye on that point.

If so, she would just have to bring him around to her way of thinking.

Chapter Seven

Routine? Why was she asking him about that? Simon had no idea what sort of routine Miss Fredrick had set for them, or even if they had one at all. "I'm not sure I understand what exactly you're asking about—what sorts of routines?"

"I would think it would be self-explanatory. I'd like to know what they are accustomed to in the area of mealtimes, bedtimes, quiet times, bath times. What portion of their day is set aside for educational pursuits such as reading, sewing, nature studies, journaling? Are they accustomed to daily readings from the Good Book? That sort of thing."

He didn't appreciate the condescending tone she'd used, but he was determined to remain civil. "Mrs. Pierce, perhaps I didn't explain my role clearly. I had no involvement in the kids' day-to-day lives prior to our boarding the train in St. Louis. I am merely the escort, charged with seeing them safely to Hatcherville and getting them securely installed in their new home. I have no idea what their normal routines are, only what we experienced during the trip, which I imagine was anything *but* normal."

"I see. Then perhaps we shouldn't worry about what

they did in the past and concentrate instead on what makes the most sense for now."

"I agree." Though he had some doubts that they would agree on just what *would* make sense.

By this time they'd stepped back inside the kitchen, and she waved a hand toward the table. "Shall we have a seat while we work it out?"

"You mean now?"

"Is there some reason we should wait?" Her expression reminded him of a severe schoolmarm who was dealing with a difficult student.

"I thought perhaps Miss Jacobs should be involved." He tried to be diplomatic. "I mean, we've both admitted to not having experience dealing with children, and she obviously has. Don't you think she could be helpful?"

Mrs. Pierce took a seat, her expression set but her copper-colored eyes flashing like a bright new penny. Was she enjoying this?

She placed her clasped hands in her lap. "For the moment I think it is more important that she continue to keep the children entertained so we can discuss this without distractions."

He tried again. "But if we don't have any point of reference to draw on—"

"Surely laying out routines and schedules has more to do with the adult's perspective than with the children's. And I am not so far removed from my own childhood that I don't remember the routines imposed on me at my boarding school." She shifted slightly, as if she'd said more than she intended.

Boarding school. So she came from money, did she? That explained a lot.

Simon moved toward the table, deciding he might as well hear her out. He took a seat across from her. "All right. I'm willing to give it a shot. Where would you like to start?"

"The first thing I think we should decide is whether everyone should take their meals together or if we should eat in shifts."

"Together," he said immediately, before she could launch into a discussion of pros and cons. "I want to maintain the feeling of family for them as much as possible."

Something flashed in her shiny-penny eyes that he couldn't quite identify, but it left him with the impression that he hadn't given her the answer she'd wanted. To do her credit, though, she nodded. "Very well, then we will need to add back the leaves to the dining room table and find three additional chairs."

"No problem. There are four perfectly fine chairs right here—we can take three of them into the dining room. And if you'll show me where you keep the table leaves, I'll take care of that, as well." Perhaps this routine-setting thing wouldn't be so bad, after all. "What's next?"

"Mealtimes. I would suggest breakfast at seven, the midday meal at noon and dinner at six, but I'm open to suggestions. However, I do feel that whatever schedule we decide on, we should make a point to adhere to it."

"I'm sure, if that's the most convenient schedule for you, it will work fine for the children."

"Good. Now let's move on to bedtimes. I believe it should be no later than eight."

"For the younger ones, perhaps, but the older ones might find that restrictive."

"I suppose, if they want to occupy themselves quietly in their rooms for the first hour then that would be acceptable."

Was she worried about them being too much of a bother for her? But they would only be here for a few days, God willing, so he supposed he could go along with her on this. "All right. What else?"

They discussed bath times, responsibilities for keeping their rooms tidy, and the level of decorum she expected them to maintain in her home.

Simon tried to keep his thoughts to himself and go along with her plans. But he had to wonder—what kind of childhood had the woman had if she thought this was an appropriate routine for youngsters? If this was how she'd spent her time at her boarding school he'd say she would have been better served staying home. "So, are we done?" He hoped his tone didn't convey any of his disdain for her plans.

"Not yet. We need to discuss the amount of time we might want them to spend learning artistic and social skills."

Enough was enough. "Mrs. Pierce, these are *children*." He didn't bother to mask his irritation. "They also need time to just *be* children, to play."

She remained unruffled. "Of course. But it is also important that they be trained while they are young so they may grow into adults who respect and value knowledge and refinement."

"What did you have in mind?" Simon reminded himself once more that this was her home and that they wouldn't be here for long. But he would draw the line quickly enough if he saw her do anything that would make the kids feel as if they didn't measure up to some arbitrary standard she might have in mind. They'd already faced enough of that in their young lives.

And quite frankly, so had he.

"I would be willing to work with them on literature, art, music and etiquette." She actually had a hint of a smile on her face, as if this was something she looked forward to.

"In addition, I could work with the girls on their household skills, and perhaps you could work with the boys on whatever skills are particular to young men."

"Mrs. Pierce, I don't—"

She held up a hand to interrupt his protest. "Of course I didn't mean to imply we would address all of these things at the same time."

Thank goodness she recognized that much at least.

"Depending on the length of your stay," she continued, "we might not get around to all of it. But we could assess what skills they already possess and what they might be most interested in learning, and work up a plan from there." She gave him an "I'm right on this" look. "Because it is always good to have a plan worked out."

He chose his words carefully, not wanting to insult her. "Mrs. Pierce, while I know you mean well, a governess is the last thing these children need right now." Or maybe ever. "I think it'll be a better use of everyone's time if we just assign them their fair share of the household chores and leave it at that."

There was the merest hint of disappointment in her expression but it disappeared quickly. "I disagree. But if that is how you feel, then of course that is what we must do." The frostiness was back in her tone.

"Maybe when they get settled into their new home and begin to establish their own routines—" he figured she'd like his use of that word "—then that will be soon enough to worry about all that. But for now they just need some calm and as much normalcy as possible in their lives."

She seemed somewhat mollified. "As I said, you are their caretaker so I will defer to your wishes. If you should change your mind, however, I stand ready to do my part."

Her capitulation surprised him. Perhaps he'd read her

wrong. "Thank you. And as I said, I'll expect them to do some chores around here."

"Such as?"

"Well, in addition to keeping their rooms neat and tidy, the girls can help with the dishes, sweeping, dusting, laundry—whatever housekeeping chores need tending to while we're here. The boys can help me with some of the yard work and outdoor chores."

"That seems reasonable." She raised her chin. "I assume, however, if there is time in their schedules, and if it does not unduly tax them, you'd have no objection to my introducing them to a small taste of the finer arts?"

So she hadn't really given up. Perhaps it would be best if he just came out and said what he was feeling. "So long as you don't use such lessons to make them feel inferior, then I don't see any harm in it."

She stiffened. "That would *never* be my intention, no matter what I was teaching them."

Not her intention perhaps, but it could still be the result if she went about it the wrong way. "I'm glad to hear it. But let's go easy with them for the next day or two. And who knows, we may even be able to resume our travels and let you return to your normal routine by then."

Her gaze softened ever so slightly. "If you don't mind my asking, what is the true situation with Miss Fredrick?"

Simon raked his fingers through his hair. "Dr. Pratt says it's all in God's hands now." He grimaced at his own words. "But that's always the case isn't it? Everything is in God's hands at all times." He refused to give up hope.

"Have you given any thought to what you will do if she doesn't get better?"

The widow sure didn't shy away from difficult subjects. "I think it's too early to be giving up on her."

Her expression changed back to that of a no-nonsense

schoolmarm. "Planning for a less than happy outcome is *not* giving up on her, and it's definitely not too soon to be thinking of such things. One must strive to be prepared for any contingency. I would think, especially in this case, that would be true."

She was right of course, at least about facing facts. But he wasn't ready to discuss going on without the children's foster mother.

"If the time comes when that becomes necessary, I'll figure something out. Rest assured, I won't abandon these children until I've made certain they'll be well cared for."

"A commendable sentiment. But again, you aren't doing the children any favors by not planning ahead."

He knew she was right but he wasn't ready to deal with it just yet. "Is there anything else you need to discuss with me?"

"I would like to know a little more about the children."

"Such as?"

"Do you know anything of their history? For instance, how did they all come to live with Miss Fredrick? And are any of them siblings?"

"I'm not well acquainted with them personally, but my sister gave me bits and pieces of their stories in the letters she wrote me. And Miss Fredrick gave me some information when I agreed to help her find a new place to set up her household." He chose his words carefully. "There are some sets of siblings in the group and some who have no blood kin here. But they are *all* siblings now, at least in spirit."

"Of course."

Perhaps it would help her feel more of a kinship to the children if she did know some personal information about them. "Fern, Rose and Lily are sisters," he elaborated. "They were the first that Miss Fredrick took in so they've been living with her the longest. They're the children of a distant relation of Miss Fredrick's. She took them and their mother in when the woman learned she had consumption. She gave the girl's mother her word that they would always have a home with her." No need to mention that their father died in jail. "They were the first Miss Fredrick took in and that was about six years ago."

"Is that when she decided to open a children's home?"

"She didn't decide, exactly. She told me that was God's idea, not hers."

Mrs. Pierce frowned slightly. "What does that mean?"

"She made no real effort to take other children in— they just landed on her doorstep, so to speak." He marshaled his thoughts, hoping he had the details right. He had to be careful not to share any of the secrets that weren't his to share.

"Less than a year after the three girls moved in," he continued, "a neighbor who'd recently lost his wife asked Miss Fredrick to look after his kids during the day while he was at work until he could make other arrangements. Those kids were Russell, Harry and Tessa. Two weeks later, the man died. The kids didn't have anyone else step forward to claim them, so she assured the children they would have a home with her for as long as they wanted one." He didn't go into how the father died. The man took to the bottle after his wife died and got himself killed in a bar fight. He wasn't sure how much the kids knew about that sad event, but he certainly wasn't going to be the one to spread the word.

"They were fortunate to have found a place with someone so kindhearted," Mrs. Pierce said.

"That they are—all ten of 'em. In the following years, four infants were left on Miss Fredrick's doorstep—I guess folks heard that they would be welcome there. Unfortunately two of the infants didn't survive long." Many of Miss Fredrick's neighbors held the opinion that it was prostitutes who abandoned their offspring at her door. And they were likely right.

"I take it Molly and Joey were the two who did survive?"

He nodded, surprised that she remembered their names.

"So they are the ones who have no siblings among the others."

He stiffened. "Like I said, something you need to remember about these kids if you want to understand them is that in every way but blood they consider themselves siblings and Miss Fredrick as their mother. She worked very hard to instill that in them—the fact that they are truly a family, I mean. I don't intend to let anyone take that bond away from them."

"Of course." She wrinkled her nose delicately. "It sounds as if people took advantage of her kindheartedness."

"I don't think she saw it that way. In fact I think she looked on it more as an opportunity and a privilege. She truly loves these children."

A slight frown line appeared above her brow. "But I believe you haven't accounted for two of them, Audrey and Albert. You mentioned in the meeting that they are your sister's children?"

He nodded. "Their mother, my sister Sally, passed away three months ago."

"I'm sorry. Was she your only sibling?"

He felt a little kick in the gut at this reminder. The memory could still hit him that way, even after all these years. "No, I had another sister, Imogene, but she died when we were children." Both of his sisters were gone. And he hadn't been there for either of them at the end.

"I'm sorry," she repeated.

He nodded an acknowledgment of her apology, then moved on. "I knew I wasn't up to the task of raising her kids, not on my own anyway. Miss Fredrick and I discussed it and she generously offered to give them a home. That's part of the reason I helped her find a new place for her and the kids to settle down in. That, and the fact that I wanted to make sure I continued to have some involvement in Audrey's and Albert's lives."

"Such as providing this escort when Miss Fredrick decided to move."

He nodded. "But it wasn't just to provide escort—I intend to move there myself so I can be close by. As I said, I want to be a familiar part of their lives. Audrey and Albert are family and I want to be close by should they ever need me for anything." He was determined to never again be too far away to help someone who needed him.

"It's good that you want to be a part of their lives. But was it so easy to uproot yourself?"

He shrugged. "I don't really have strong ties to St. Louis. No family left there now, and I work for myself doing carpentry and occasional odd jobs here and there. Hatcherville has a brick-making facility that I could hire on with if nothing else works out." He was determined to do whatever he had to do to take care of Sally's kids.

But Mrs. Pierce wasn't finished with her questions. "Was there a particular reason Miss Fredrick decided to move so far from her established home? Surely, if her household had outgrown her current residence, there were options closer to home. One would assume she already had friends and connections there that she could call on for assistance should she need it."

"She had her reasons." Reasons he wasn't going to go into, especially with someone who seemed as straitlaced as Mrs. Pierce. These children needed a clean break from their past, and he wasn't going to do anything to jeopardize that.

To do Mrs. Pierce credit, though, she didn't press or seem unduly put off by his answer, or rather, lack of one. Instead she moved on. "Which brings us back to the question of what you will do if Miss Fredrick is no longer able to take care of the children." She said this as matter-of-factly as if saying they had run out of flour. "We will, of course, continue to pray that she recovers fully, but even so, with a stroke there is likely to be a long recovery period."

That was something he hadn't considered. If Miss Fredrick became a convalescent, would her brother put aside this bickering between them and take care of her? And the children?

But that wasn't something to discuss with his hostess. Then it struck him that she might be worried he would try to overstay his welcome. "The house in Hatcherville is already paid for and most of the furnishings from her previous house have been shipped there, so having a place for the children to live won't be an issue."

He was thinking things through as he talked. "I suppose, if the worst *does* happen, I can hire someone responsible, perhaps a married couple, to serve as the children's caretaker while I keep an eye on them as I'd originally planned."

"Then you *have* put some thought into this—good." She stood. "If you will excuse me, there are some things I should take care of before we serve the evening meal."

He stood as well, knowing a dismissal when he heard one. "Of course. And I want to check in on the kids to see if Miss Jacobs needs rescuing."

"I imagine she is in her element."

He agreed. "But still, I don't want to take advantage of her kindness."

"As you wish." She turned toward the cupboard, apparently assuming they were finished with the conversation.

Simon headed for the parlor, still trying to figure out Eileen Pierce. The woman was much too rigid in her thinking—that much was obvious. It was also obvious she hadn't been around children much, and her ideas of how they should be treated were of the ivory-tower as opposed to the down-to-earth variety.

But to be fair, she did have some good qualities. It seemed she'd gone to the trouble of learning everyone's names. And her method of settling them when their baggage arrived had been surprisingly effective, proving that there was a place for discipline, as long as it wasn't taken to extremes.

She'd also shown both resourcefulness and concern when she'd turned her porch swing into a rocking chair to accommodate Molly. That soft expression on her face when she'd thought herself alone with the toddler had been sweetly transforming, as if she *did* have some semblance of maternal instincts.

He could forgive her her routines and other rigid nonsense if he was certain that deep down she really did have the kids' best interest at heart.

But how could he be sure?

Chapter Eight

Eileen moved to the cupboard to take stock of her place settings once more. Mr. Tucker's insistence that the entire household eat at the same time was regrettable, but she would have to make it work. To her relief she did have the right number of place settings, but only because Daisy and Regina had thought ahead and sent her some extras. Not everything would match, of course, and some of the children would be drinking from mugs rather than glasses, but there was no help for it. She cringed at setting such an unharmonious table, but she would just have to put the best face on it she could.

She momentarily considered eating separately. With Ivy and Dovie she had been able to justify keeping her distance. They were boarders and there were boundaries to be maintained. She hadn't wanted to invite familiarity, hadn't wanted to invite the kind of closeness that would make her boarders feel comfortable prying into her personal life. If that made for a lonely life, so be it—she'd had enough of being judged and found wanting.

But *these* were not boarders—Mr. Tucker and the children were guests. Which meant she had obligations as their hostess. And that included presiding over the meals.

Besides, she'd told Mr. Tucker she believed the children should be trained in the proper way to behave. She had a duty to teach them, and how better than by example?

Eileen counted the dishes and silverware one more time. She hoped the children would be careful—if any of these plates were broken she had nothing to replace them with.

As she crossed the room, her thoughts shifted from the dishes to Mr. Tucker. What a strong sense of family he had. It was as admirable a quality as it was foreign to her. She had two younger half sisters, but she hadn't been raised with them, and her mother and stepfather had been distant. So this bond he was so passionate about was difficult for her to understand.

But it sounded like something she might have enjoyed.

Perhaps there was a reason these children—and Mr. Tucker—had ended up in her home. They obviously needed some order and discipline in their lives, and that was something she could definitely provide. It had taken a bit of persuasion, but Mr. Tucker seemed to have finally understood that.

And it had not escaped her notice that he hadn't spent any time thinking through his options given the situation. Of course, said situation was recent and he'd had other things to contend with in the meantime.

Still, she received the distinct impression that he wasn't the sort to do much planning. Which might be something he could get by with in the usual way, but this was hardly a usual situation. And one should always strive to do more than merely *get by*.

Eileen headed down the hall to the bathing room. She carefully took stock of her towels and the supply of firewood. She'd taken several cold baths lately to conserve the wood, but a good hostess wouldn't expect her guests to do the same. She had a vague idea that little children caught chills easily, and the last thing she needed was to have to deal with sick children.

In this room, at least, she had no need to worry about what her visitors might think of her social status. The washroom was one of the luxuries Eileen had insisted on when she'd first moved to Turnabout as a new bride, and Thomas had indulged her, lavishing on her whatever she wanted. She still felt that sense of being pampered when she walked in here. The floor was beautifully tiled; the water was piped into a receptacle that sat on a low stove-like apparatus for heating. The partially sunken tub, which she had had specially shipped in from New Orleans, was opulently large and carved from a single block of marble. It had taken a whole team of men to move it in here. It was why it was still part of her home and had not been sold off with some of her other furnishings—it would have been too difficult to remove.

She let her eyes scan the rest of the room. To one side, a beautifully carved four-panel screen stood ready to provide the bather with additional privacy. Brass hooks lined the wall for keeping one's clothing off the floor. A door on the far end led outdoors.

Then her gaze came to rest on the less indulgent aspects of the room. She'd had to make a compromise or two in the past couple of years. When her housekeeper had been let go and she had to start doing her own laundry, Eileen had brought the washtubs in here and strung a clothesline across one end of the room so that she could do her menial work in private.

Dovie and Ivy knew it was in here, but she never did her laundry while they were around. Just because she had been reduced to doing her own housework didn't mean she had to put herself on display while she played the part of washerwoman.

Of course some of that would have to change now. The sheer volume of laundry the residents in her house would generate would dictate that the clothes be hung outside to dry. She'd have to speak to Mr. Tucker about stringing an additional line for her.

And she had to stop waiting until problems fell in her lap and start planning ahead, just as she had pressed Mr. Tucker to do. What other issues related to her new house-guests was she likely to encounter?

It was time she found a quiet place and thought through the possibilities so she would be prepared.

At dinnertime, Dovie recruited the children to help set the table. Eileen no longer owned the elegant wrought iron cart that her housekeeper had once used to transport the dishes and food from the kitchen to the dining room, so it was necessary to hand carry everything. Eileen didn't take an easy breath until everything had been transported without incident.

As they prepared to take their seats, Dovie looked around the table. "The little ones will need risers on their chairs," she said thoughtfully.

Risers? Eileen looked at her chairs. Entertaining children in her dining room had never been a consideration before. What could she use to improvise?

But before she could formulate a plan, Mr. Tucker spoke up. "I'll take care of finding or making something to serve the purpose tomorrow. For now, if you or Mrs. Pierce will hold Molly in your lap, I'll hold Joey in mine."

Apparently reading the panic in her face, Dovie quickly spoke up. "I'll be glad to hold Molly, if Eileen will allow me the honor."

Grateful for the woman's offer, Eileen gave a regal nod. "Yes, of course."

"Then that leaves you to serve everyone's plate," Mr. Tucker said, smiling her way.

Eileen hesitated, then stood. She supposed if she had to choose between server and nursemaid, she preferred the role of server. The memory of how Molly had felt snuggled up against her flitted through her mind, but she shoved it away. Such things were not for her.

As Fern no doubt agreed.

"So how shall we do this?" she asked. "Would it be better for you to pass up your plates for me to serve? Or for you to each bring me your plates to fill?"

"I would suggest they bring you their plates," Dovie answered. "Less handling and confusion that way."

She nodded, seeing the logic in that. "Very well. Children, take your plates and line up. And do take care to hold them straight so nothing slides onto the floor."

Eileen served the first two plates without incident. Then it came to the third child, Rose. She placed a generous slice of ham on the plate then ladled up some of the butter beans.

"No!"

Eileen froze, startled by the little girl's vehemence.

"Rose doesn't like for her food to touch." Fern said. The older girl's lips were pinched in disapproval, as if Eileen had been sloppy, or worse yet, had done it on purpose.

Why did Fern seem to dislike her so much? But now was not the time to worry about that.

"My apologies." She set the plate with the offending contents aside and picked up her own. She very carefully dished up the ham, squash and butter beans so that very little liquid made it to the plate and then placed them so nothing touched.

Rose studied the plate suspiciously, then smiled, nodded with a thank-you and moved to her chair.

The next three children were served without incident, and Eileen began to breathe easier. She wasn't sure why she'd been so nervous; this was a simple task after all.

Then Harry stepped up for his portion. Just as she put the last spoonful of vegetables on his dish, it happened—Harry dropped his plate. The food splattered everywhere, including the bottom of her skirt. And the plate—one of the precious few remaining from her good china service, broke into three pieces.

Eileen stared at the mess, unable to move, horrified by the extent of the disaster. It wasn't the mess; it wasn't even the possibility that her dress was stained. That broken dish meant someone would not have a plate to eat from for this meal or any subsequent ones while her newfound guests remained in residence.

She turned her gaze on the offender, prepared to scold him for his clumsiness. Then she spotted his stricken and mortified expression and the words dried in her throat. Their eyes locked for a moment and Eileen found herself searching for the right words to defuse the situation.

She managed to drag out a smile and keep her dismay out of her tone. "No harm done."

Dovie set Molly down in the chair and bustled over. "Harry, why don't you let me help you clean up this mess while Mrs. Pierce finishes serving the others."

Grateful for Dovie's intervention, Eileen took a quick glance at the others in the room and saw expressions displaying various degrees of wariness. Were they worried there would be repercussions?

She took care to smile at the next child in line. Keeping her expression and movements calm and unruffled, she mechanically placed the food on Tessa's plate and each of the others that followed, making sure she said something to each of them. But her mind kept spinning over what she would do to replace the broken dish.

By the time she filled the last plate, the mess on the floor had been cleaned up and she handed Harry the plate she'd fixed earlier for Rose. Hopefully the boy wouldn't mind that the food touched.

And she still hadn't come up with a solution to being short by one plate.

Time to make a graceful exit—or as graceful as possible given the circumstances. "If you will excuse me, I have something to attend to. Please go on with your meal without me."

Her announcement was met with an awkward silence and some of the wary glances returned. Her gaze snagged for a heartbeat on Mr. Tucker's frown, but then she turned to make her exit. Leaving her guests to their own devices seemed preferable to making a spectacle out of her lack of a place setting.

But before she could get away, Mr. Tucker spoke up. "Mrs. Pierce, whatever it is you need to take care of, surely it can wait until after we eat." His gaze practically demanded she stay.

But she ignored both the gaze and the words. "I'm afraid it cannot." And with that, she left the room without a backward glance.

When Eileen reached the kitchen, she looked around as if a plate would appear out of thin air. The only thing that seemed remotely appropriate was the meat platter, but it was big enough to serve a full-grown turkey. Even the saucers were on the side table in the dining room, awaiting time to serve the pecan pie.

She gave a mental shrug. That was irrelevant. The fresh

food was back in the dining room and she didn't plan to go back out there before the others were done eating.

Eileen moved to the sink and wet a rag. She lifted her hem and began scrubbing at the food spatters on her skirt with firm, even strokes. Too bad she hadn't been wearing the black skirt. She no longer had so much clothing that she could afford to discard something merely because it was stained.

Her stomach rumbled—she'd had a very light lunch. She supposed she could always open one of the jars of vegetables she'd put up from her garden. But after the savory meal she'd just dished up for the others, she had very little enthusiasm for such fare.

Perhaps she would just wait. Once the dishes were washed and the children were put down for the night she could come back here and snack on whatever leftovers were available.

The door opened behind her and she quickly dropped her skirt. Then she turned around with hastily mustered dignity. Mr. Tucker stood in the doorway, looking oddly diffident.

She managed a haughty look. "I will thank you, sir, to knock when entering a room with a closed door."

"My apologies, ma'am. I guess I'm just not used to knocking before entering a kitchen."

He was quite right, but she ignored both that and the hint of amusement in his tone. "And just what are you doing following me in here? Shouldn't you be keeping an eye on the children?"

"The better question is, what are *you* doing in here. After we said the blessing I told the kids I'd check on you. They all think you're angry with them, or at least with Harry."

It seemed she was failing in at least one area of her

duties as a hostess. "Please put their minds at ease." She brushed at her skirt, keeping her expression politely distant. "You may assure them it is only that I prefer to take my meals in private."

"Nonsense."

She stiffened. Had he just called her a *liar?*

"You were all set to eat in the dining room before Harry's accident."

He had her there, so she held her tongue.

"Accidents happen—" his voice had taken on a more cajoling tone "—especially when children are involved. But as adults we need to be understanding and forgiving. They shouldn't be made to feel that they've been found lacking."

Time to put an end to this. She tilted up her head and gave him a direct look. "Again, I apologize if they misread my mood. Was there anything else?"

Her words only seemed to intensify his irritation. "Reassurances from me won't help the situation—they need to see it for themselves. You can't really want to have the children think you don't care for their company."

Why couldn't the man just drop the subject and go away? "The children have you and Miss Jacobs to help build their self-esteem. My function is to provide shelter, and perhaps also provide them with instruction on matters of propriety and taste."

"And do you consider your current actions a good example for them to follow?"

She had no answer for that.

"Just put aside your own feelings for a moment and think of theirs. Surely you can do this one thing, just to put their minds at ease."

She knew he was trying to manipulate her by playing

on her sympathies. But that didn't stop her from feeling a pang of guilt.

"Afterward," he continued, "if you want to eat every other meal for the rest of your life in total isolation, then I won't interfere."

His sarcasm was easier to deal with than his cajoling. "And what makes you think you have the right to interfere now?"

He threw up his hands. "Have it your way."

He pushed out of the room in a huff, and Eileen heard him mutter something that sounded suspiciously like *impossible woman*.

She sagged against the counter, feeling more than a bit sorry for herself. There were tears pressing against the back of her eyes, but she refused to let them fall. Better he think her selfish than that he learn the pitiful truth.

Without warning the door swung open again.

"I don't think you truly under—" Mr. Tucker paused midsentence, studying her face. Then he gave a short bow. "Forgive me for being such a thoughtless lout. I'm sorry if I upset you—of course you have every right to your privacy."

It was his unexpected kindness that did her in. "I don't have another plate!" She clapped a hand over her mouth. She hadn't meant to blurt that out—she *wasn't* a blurter. But at least she had the satisfaction of seeing surprise replace the sympathy on his face.

He recovered a moment later and gave her an incredulous smile. "Is that all?"

"Is that *all*?" She took a deep breath, calming herself and trying to reclaim her dignity by brute force. "Mr. Tucker, it seems to me a plate is an essential part of the meal process."

"Well, sure, but one can get creative and improvise."

Without waiting for her response, he moved to her cupboards and shifted a few things around.

She watched him, trying to figure out how to get the situation back under control after her pitiful confession. What must he think of her now?

"Ah, here we go." He turned back to her in triumph. "Two shallow bowls."

Did he really expect her to eat from a bowl while he and the others ate from plates? That would be so undignified. "Bowls are for soups and stews."

His cocky attitude didn't falter. "What I was *actually* thinking was that in the future, we can serve Molly's and Joey's food in these while the rest of us eat from the plates." His pleased-with-himself grin should have irritated her, but for some reason it didn't.

"I see." She supposed that could work. But it didn't take care of tonight's meal.

"As for today," he said as if reading her thoughts, "I can't eat my meal knowing you are back here alone and hungry. Please return to the dining room with me."

His smile was disarmingly charming, but she stiffened her resolve. "Mr. Tucker, please don't waste your time worrying over me—I am neither lonely nor unduly hungry. I have told you that I will not eat my meal from one of those bowls. And I can hardly swap dishes with one of the children now that they have already started on their meals. Feel free to make what excuses you feel necessary to relieve their anxiety." She marched to the pantry and snatched up a jar at random. "I will open this jar of—" she looked at it more closely "—speckled butter beans. It will do quite well for my dinner." Hopefully she put more enthusiasm in her voice than she truly felt for the bland fare.

Did he actually roll his eyes at her?

Chapter Nine

Simon couldn't believe Mrs. Pierce would rather go hungry than sacrifice her dignity. But he was relieved to discover that *that* was her issue rather than a selfish desire to make Harry feel bad.

If the infuriating woman would just relax and handle the situation with a touch of humor, no one would give it a second thought. But humor didn't seem to be a strength of hers—he'd have to come up with something else— something that would allow her the cold comfort of her dignity. "All right, if you won't eat from a bowl, perhaps you can claim to have a light appetite and eat from one of the saucers."

There was no thawing in her demeanor. "Those saucers are for the dessert. If I take one for my meal, then we will be short one when it comes time to serve the pie."

That was an easy fix. "Not necessarily. I'll just eat my dessert from my dinner plate. No one will think anything of it."

Still she hesitated, so he tried another approach. "If you won't do it for yourself, then do it for the children. Right now they still think you're angry with Harry. And the lon-

ger we stay back here, the stronger that feeling will grow."
He gave her a direct look. "*Are* you angry with Harry?"

"I've already told you I wasn't," she said stiffly. Then
she unbent slightly. "Actually, I suppose I *was* angry at
the time."

He was pleasantly surprised by her honesty. It con-
firmed his belief that she was a woman of integrity.

"But only for a moment," she continued. "Anger is a
useless emotion that accomplishes nothing."

At least they agreed on that point. He gave her what he
hoped was a persuasive smile. "I know eating from a sau-
cer is not the most dignified way to take your meal, but
I'd consider it a great favor if you'd do so just this once.
Come on and rejoin us in the dining room so the children
can see for themselves you're not angry."

He thought he could detect some of her resolve slipping and searched for a way to press his advantage. "You
said earlier that you wanted to give the children instruction on social skills. Isn't showing grace under pressure
one of those skills?"

She didn't say anything for several heartbeats. Then
she nodded. "You are correct. And if it truly means that
much to you and the children, I suppose I could make do,
just this once."

"Thank you. Your selflessness is a wonderful example
for the children."

She moved to the door, her expression composed. She
either hadn't heard the teasing note in his words or chose
to ignore it.

When they entered the dining room, all discussion
stopped and the children studied them with wary expressions.

"My apologies for being gone so long," Mrs. Pierce said
pleasantly. "I wanted to clean my skirt before the stain

set." She casually reached for one of the nearby saucers, then sat down with a graceful movement.

Simon studied her relaxed demeanor with approval. One would think her the hostess to a gathering of welcome friends rather than unanticipated houseguests, most of whom were children.

She looked around the table. "I declare, it's been more than two years since I sat with so many for a meal in here. It feels almost like a dinner party."

"I like parties," Molly said hopefully. "Me and Flossie have tea parties sometimes."

"Tea parties are quite nice," Mrs. Pierce agreed. "Perhaps we can have one while you are here."

Simon felt some of the tension ease from the room.

"I understand you had the opportunity to visit the Blue Bottle Sweet Shop this afternoon," she said to Harry. "Were you able to sample any of Mrs. Dawson's fine treats?"

"Yes, ma'am." The boy sat up straighter. "I never tasted such fine caramels in all my born days."

She smiled. "Caramels were always my favorite treat as a little girl, as well."

Then she turned to one of the other children to ask a question about their meal at Daisy's restaurant.

Throughout the meal she was a gracious hostess, making certain the conversation didn't lapse or grow stale and trying to draw everyone out. She might not have much experience with children, Simon reflected, but her social skills were excellent.

Once the meal was over, Simon stood. "All right, it's time for us to show Mrs. Pierce how much we appreciate her hospitality. Audrey and Albert, you clear the table. Rose and Lily, you take care of washing, drying and putting away the dishes."

"I'll help with that," Miss Jacobs offered as she stood.

With a nod, he turned to Fern. "If Mrs. Pierce would be so good as to show you where things are, you can help Molly and Tessa take their baths. Harry, Russell and Joey, let's bring in some firewood for the morning."

Mrs. Pierce stood, as well. "We'll also need some wood for the firebox in the bathing room."

"Then we'll take care of that first thing. Come on, boys."

Fern took Molly and Tessa by the hand. "Let's go get your nightclothes." She didn't so much as look at Mrs. Pierce.

Simon swallowed a sigh. He didn't know whether to say something to Fern or just hope things worked out on their own—he was no good at that sort of thing.

Dealing with the children's squabbles and emotions was something he'd expressly told Miss Fredrick he didn't want to get involved in. She'd assured him she was quite capable of handling that aspect of the trip herself. The possibility that she would become incapacitated had never crossed his mind.

Simon instructed his helpers on how much wood to bring inside and where to put it, then gathered up an armload to carry into the bathing room himself.

He'd realized her woodpile was nearly depleted when he'd checked it out earlier and had hiked along the nearby tree line to gather what he could find quickly. Tomorrow he and some of the boys would do a more thorough job. If possible, he wanted to lay up enough wood to last the widow through the winter before he left.

Simon stepped into the hallway a few minutes later just as Mrs. Pierce was leading the three girls toward the washroom.

"Good," she said when she saw him. "You can follow us."

She led the way to a room at the very back of the house. When she pushed the door open and allowed the girls to precede her he heard the little gasps of pleasure from Molly and Tessa.

"It's beautiful," Molly said. "This house really *is* a castle."

When Simon entered he saw what had triggered that reaction. The surprisingly large, beautifully tiled room was the picture of opulence. The impressively large, heavy-looking carved tub must have taken an army of men to install, not to mention they had to have built the room around it. A bench, made of cypress wood, sat to one side of the tub, awaiting the bather's needs.

Even the squat, cast-iron stovelike fixture near the tub had gleaming brass fixtures and fancy enameled face plates. As he stoked the fire, he took in the large reservoir built onto the top of the firebox.

Mrs. Pierce moved to the tub and turned on the water. "We'll let a little bit of cool water in here while we wait for the water on the stove to heat." She then stepped over to the stove to turn on the faucet there, letting in the water to be heated. At the same time he finished lighting the stove and stood. The action put them in unexpectedly close proximity for the second time today.

Not that he minded.

Not even a little bit.

Eileen's breath caught in her throat as she got an unexpected close-up look at his eyes. His flashing forget-me-not blue eyes that seemed to see so much more of her than anyone had before.

Shaken by that thought, she took a hasty step back and nearly tripped over her own feet.

He shot out an arm to steady her and she actually felt a tingle at that contact. This was ridiculous. She was no starry-eyed schoolgirl and he was no knight in shining armor. But her treacherous pulse seemed to think otherwise.

Her cheeks burned as Mr. Tucker gave her a knowing smile.

Fortunately, he didn't put her on the spot. "Since there are so many baths to be had," he said instead, "I'll get another armload of firewood.

Eileen watched him leave, still feeling oddly unsettled.

She turned to see the three girls watching her curiously and quickly pulled herself together. "It's going to take a little while for the water to heat up, so let me show you where everything is while we wait."

She turned off the tap on the tub, then quickly showed the girls where the towels and soap were stored. With their help she moved the screen so that it shielded the tub from the door. She also showed them where they could hang their garments while they were bathing.

She stepped out into the hallway and leaned back against the closed door, trying to gather her thoughts.

What was wrong with her? She hadn't even known this man for a full day, yet he was affecting her in an altogether uncomfortable manner.

It had to be only because it had been so very long since anyone had paid her this kind of attention. The unapologetic interest and appreciation were a heady tonic to her flagging morale. Even when he argued with her, he did it in a manner that made it clear he had really listened to what she had to say; he just didn't happen to agree with her.

But she was honest enough with herself to realize he probably treated everyone this way. It had nothing to do with her.

It would be a huge mistake to give in to the temptation to believe otherwise.

Chapter Ten

According to the children, it was a standard practice for all of them to gather together in the parlor before bedtime and have some family discussion time.

After everyone was seated, Simon looked around. "How do you usually spend this family time?" he asked.

"Gee-Gee has us each mention something that happened during the day that we're thankful for," Russell said. "She says it's important that we go to bed thinking on blessings, not complaints. And then we say a group prayer—we each take a turn voicing it."

The more Simon learned of Miss Fredrick, the more he appreciated how special she was. He nodded to the child on his left. "Would you like to start us off Audrey?"

The seven-year-old didn't hesitate. "I'm thankful that today I got to visit a candy store that was in a toy shop."

They moved clockwise around the room. Some of the children had to think harder than others—given the day they'd had, Simon wasn't surprised.

When they reached Dovie, she didn't question whether or not she should participate. "I'm thankful to have met such fine children," she said without hesitation.

Simon wasn't sure about Mrs. Pierce, but to his relief,

when her turn came up, she lifted her chin. "I am thankful for the generosity of my neighbors who provided the meal for our supper and other household items for our use."

He gave her a smile of approval before turning to the next person in their circle. Eventually they made it all the way around the room and back to him. "I'm thankful for many of the same things you all have already mentioned," he said, "but I'm also thankful that I have met these two wonderful ladies—Mrs. Pierce and Miss Jacobs."

Russell indicated it was his night to voice the evening prayer and the boy did it with a quiet poise and articulateness that surprised Simon.

After the final amens, Simon stood. "Now, it's been a long day, for all of us. I think it's time we turned in for the night."

"But we haven't had our bedtime story yet," Joey said.

Simon barely managed to suppress his grimace. "Bedtime story?" Surely they didn't expect *him* to take Miss Fredrick's place in that ritual.

"Gee-Gee *always* tells us a story before we go to bed," Molly explained.

Simon rubbed the back of his neck. "I don't think I know any bedtime stories to tell you." He turned, intending to ask Miss Jacobs for help. But before he could do so, Molly hopped up and went to stand in front of Mrs. Pierce.

"Do *you* know any bedtime stories to tell us?" she asked.

Mrs. Pierce looked startled, then she nodded. "When I was a little girl," she said slowly, "my father had a book of stories that had wondrous tales of adventure. I still remember some of them. I can tell you one if you like."

Molly nodded vigorously enough to make her braids dance. "Oh, yes, please."

"Very well. Take your seat."

Molly plopped down on the floor at Mrs. Pierce's feet and stared up expectantly.

Mrs. Pierce stared at the little girl a moment with one of her unreadable expressions, and he wondered for a moment if she would make the little girl move to a chair.

But she finally looked up and glanced around the room to include all the children. "Long ago in a faraway land, there was a mother duck who sat on her nest, eagerly awaiting the hatching of the six eggs resting there. She sat, and she sat, and she sat, until finally, one by one, they all hatched—all, that is, but the very largest egg."

Simon listened as she told the story of the ugly duckling who tried and tried to fit in with his hatch-mates, but never did. He was surprised at how animated she became, conveying emotion and character through her voice and gestures. It was almost as if she were a different person from the stiff, reserved woman he'd been dealing with all day.

Well, perhaps not *all* day. There'd been those two moments when they'd connected in a very personal way. There'd been nothing stiff about her then.

Whatever the case, she had the children completely enthralled. And as he listened to the story, she had him captivated, as well. It was as if that particular story had been written for him.

Like the ugly duckling, he'd been placed in the wrong nest and didn't fit in with the others there. Orphaned at nine, he'd ended up in his uncle Corbitt's home. Uncle Corbitt's son, Arnold, was a year older than Simon and could do no wrong. The comparisons between the two boys were as inevitable as they were harsh.

In the beginning, Simon had strived to please his uncle. He gave up his love of working with wood when his uncle sneered at such an occupation. Instead, when he'd turned thirteen, he'd apprenticed alongside Arnold at his uncle's accounting firm. He'd hated it—hated being hunched over a desk indoors all day, hated working with figures and files, hated the fact that no matter how hard he worked, how painstaking his efforts, his uncle always found something lacking.

He had spent four miserable years in that office, and had watched other young men move up the ladder past him, before he came to his senses and realized that he would never be good enough to please his uncle.

He moved out, apprenticed himself to a master cabinetmaker and never looked back. Like the ugly duckling, he'd discovered who he was meant to be.

When at last the story was over, there was a moment of silence when no one spoke and no one moved.

Molly, still wide-eyed, was the first to break the spell. She let out a big, happy sigh. "Have you ever seen a swan before?" she asked.

Mrs. Pierce shook her head. "Not in person, but I've seen pictures of them and they are truly beautiful, elegant creatures."

"I'm so glad the little duckling found some friends," Tessa said dreamily.

"As am I." Mrs. Pierce stood, her control now firmly back in place. "I believe it is time for you children to go upstairs and turn in for the night."

Molly jumped up. "But first you have to rock me in your com-prize rocker."

"What's a prize rocker?" Joey looked at Molly as if he thought she was getting away with something.

Mrs. Pierce answered before Molly could. "Since I don't have a regular rocking chair, Molly and I sat out on my porch swing this afternoon."

"A swing." Joey was immediately intrigued. "Can I see?"

Molly frowned at him. "I get to sit on her lap."

Joey frowned right back. "Says who?"

Audrey and Tessa chimed in with requests to join them, as well.

Simon intervened. "I don't think that swing could hold all of you at the same time. If Mrs. Pierce is willing, those of you who want to be rocked can go two or three at a time. But only for a few minutes, mind you. We don't want to wear her out." He shot the widow a teasing grin. "Not on our first day here anyway."

She didn't acknowledge his teasing, but he thought he detected just the tiniest smile trying to slip past her controlled demeanor.

Turning away from him, she nodded toward the kids. "Of course. We'll start with the youngest since they should be tucked in first. The rest of you will sit quietly here in the parlor until it is your turn."

Yes, she was most definitely back in control of herself.

"The night air can have a bite to it this time of year," Dovie said. "Wait here and I'll get a blanket for you."

While they waited, Mrs. Pierce gathered Molly, Joey and Tessa together, and then assured Audrey, Albert and Lily that they would be next.

"Mind if I join you?" Simon wasn't sure exactly why he'd asked her that. Except that he wasn't ready to turn in just yet. And that he found her company, if not pleasant, very intriguing.

At her surprised look he hastily raised a hand to forestall her response. "Not on the swing. I meant I'd like to sit out on the bench by the door. Just thought I'd enjoy the night air and do a bit of whittling."

Miss Jacobs showed up with the blanket just then so the widow gave him a short nod as she turned to take it from her. "As you wish."

Eileen escorted the three children outside. As they headed for the swing, she was grateful for the blanket. Now that the sun was down there was a definite chill in the air.

Almost before she had settled into her seat, Molly clambered up into her lap as if it were a prized position that one of the others would try to snatch from her. Tessa and Joey took a seat on either side of her and Eileen was startled to have Tessa burrow under her arm and Joey hang on to her other one.

By the time they were all settled under the blanket, Mr. Tucker had stepped outside carrying a pocketknife and a chunky piece of wood. She watched him for a moment, admiring the strength and confidence in his movements as he freed playful curls of wood from the stodgy block of pine. It was almost hypnotic.

"Sing me a song."

Molly's sleepily uttered request broke the spell, and Eileen guiltily turned her attention back to the children, glad Mr. Tucker hadn't caught her staring.

She felt self-conscious at the thought of singing with him there, but he seemed to be focused entirely on his whittling.

After a moment, Eileen set the swing in motion, and the children let out a collective sigh of pleasure.

Not wanting to spoil this fragile peace, she dredged up the memory of a song from long ago, one her father had sung to her. She began to softly sing the strains, halt-ingly at first, still very aware of Mr. Tucker's presence. Then more confidently as he showed no signs of paying any attention.

* * *

Simon kept his gaze focused on his whittling, but every other part of him was acutely aware of the woman seated just a few feet away. He'd felt her stare on him like a feather on his neck. He'd heard the hesitation in her voice as she began the lullaby and known it was because of him.

Then, when she'd settled into it more comfortably, he'd felt as if she'd accepted not just his presence but *him*.

Which were all just fanciful notions, and he wasn't normally given to fancifulness.

Listening to her now, he had to admit that she had a very nice voice—soothing and something he thought of as smoky at the same time.

It was the same with the story she'd told the kids earlier. She'd had them—even the older ones—eating out of her hand. It was as if, when she lost herself in story—spoken or sung—she became someone different, someone warmer and more approachable.

It had him seeing her in a whole different light. She might not have the friendliest of demeanors, and she obviously wasn't accustomed to dealing with kids. But there was an instinctual tenderness and caring below the surface that the children were beginning to respond to.

The puzzle was, why did she try to keep those virtues so well hidden? Because she obviously put up that cool, reserved front deliberately.

She finished the little lullaby she'd been singing and flowed seamlessly into a soft humming, keeping the swing in motion. He chanced a glance her way and saw Molly had fallen asleep and Tessa and Joey were yawning. Mrs. Pierce was stroking Tessa's hair with the gentleness of a loving caress.

Her demeanor seemed dreamy, unfocused—until she

glanced his way. Then her eyes widened as if she'd just remembered he was there.

Simon set his whittling aside and stood. "It's time to get this crew to bed," he said softly as he approached the swing. He reached down to take Molly and for just a heartbeat she resisted. Then she released her hold and he scooped the sleeping toddler up.

Mrs. Pierce straightened and patted Joey and Tessa's legs. "Come along, you two. Time for bed." She took each by the hand and followed Mr. Tucker into the house.

Fern met them at the foot of the stairs. "I'll take Tessa and Joey to their rooms and tuck them in."

To Simon's surprise, Mrs. Pierce didn't react to the challenge in Fern's tone. She merely surrendered the children's hands. "Thank you, Fern," she said politely. "I'll take Audrey, Albert and Lily out to the swing while you're doing that."

Simon followed Fern and her two charges up the stairs, but his thoughts were still with their hostess. Was she unaware of Fern's puzzling hostility, or had she just chosen to ignore it?

He remembered how woebegone the widow looked when he'd returned unexpectedly to the kitchen earlier. It had made her seem more approachable, somehow, more human.

More attractive.

Still, the idea that she could remain so calm over everything else that had been thrown at her today and then fall to pieces over being short by one place setting made no sense to him.

One thing was becoming obvious though—the ice queen was beginning to thaw. If he stayed here long enough, would he see her melt completely?

Chapter Eleven

Eileen headed downstairs earlier than normal the next morning. Truth to tell, she'd had trouble getting much sleep at all last night. So much had happened in just one day. To think, this time yesterday she hadn't even heard of Mr. Tucker and his charges.

And to be perfectly honest, it was Mr. Tucker himself who'd been responsible for her restlessness. In just one short day he'd managed to put her on edge, make her question her way of looking at things and generally upset her well-ordered life.

The fact that she had taken a little extra care with her appearance this morning and that she found herself eager to see him were proof that he was not good for her equanimity.

And, to be honest, she wasn't exactly sorry the children had descended on her house, either. Despite some of the problems having so many unexpected houseguests had introduced into her life, it actually felt good to have a purpose other than just surviving day to day, and to have people around her who looked to her for help.

And perhaps, once this little interlude was over and

her guests had departed, her neighbors would look on her with a friendlier eye again.

But for right now, there was much to be done. She had convinced Mr. Tucker yesterday that they should set a routine for the children, so now she must follow through with her plans.

Her foot had barely touched the bottom stair when she heard a light knock at the front door.

Wondering who would be calling at such an early hour and why they hadn't rung the bell, Eileen headed for the door. She opened it to see Hortense Peters's oldest son halfway down the front walk.

He turned back. "Hello, Mrs. Pierce. Hope I didn't disturb you or the other folks inside. Ma told me to just leave the baskets on the front porch if no one was up and about."

Eileen looked down and sure enough two large cloth-covered baskets sat there.

"Thank you—Dwight, is it? And thank your mother for me, as well."

"Yes, ma'am." And with a nod of his head, the lanky youth turned and continued on his way.

Eileen took hold of both baskets and headed for the kitchen. She pushed the door open with her hip, then paused on the threshold. Mr. Tucker was already there, getting the stove stoked and ready

He glanced over his shoulder and gave her a broad smile. "Good morning. Looks like I'm getting your stove heated just in time."

She moved to the table to set the baskets down, determined not to let him see how much he rattled her. "I see you're an early riser." She lifted the cloth on the first one to find it contained eggs, very carefully packed. A quick count revealed there were seventeen of them—quite a generous gift.

"One of the best parts of the day is watching the sun come up." Mr. Tucker stood and brushed his hands against each other. "I've actually been up for a while—I went over to check on Miss Fredrick first thing."

She met his gaze, trying to discern how it had gone. "How is she?"

"No change." He nodded toward the basket. "What do you have there?"

Eileen accepted his change of subject. "The ingredients for our breakfast." She checked inside the second basket and found it contained a length of summer sausage and two small loaves of fresh-baked bread. There was even a jar of what looked like pear preserves. She met his gaze again. "There is enough here to make a hearty breakfast for everyone."

Dovie bustled into the room just then. "Good morning, you two. I guess I'm the slugabed today."

"I believe it's more that we are up extra early." Eileen waved toward the baskets. "I figured with so many to cook for, it might be wise to get an early start."

"It 'pears like Mr. Tucker has spoiled us and gotten the stove going." Dovie peered into the baskets. "Oh, my, yes. We can whip up a fine breakfast with these ingredients."

Dovie crossed the room to pluck an apron from a peg by the door. "Why don't you two see about getting the children up while I start cooking these eggs."

Get the children up? Eileen wasn't sure she liked the sounds of that. What all was involved?

But Mr. Tucker was already nodding agreement and holding open the kitchen door for her so she swallowed her protest. She was very careful, though, not to brush against him as she stepped past him to make her exit.

"If you get Fern up first," he said as they moved to

the stairs, "she'll help you with the others. I'll take care of the boys."

He seemed all business this morning. Which was perversely disappointing. "Very well." Eileen gave him a stern look. "But please make it clear that they should straighten their beds and put their nightclothes away neatly before they come down."

He frowned at that, but then nodded and executed a short bow. There *might* have been a touch of sarcasm in the gesture, but she chose to ignore it.

When Eileen knocked on Fern's door, she discovered the girl was already awake. Had she had trouble sleeping, as well? Eileen felt her first touch of kinship with the prickly girl.

"Miss Jacobs is cooking breakfast," she said. "Time for everyone to get up and get dressed. Do you need help with anything?"

"No." Fern's tone was stiff. "And I'll help Molly."

Fern's tone indicated she thought Eileen would argue the point with her.

But she was mistaken. "Very well." Eileen moved back to the door. "I'll check in on the others. You two can join us downstairs when you are ready. And don't forget to straighten your room."

Eileen got the other four girls moving, helping them start on their morning ablutions before she headed back down the stairs to help Dovie in the kitchen.

Breakfast went much smoother than last night's supper had. Molly and Joey were given the shallow bowls to eat from rather than plates, which meant not only were there enough plates for the rest of them there was even one to spare if it should be needed. And rather than Eileen serving the plates, Dovie filled each plate with eggs and sausage from the stove and transported them to the dining room already filled. There was only the bread and jelly to be passed around at the table itself.

Mr. Tucker offered the blessing, including a prayer for Miss Fredrick's recovery.

After the amens were said, Fern spoke up. "May we visit Gee-Gee today?"

Eileen paused in her eating, curious to hear how Mr. Tucker would handle the question.

He hesitated, then set his fork down. "I'm afraid there's not much visiting to be done. I checked in on her this morning. She hasn't awakened yet. I think it might be better to wait another day or so before you try to see her."

"But she *will* get better, won't she?" Fern pressed.

"That's for the Good Lord to decide." Mr. Tucker glanced around the table. "The best thing we can do for her is to continue to pray."

The kids sobered and began eating their breakfast in silence.

Despite the somber mood his words had evoked, Eileen admired Mr. Tucker's ability to speak honestly but with great empathy to the children.

Miss Fredrick had chosen well when she asked him to accompany her.

After breakfast, as they pushed away from the table, Simon decided to speak up before Mrs. Pierce could bring up the subject of routines. "Girls, please take care of the table and the dishes this morning. Boys, you're going to come outside with me and help with some chores I have lined up."

"What kind of chores?" Harry asked.

"There are leaves to be raked, firewood to be gathered and some repairs to be made." He turned back to the girls. "Once the table is cleared and the dishes are done, I'm sure you'll want to help with whatever household chores Mrs. Pierce or Miss Jacobs assign you. Isn't that right?"

Heads nodded and a few "yes sirs" echoed across the room. He glanced Mrs. Pierce's way, but couldn't gauge her reaction. She certainly wasn't shy about speaking up, so he was sure she would tell him if she disagreed with his approach.

He turned back to the boys. "Come along, men. Let's get to it."

When they stepped out onto the back porch, Simon rubbed his chin a moment, trying to decide where to start. Then he pointed to the carriage house. "I think the first order of business is to take a look inside there and see what kind of materials and tools we have to work with."

"Sorta like a treasure hunt," Harry said.

Simon grinned as he led the way. "Exactly. Only we're looking for useful tools and supplies rather than jewels and coins." When they reached the structure, he had the boys help him open all the doors and shutters to let in as much light as possible.

There were two windows on both the east and west side, as well as a smaller door straight ahead on the back wall. That should have been enough to provide light to the entire interior. But vines had grown up over some of the windows and the rear door would only open partway. Which meant the light from outside was only able to penetrate about two-thirds of the way in—the rest of the interior was just shadows and musty odors.

Near the entrance was a collection of gardening tools that looked well used and well cared for. It included a wheelbarrow, which he figured would definitely come in handy.

As he examined the tools, he tried to picture the reserved widow using the hoe and other implements to work the soil in her garden, but his imagination failed him. What was her story anyway?

Her bearing and manner spoke of a privileged upbringing. And this home she lived in spoke of wealth. But she had no servants, and the house showed signs of having been stripped of many of its furnishings. And he had sensed some kind of tension between her and the other townsfolk yesterday at the meeting.

Had she fallen on hard times recently? But why would that have put her at odds with the community?

"What exactly are we looking for?" Russell asked, bringing his thoughts back to the present.

"An ax, ladder, nails, paint." Simon shrugged. "Anything that might come in handy for chopping firewood or fixing up the place."

"There's an ax," Russell said as he crossed to the left wall. "And a ladder, too."

"Careful." Simon quickly followed the boy. "Better let me get the ax down."

Russell frowned. "I know how to handle an ax."

Conscious of the boy's feelings, Simon nodded. "I'm sure you do, but I need you to help the other boys get that ladder down and drag it outside. Stretch it to its full length on the ground and then check the rungs for soundness." He placed a hand on the boy's shoulder. "I'm counting on you to make a thorough check."

Appearing slightly mollified, Russell took charge of the ladder and his small team, and they had the ladder outside in short order.

Simon took the ax down and examined it closely. It needed sharpening, but that was something easily handled. Otherwise it was in good shape. And he spotted a heavy mallet and wedge, as well. Both would come in handy when splitting firewood.

He joined the boys outside and was pleased to see the ladder was in good shape, too. One of the lower rungs had a small crack in it, but he could fix that. And, once extended, it would easily reach the gutters.

He'd have Mrs. Pierce's house and yard fixed up in no time. It was the least he could do for her.

And hopefully it would gain him one of her rare smiles in the process. Something he found himself looking forward to more and more.

Midmorning Eileen stepped out on the back porch and saw Russell and Harry hard at work corralling the sodden mass of leaves and twigs that had overtaken her lawn into large piles.

There was no sign of Mr. Tucker or the other boys.

The two boys paused when they saw her, and she stepped up to the porch rail. "Miss Jacobs has made some lemonade. She thought you gentlemen might want to take a break."

"Yes, ma'am!" The leaves were immediately abandoned as both boys headed for the porch.

"Where are the others?"

Before they could answer her, Mr. Tucker and the two younger boys appeared around the corner of the house. "Somebody looking for us?" he called out cheerfully.

"Just wondering where you'd disappeared to." Eileen noted the wheelbarrow loaded with firewood he was pushing. It seemed he'd had a very productive morning.

"I was just letting Russell and Harry know about the pitcher of lemonade inside. There's enough for you three as well, if you're interested."

"Yes, ma'am." The younger boys started for the porch, but Eileen raised her hand, stopping all four boys.

"Before you come inside you might want to wash up. There is a water pump by the carriage house."

The boys didn't seem overly pleased with her suggestion, but they obediently turned and headed for the pump.

Instead of joining them, Mr. Tucker started unloading the wheelbarrow.

She remained where she was rather than head back inside. To make sure the boys washed up properly, she told herself.

So why did her focus seem to remain on the man working at the foot of the steps?

"By the way," he said, wiping his brow with the back of his hands, "I took your advice."

She was surprised by the unexpected comment, but at the same time felt a little touch of pleasure. "And what advice was that?"

"To plan for the worst-case outcome." He stacked another large branch on the pile.

So she *had* gotten through to him. "What did you decide?"

"When I went by Dr. Pratt's office to check on Miss Fredrick this morning, I spoke to his niece, Mrs. Leggett, about possibly traveling to Hatcherville with us if we should need her services. She has some medical experience, so she could provide care for Miss Fredrick until she can resume her normal routines. And Mrs. Leggett is a mother herself, so she knows how to deal with children."

A surprisingly practical choice. "She sounds like an ideal candidate. I take it she said yes."

He nodded. "She did. I just hope her services won't be required."

"As do I."

He unloaded the last bit of wood and straightened. "I'll just put this wheelbarrow away, then I think I'm ready for that promised glass of lemonade." He flashed a grin. "But don't worry—I intend to wash up proper first."

He whistled as he headed for the carriage house, leaving Eileen staring after him. Being teased was an entirely new experience for her, and she wasn't sure what to make of it. On the one hand, it was a very undignified way to treat her, one she should object to. But on the other hand, when he spoke to her like that, when he gave her that look that seemed to imply a certain level of friendship, it made her feel warm and soft inside.

She had to keep reminding herself, though, that feelings were fleeting and could betray you. In the end it was respectability and prominence that mattered.

As the boys climbed up the porch steps she cautioned them to wipe their feet, then followed them inside.

And forced herself not to turn around to see what Mr. Tucker was doing.

Chapter Twelve

After the lunch table was cleared and the dishes cleaned and put away, Eileen announced it was rest time. The children were instructed to go to their rooms for an hour either to nap or amuse themselves quietly. As she had the day before, Eileen took Molly and Flossie out to the swing to be rocked before her nap. But this time she made certain Fern knew where Molly would be.

Rather than taking the opportunity to rest, Mr. Tucker slipped out to pay another visit to the clinic to check on Miss Fredrick.

He returned in time to carry a drowsing Molly up to her room.

"How is Miss Fredrick?" Eileen asked when he returned downstairs.

"There's been no change."

She noted the ever so slight droop to his shoulders. Knowing he didn't need empty reassurances, she held her peace.

He scrubbed a hand across his jaw. "I'm not sure how I'm going to tell the kids."

"Tell them that it is in God's hands, as is their own future."

"And if she dies?" The harshness in his tone hit her like a slap. "Are they to believe that was God's doing, too?"

The emotion in his voice was so raw, she wondered if he had struggled with this issue in the past. "Everyone dies, Mr. Tucker," she said gently. "These children should be well aware of that. But what you must be sure they understand is that, if she doesn't recover it doesn't mean God doesn't hear their prayers nor does it mean He doesn't care. It simply means He had something else in mind for Miss Fredrick and was ready to call her home."

He looked at her, and she watched as the tension in his jaw sloughed away. "I'll look to you to help with that discussion should the time come." Then his crooked smile returned. "You do realize that this also means we'll likely be trespassing on your hospitality a bit longer."

She lifted her chin. "On the contrary, it merely means you still do not know the end date, no more than you knew it before you checked in on the patient."

He shook his head with an exaggeratedly solemn expression that was belied by the twinkle in his eyes. "I've always heard one should be cautious when dealing with a woman who insists on having the last word."

"As you should be. Most women with that trait tend to have a quick mind and a sharp wit."

He chuckled. "I'll keep that in mind."

She let that go without comment.

"I think I'll go finish getting the carriage house set to rights," he said. And with a wave, he turned and sauntered away.

Had they actually been flirting? It was an activity she'd once excelled in, but it had been so long...

Pushing those memories away, she turned and headed for the parlor. Time to focus on something productive, like the mending that sat in her sewing basket impatiently awaiting her attention. She would most definitely *not* be focusing on that smile of his.

Strange, though, how difficult it had become to focus on even the simplest of tasks. Surely it was due to nothing more specific than the presence of so many houseguests.

As she accidentally jabbed the needle into her thumb she acknowledged that perhaps there just might be something slightly more specific tugging at her attention.

Mr. Tucker's visit to Dr. Pratt's clinic the next day bore no better news than it had the day before. Much as they tried to keep the children busy to distract their thoughts, a thick, somber cloud seemed to settle over the entire household.

That evening, when the last of the children were settled in their beds, Eileen sought out Mr. Tucker. She found him on the front porch. But he wasn't whittling. Instead he stood near the steps with his elbows planted on the porch rail, apparently just staring out at the sky.

She hesitated, not sure whether to approach him or slip back inside. Before she could make up her mind he glanced over his shoulder and gave her a smile. "Care to join me?"

With a nod, she closed the door behind her and joined him at the rail. They stood side by side, close enough to touch if they cared to, staring out at the night sky, not speaking.

The silence drew out but it wasn't awkward or uncomfortable, in fact it felt quite…companionable. He had burned the leaves the boys raked up earlier, and the smoky scent still hung in the air. A dog barked in the distance, and she thought of Joey and his desire to have a pet of his own. Which reminded her of her own desire for a pet growing up.

No, best not to think of the past.

Time to get back to business. "There is something I need to speak to you about."

"Oh?" He turned his head toward her, keeping his elbows planted on the rail. "Is there another chore you thought of that I can take care of for you?"

"Oh, no, nothing like that." Did he think her so mercenary? She was silent a little longer. "This is not exactly my story to tell, but I felt it important you understand, not only for your own information, but also to help answer any questions the children may have."

He turned completely around this time and leaned back against the rail, folding his arms across his chest. "I'm listening."

Having those blue eyes of his focused so intently on her like that was more distracting than she wanted to let on. "It concerns Dovie. When we head for church service in the morning, she won't be joining us."

Simon frowned. "Don't tell me she's not a believer. I've heard her pray and she seems quite sincere."

"No, that's not it. I guess you could say she has a malady of sorts that prevents her from going out amongst people."

A wrinkle furrowed his brow. "What kind of malady?"

"I don't really understand it. Ivy tried to explain it to me once. It seems Dovie gets agitated and physically ill if she tries to leave the immediate vicinity of the house. Apparently she needs to feel her room is nearby so that she can retreat to it if she feels overwhelmed."

"How unusual." He seemed more intrigued than skeptical. "So, has she always lived here with you?"

"No, she moved in this past summer. She actually lived in another town before that. But she lost her home and moved here to be closer to Ivy."

"If she can't leave the area around her home, then how did she make that trip?"

"My understanding is she took a sleeping draught and then Ivy and her husband took care of getting her here while she slept."

"That's incredible." His hand moved as if to touch her, then halted. But her own hand tingled as if realizing its loss.

"Thank you for explaining the situation." He turned back around to stare out into the dark. "You're right—the children probably *will* have questions. I'm not sure exactly what to say to them."

"You accepted the truth. Why shouldn't they?"

He lifted an eyebrow, an amused glint in his eye. "Is everything always so black-and-white for you?"

Did he think her too narrow-minded? She turned to face out into the night, as well. "Gray does exist, of course, but it's the color of shadows and fog. I find it best to stay away from it, if possible."

He didn't look her way, but she had no doubt he intended her to see the teasing smile that tugged at his lips. "An answer for everything."

As earlier, they were both silent for a while, staring out at nothing in particular. But this time it wasn't quite so comfortable. Was he as aware of her presence as she was of his?

"It's nice out here this time of evening."

His tone had been soft, but she'd been so lost in her own tangled thoughts that she barely controlled the start at the sound of his voice. Luckily he didn't seem to notice.

"The streetlamps are lit," he continued, "most everyone is in their homes, the stars are shining bright."

"One could almost imagine that the slate has been wiped clean and that tomorrow will bring a fresh beginning." As soon as she'd said the words she wished them back. Such thoughts were not meant to be shared.

But he'd already turned to look at her, a puzzled smile on his face. He brushed a stray hair from her cheek. "And what is on your slate that you wish wiped clean?" he asked softly.

That touch sent a shiver through her. For just a moment, she was tempted to tell him everything.

Then reason reasserted itself. She drew herself up and removed any hint of emotion from her face. "I believe everyone has some fault or other they'd like to rid themselves of, don't you agree?"

"I suppose. After all, only one man has ever led a perfect life."

She nodded. "Exactly. Now, if you will excuse me, I think I will retire for the night." And before he could ask her any more probing questions, she turned and went inside.

Simon watched her go. He'd thought, for just a moment, that she'd thawed toward him. But no doubt it had been the hour and the events of the day that had caused her to let down her guard. It had certainly snapped back into place quickly enough when he'd touched her. But he didn't regret the act. He'd been wanting to touch her hair all day. And it had been every bit as silky as he'd imagined. For a moment he tried to picture how it might look loose, tumbling over her shoulders.

Abruptly, he pushed away from the rail. Getting involved in this woman's business would be a mistake. His focus should be on fulfilling his obligations to the children and to Miss Fredrick.

And that meant getting them to Hatcherville as soon as possible, *not* dallying here in Turnabout. Hopefully, in no time at all this town, and this warm-below-the-surface ice queen, would be nothing more than a fond but quickly fading memory.

But as he climbed the stairs he had a feeling that the memory of this particular woman wouldn't fade quite so quickly.

The next morning was a whirlwind of activity as they worked to get all ten children ready for church. There were lost ribbons to be found, loose buttons to be reattached, shoes to be found, hair to be braided or combed just so.

By the time everyone was ready and lined up by the door, Eileen felt her hostess skills, not to mention her patience, had been tested to their very limits. But at last they were ready to make the three-and-a-half-block walk to church.

Before they could step out the front door, however, Tessa looked around with a puzzled frown. "Aren't we going to wait for Nana Dovie?"

"Miss Jacobs is not going with us," Eileen answered.

"Why? Is she sick like Gee-Gee?" Joey asked anxiously.

"No," Eileen hastily reassured him, "at least not like your Gee-Gee."

"So she *is* sick?" Tessa pressed.

Eileen cast a quick glance Mr. Tucker's way, but he was apparently leaving it to her to do the explaining. Very well. "Miss Jacobs never goes very far from this house— not to go shopping, not to visit friends, not to take walks, not even to go to church."

"Why?"

To Eileen's relief, Mr. Tucker finally decided to speak up. "Because something inside her won't let her. The same way Rose can't eat foods that touch, or Molly can't go to sleep without Flossie. Nana Dovie's heart won't let her leave this place. She can't help it, and we shouldn't think ill of her for it."

That seemed to satisfy the children. Without another word they exited the house and headed for the front walk. Eileen cast an approving glance Mr. Tucker's way, then thought better of it when she saw his self-satisfied grin.

That man didn't seem to have a humble bone in his body!

She stepped forward and took the lead with Molly and Tessa, while Mr. Tucker brought up the rear. It felt as if they were in a parade. Then she corrected herself. No, it was more like a mother duck trying to get her hatchlings safely across the lane and to the pond.

Pushing aside that unflattering image, she tried to think ahead to what they would do when they arrived. Her first thought was the realization that they would never all fit in one pew. Should they divide up the boys and girls as they had the floors, or should they put the older children together and the younger ones together? And however they did this, would Mr. Tucker expect her to oversee one of the groups?

In the end they went with the latter arrangements. The six older children sat in one pew while the four younger ones sat behind them with Eileen and Simon bookending them.

It wasn't until everyone was finally seated that Eileen breathed a sigh of relief. How had Miss Fredrick handled all of this on a daily basis, and without the assistance of Dovie and Mr. Tucker?

A moment later she began to sense something different. It took a moment for her to figure out what it was, then it hit her. There were people actually sending smiles of greeting her way.

She had so perfected the art of not meeting anyone's gaze these past two years, and not showing any outward sign of emotion of any sort, that she'd almost missed it.

It wasn't coming from everyone, of course. But there were enough that it was unmistakable. And only now, when some sense of welcome had returned, did she admit to herself how much she'd missed it.

Simon found the children surprisingly well behaved throughout the service, with minimal fidgeting on the younger ones' part.

After the service, several of the local children introduced themselves to the newcomers. If at least part of the reason was because they had been prompted by their parents, Simon had no problem with that. He let the kids tarry and visit for a while. It would be good for them to mingle with others their own age.

Mrs. Pierce stood next to him, her unapproachable ice-queen mask now firmly back in place.

Was it her choice not to mingle with her neighbors or had she been ostracized for some reason? Before he could speculate further, they were approached by a trio that included two women and an impressively large gentleman.

The man greeted Mrs. Pierce with a tip of his hat. "Good day to you."

She returned his greeting with a nod of her head. "And to you, Mr. Parker." Her expression never wavered.

Mr. Parker then extended his hand to Simon. "Hello. I'm Mitch Parker. I believe you've already met my wife, Ivy. And this is Miss Janell Whitman."

Simon acknowledged the introductions and then Mr. Parker spoke again. "Miss Whitman and I are the school-teachers here in Turnabout. We wanted to let you know the children are welcome to attend school while you're here in town."

Simon immediately liked the idea. It would be good for the children to be around others their age on a regular basis, and it would also give them something besides their uncertain futures to focus on. Not to mention that it would give Mrs. Pierce a break from having them underfoot.

"Thank you. If it turns out we have to make an extended stay here, I might take you up on that offer."

"Just let us know when you're ready," Miss Whitman added. "Do you know what sort of education they've had up to this point?"

"I believe Miss Fredrick taught them herself."

"Well, we can certainly work with them to see how far she's gotten with them. Are any of them eleven or older?"

"Fern is thirteen and Russell is eleven."

"Then they'll go into my class," Mitch said. "The rest, at least those six years old and older, will join Miss Whitman's class."

That would leave just Molly and Joey at home during the day. Surely that would make things easier on Mrs. Pierce. And, he had to admit, himself, as well.

Before the trio excused themselves, Mrs. Parker turned to Mrs. Pierce. "I know you have a full house, but I hope you don't mind if we make our usual visit with Nana Dovie this afternoon. I promise we'll stay out of the way."

Mrs. Pierce's demeanor thawed the tiniest bit. "Of course. Dovie will be expecting you."

"Thank you. Then we'll be by at the regular time."

As they moved away, Eileen spoke up. "Ivy is Dovie's foster daughter. She and her husband normally visit with her on Sunday afternoons."

Glad of the explanation, Simon nodded. Then he spotted Mrs. Leggett and Mrs. Pratt and excused himself to speak to them. "Is there any news?"

"My husband is sitting with her now," Mrs. Pratt said. "But I'm afraid there's been very little change." She glanced toward the children across the way. "Poor little dears—they're having a hard time of it, I imagine."

He thanked her for her concern, then smiled at the two women. "Whatever happens, I want you to know that I absolutely believe the doctor is doing everything he can. And that I appreciate all the care the three of you are giving her."

Mrs. Pratt patted his arm. "You're a good man, Mr. Tucker. The children are lucky to have you looking out for them."

Simon wished he felt as confident of that as she seemed to be.

He turned to find Mrs. Pierce standing apart from the others, a remote expression on her face, an expression that seemed aimed at no one in particular and everyone here at the same time.

It was eerie to witness, and more than anything else it made him wonder why she found it necessary to shield herself that way. Who or what in her past had done that to her?

Chapter Thirteen

When they returned to the house, Dovie had the table set and the food warmed up.

As they ate their meal, Eileen again did her best to keep a pleasant conversation going. But it was difficult when she felt herself being scrutinized by Mr. Tucker. It had started in the churchyard, his studying her as if he was trying to discover her secrets. And that was something she absolutely would not allow.

Mr. Tucker cleared his throat, and for a moment she thought he was going to address her. But instead he looked around at the children.

"I met Turnabout's schoolteachers today," he announced.

The children all paused and stared at him questioningly.

"They were kind enough to invite you all to attend school while you're here."

"What did you tell them?" Harry asked. "Are we really going to school here?"

"I told him I'd consider it. If we end up staying for any length of time, though, I think it would be a good idea."

"Then there's no point in sending us there," Fern said

firmly. "Gee-Gee is going to get better soon and we'll be on our way to Hatcherville again."

Eileen saw the small tic of emotion in Simon's face and decided to speak up and shift the focus off him. "I'm certain Miss Fredrick would agree that it's important for you to keep up with your studies."

"You don't know her," Fern said, "so you don't really know how she'd feel about it."

Simon gave her a lowered-brow look. "Mind your manners, young lady."

Fern leaned back sullenly and stared down at her plate.

"There are a lot of good reasons to enroll you," he said to the group at large. "As Mrs. Pierce pointed out, you need to keep up with your studies. It will also give you an opportunity to meet new friends."

"But we're just going to leave Turnabout eventually," Russell said. "So what good is it to make friends here?"

"Making friends is never a waste of time," Dovie said quietly.

"But—"

Simon raised a hand. "As I said, I haven't made a decision yet, but when the time comes, the decision will be mine to make and I expect you to abide by it. Is that understood?"

There was a chorus of "yes sirs" from the children, some less enthusiastic than others.

All in all, Eileen was impressed with the way Mr. Tucker had handled the situation. He'd certainly shown that he was able to use a firm hand with them when it was called for.

Simon pushed his chair back from the table. He'd eaten a bigger slice of pie than he should have but that apple and pecan filling under the golden crust had been too good to pass up.

Before he could stand, though, the door chimes sounded.

Mrs. Pierce looked up with a frown. "Now whoever could that be? It's too early for Ivy and Mitch to arrive." She stood and moved to the front hall.

While she was gone, the rest of them began clearing the table. When she returned a few moments later her gaze went right to him. Something in her expression alerted him that something wasn't quite right.

"Mr. Tucker, may I speak to you for a moment?"

"Of course."

He saw a look pass between her and Dovie, and immediately Dovie got the children busy with kitchen duty.

With a slight nod of her head, the widow indicated he should follow her into the hall.

"What is it?" he asked as soon as they were out of earshot of the children.

"Dr. Pratt is here to speak to you. He is waiting in the parlor."

There was only one reason the doctor would have come to him this afternoon. Simon steeled himself for the worst. Mrs. Pierce watched him, her expression impassive, but he thought he detected a note of sympathy lurking in her eyes. She either knew the reason for the doctor's visit or suspected the same thing he did.

Impulsively he touched her arm. "Would you mind joining us for this conversation?" He wasn't really sure why he'd asked her that, and from the momentary flicker of surprise in her eyes, she wasn't either, so he added quickly, "Whatever the news, it will likely affect our stay here, so you may want to hear what he has to say firsthand."

She nodded, her expression impassive once more. "Of course." Then she turned and led the way to the parlor.

When Simon entered the room, Dr. Pratt was standing, his coat over one arm and his hat on a chair beside him, as if he wasn't planning to stay long.

The physician stepped forward and shook Simon's hand, then wasted no further time in getting to the point. "Mr. Tucker, I'm afraid it's my sad duty to inform you that Miss Fredrick passed away a short time ago."

Simon raked his hand through his hair. He thought he'd prepared himself for this news but it hit hard just the same. While he hadn't known her long, Miss Fredrick had been a truly good woman whom he'd come to admire and respect. Even more so now that he'd had charge of the children for just a few days.

As for the children themselves, not only had they known her longer, but the woman had been a mother to them. How was he going to tell them they'd lost her? And what sort of reassurances could he offer them about their future?

They still had the house in Hatcherville, of course, and he could escort them the remainder of the way as planned. But then what?

"What sort of arrangements do you want to make for her remains?"

Simon hadn't even thought that far. "I'll contact her brother right away to see what his wishes are." Would Wilbur Fredrick regret that he hadn't tried to get here sooner?

Dr. Pratt nodded. "In the meantime I'll contact Mr. Drummond, the undertaker, on your behalf."

Mrs. Pierce turned to him and cleared her throat delicately. "If you like, I can go through her bags to find a suitable garment to send to Mr. Drummond for her to be laid out in."

He was both surprised and touched by her offer. It was something he wouldn't have even thought about doing. "Yes, thank you." He turned back to Dr. Pratt. "If you'll excuse me, I need to figure out how to break the news to the children."

"Of course, I'll leave you to it. Again, you have my deepest sympathies. And know that Mrs. Pratt and I will keep you and the children in our prayers through the coming days." He slipped his arms into his jacket and picked up his hat. "Don't worry about showing me out. I know the way." And with that, he left the room.

When they were alone, Mrs. Pierce eyed him with obvious concern. "Are you all right?"

He was touched by her concern. Having her here made him feel less alone, more able to deal with what was to come. "I'm still trying to get my bearings," he admitted. Then he tried for a bit of levity. "Are you going to say 'I told you so'?"

She gave a faint smile. "I wouldn't do that. Especially at a time like this."

He turned serious again, rubbing the back of his neck. "Do you have any suggestions for how to break the news to the children?"

"There's nothing that will soften this news, so I believe the straightforward approach would be best. The important thing is to be ready to answer their questions—both those they ask and those they don't."

She gave him a sympathetic look. "And there will undoubtedly be tears."

He cringed. He'd much prefer dealing with outbursts than with tears.

"Remember, other than Molly and Joey, they've all been through this once before."

"I know." And for his niece and nephew it had been barely three months.

He straightened his shoulders. "I'd best go ahead and get this over with."

She gave him a look he could almost believe was approval. "Would you like to do this alone?"

"No," he said without hesitation. "In fact I'd very much like for you to be there."

Eileen stood in the doorway of the parlor, watching as the children filed in and arranged themselves on the available seating. Dovie was there, as well. Mr. Tucker, who'd called them together, remained standing, his expression solemn. She didn't envy him his upcoming task.

She found it edifying, however, that he'd wanted her there, both when facing Dr. Pratt and now. Was it just for moral support? Or had he wanted her beside him for another reason?

But she would ponder that another time. Right now the important thing was helping the children deal with the news they were about to hear.

Fern pulled Molly up on her lap and had Joey sit close beside her. From the expression on the older girl's face, Eileen could see she had a good idea what was coming. The rest of the children sat willy-nilly on the sofa and chairs. Some even sat cross-legged on the floor.

When they were finally all settled, Mr. Tucker took a deep breath, and she could almost feel him gather his strength to speak. She had to anchor her feet to the floor to keep from crossing the room and lending him the support of her presence. She would have to settle for helping him deal with the aftermath.

"The visitor who came by a little while ago was Dr. Pratt," he began without preamble. "He had some sad news to deliver. I'm afraid Miss Fredrick has passed away."

Emotions zinged around the room like beads from a broken strand. Confusion, denial, grief, anger, fear—she felt the plunk of them all against her skin.

"Does this mean we won't see Gee-Gee anymore?" Joey asked.

"I'm afraid so."

Audrey ran up and latched onto him, her lip quivering. "But, Uncle Simon, we've all been praying so hard."

He placed a hand on her head, his expression twisting a moment before he spoke. "I know you have, sweet pea, but it was time for her to go home to heaven."

As if they'd been waiting for a signal, several of the other children swarmed around him. It was as if they were drawing on his strength to give them comfort.

But whose strength could he draw on?

Seeming to read her thoughts, he cast a quick glance her way. Then, with an inhaled breath and crooked smile, he turned back to the children.

Eileen noticed that Fern hadn't moved from the sofa, but there was a new tautness about her, as if she were trying to hold every bit of emotion tightly inside herself.

"You should have let us visit her." Fern's voice was tight with accusation. "We could have at least said goodbye."

"I'm sorry, Fern. But she never woke up. She wouldn't have known you were there."

"But *I* would have known."

The words were low—almost whispered—and for just a moment Eileen could see the hurting child inside her.

Then Fern straightened, and the hard shell was back in place. "What happens to us now?"

Mr. Tucker faced her over the heads of the other children. Did Fern see his sympathy as clearly as she did?

"The house in Hatcherville is still there waiting for you all," he said. "And don't worry, no one is going to split you kids up—I won't let them. We'll find someone very nice and loving to take care of you."

"There isn't anyone else as nice as Miss Fredrick." This comment came from Lily.

"Perhaps not, but we'll do our best."

"But what if you can't find anyone?" asked Joey.

"I will," he said firmly. "I promise you—" he glanced around the room "—*all* of you, that I will find someone who will not only love you but whom you can learn to love, as well."

Eileen was surprised by the promise. She had no doubt he meant it. But did he know what he'd just committed himself to?

"For now," he continued, "a very nice lady named Mrs. Leggett has agreed to travel with us to Hatcherville and stay in the house with you until we find that special someone to care for you permanently."

The children didn't seem entirely reassured by that news. Eileen could understand that, given all they'd been through. In fact, she would like to know more about this Mrs. Leggett herself. Would the woman understand these children and care for them as—

"Can't we just stay *here?*" Molly asked.

Eileen froze, unsure how to respond to that. For a fleeting moment she wondered how it would be to—

"No, Molly, this isn't our home." Simon's words and firm tone brought Eileen back to her senses.

Of course they couldn't stay here permanently. What had she been thinking?

"But there's plenty of room," Molly insisted. "And Nana Dovie and Mrs. Pierce like us." She turned to face them, her expression reflecting a sudden doubt. "Don't you?"

Dovie gave her a broad, reassuring smile. "Of course we do."

Eileen chose her words carefully. "I do indeed like you, Molly. But there is another house waiting for you, the house your Gee-Gee purchased especially for you. And of course you must do as your uncle Simon says, because he only wants what is best for you."

And staying here under her roof was obviously not what anyone would consider best for them.

Including her.

As the children headed upstairs for their afternoon quiet time, Simon reflected that for once he was glad Mrs. Pierce had set up routines for them to follow. In fact, he could use some quiet time of his own right now.

Unfortunately there was still a lot to be done.

He stepped out onto the front porch, feeling the need for fresh air and open spaces.

"So what will you do now?"

He looked over his shoulder, surprised to see Mrs. Pierce standing in the doorway. He hadn't even heard the door open. Was that sympathy in her expression?

He turned back around to study the live oak that shaded one side of her front lawn. "After the funeral I'll go on to Hatcherville with the children." The enormity of that was still sinking in. "Hopefully Mrs. Leggett is still willing to accompany me to help with the children while I look for a permanent housekeeper and caretaker for the children."

She joined him at the rail without saying anything.

Strange how today he found her reserve and quiet dignity rather soothing. "Do you know Mrs. Leggett?"

"Not well. I understand she grew up here in Turnabout,

but moved away when she married her uncle's apprentice. But all of that took place before I moved here. She moved back to Turnabout recently when her husband died."

He nodded, understanding the woman's need to be around family while she adjusted to the tragedy.

"How soon will you be leaving?" Mrs. Pierce asked a moment later.

Her tone and expression gave nothing away so he couldn't tell what she was feeling. Was she merely curious? Or eager to see the last of them? "As soon after the funeral as possible."

As he said the words it hit him that in a few days he'd not only be leaving Turnabout, but he'd be leaving *her* and would likely never see her again.

And that bothered him much more than it should have, given the length and nature of their relationship. But she'd somehow insinuated herself into his world, had tickled his curiosity to unlock her secrets. He wanted to figure out why she was the way she was, why preparing for any situation and having rigid routines were so important to her, why she seemed at odds with her neighbors—folks who from all appearances were good-hearted people.

And above all, he wanted to find out how to put a permanent dent in her remote, ice-queen guise.

None of which he could pursue now.

Before either of them could say more, the front gate opened, and Ivy and Mitch stepped onto the walk. He'd forgotten that they'd mentioned coming by to visit Dovie.

As soon as the greetings were exchanged he excused himself to head over to the depot. He felt guilty for leaving Mrs. Pierce to make the explanations and deliver the news without him, but he wasn't in the mood to be around people right now.

Besides, he needed to get the telegram off to Miss Fredrick's brother right away. He supposed, if the man wanted to bury his sister back in St. Louis, it would mean making that return trip himself. Miss Fredrick deserved the escort, even in death, and it was only right for the children to attend the funeral, whether Mr. Fredrick would welcome them there or not.

Would Mrs. Leggett agree to accompany them on that trip, as well? But it was the image of Mrs. Pierce getting on that train with them rather than Mrs. Leggett that flashed through his mind.

And why that had happened was something he didn't want to explore at the moment.

Edgy and restless, Simon decided to take a walk when he left the depot. Hands jammed in his pockets, he wandered through town. Ten kids, and all of them his sole responsibility. This wasn't what he'd signed on for when he agreed to escort them to their new home. He'd asked Miss Fredrick to take Audrey and Albert in because he couldn't handle taking care of *two* kids.

And he'd made those kids promises just now, promises that he had no way of knowing if he could fulfill. What kind of man did that?

He looked up to find himself on the outskirts of town. He hadn't been out this way before. With a shrug, he continued walking, this time paying a little more attention to his surroundings.

He made a mental note of a spot he passed that looked promising for gathering more firewood. A little farther along stood a trio of persimmon trees that were heavy with fruit. He could tell that as soon as they had the first frost here, the fruit would be ready to pick. Maybe they could make an outing of it. He could bring the kids here to help him pick a bucketful or two. It would make for a tasty addition to Mrs. Pierce's pantry.

Then he remembered they wouldn't be here for first frost.

Simon halted abruptly. What was he doing? He should be back at the house before the children came downstairs.

No matter whether he wanted it or not, they were his responsibility, not that of Dovie or Mrs. Pierce.

He did an about-face and marched quickly back in the direction of town.

Eileen sat in the parlor, adjusting the hem and seams of the skirt from one of her mourning dresses. Providing the children with appropriate mourning clothes for Miss Fredrick's funeral seemed the least she could do.

Her mind, however, was on Mr. Tucker.

Where was he? He'd said he had to send a telegram, but he'd been gone for over an hour now. Ivy and Mitch had already taken their leave. The children had come downstairs a few minutes ago. They were more subdued than normal but that was to be expected. When they'd asked after Mr. Tucker and learned he was out, however, she'd seen several exchanged glances among the older children. It hadn't helped that they'd heard the blast of a train whistle soon after.

Were they worried he'd abandoned them? She was absolutely convinced that Mr. Tucker would never do such a thing, but she was irritated that he wouldn't realize that his disappearance at a time like this would affect the children in that way.

And she intended to tell him so.

Just as soon as he returned.

Chapter Fourteen

As it turned out, when Mr. Tucker returned, Eileen didn't have the heart to scold him. Though he wore his usual smile and had the same easy manner with the children, she could see the small lines around his eyes that spoke of worry or weariness, or both.

An hour or so later, Lionel showed up with a telegram for Mr. Tucker.

She watched as he read it. He clenched his jaw as tight as a bully's fist. Then he handed her the telegram without saying a word.

Eileen shifted her gaze from his face to the paper in her hand and read the terse missive.

BEST TO BURY HER THERE. PLEASE SEE TO ARRANGEMENTS.
WILL ARRIVE TUESDAY TO ATTEND FUNERAL.
W. FREDRICK

When she looked up again, he was pacing.

"A surprising decision," Eileen said carefully, "but I'm

sure he has his reasons." Though she couldn't quite curb her curiosity about what those reasons might be.

His pacing didn't slow. "I'll admit that it does simplify matters for me. But it just seems wrong to make this her last resting place, a town where she has no ties and there will be no one to mourn her."

"It is her body that is being laid to rest," Eileen said gently, "not her spirit. Those who loved her don't need a headstone to remember her by."

He finally stopped pacing and met her gaze. "You're right, of course. And I don't have a right to judge—her brother *does* plan to attend the funeral after all." His expression eased. "This also means I won't have to put the kids through a return trip to St. Louis."

He nodded his head as if coming to a decision. "But whatever her brother's plans, I intend to make certain Miss Fredrick has the best funeral service I can arrange."

She believed him. "Have you ever met Mr. Fredrick?" she asked.

"No. But Sally told me about him in her letters. He apparently didn't approve of his sister taking in all the children. There were some…issues. The two of them had harsh words over it and were barely on speaking terms."

She wondered what he meant by *issues*. But she respected his reluctance to spread gossip so she let the subject lie.

"That's a shame," she said instead. "Especially since his sister went to such great lengths to build a family for these children." Then she had another thought. "Do you think he'll want to take in the children now—he is related to three of the girls, isn't he?"

"I doubt he'll want to take them in."

That wasn't really an answer. "But if he *does,* will you allow them to be split up that way?"

"I don't know that I could stop it. He is, after all, their closest relative."

"Oh."

He must have heard the concern in her voice because he gave her a reassuring smile. "As I said, that's one thing that I *don't* have to worry about—I'm sure he won't want to take them."

Eileen wasn't entirely reassured but she let the matter drop. After all, the matter was really none of her concern.

So why did she feel so personally touched by their situation?

Simon received a second telegram from Wilbur Fredrick the next morning. This one asked him to have Miss Fredrick's personal effects gathered up to be given to him when he arrived. He also wanted to make certain the funeral was scheduled for Tuesday afternoon, the day he and his wife were due to arrive.

It appeared the man didn't plan to spend more than the one night in Turnabout. Which was fine by Simon. The less the children were exposed to the man, the better.

He spoke to Mrs. Leggett again, and she assured him she was still willing to go with him to Hatcherville to take care of the children.

With Mrs. Pierce's permission, Simon invited her and her daughter over to allow them and the children to get acquainted.

All in all it was a good meeting. Mrs. Leggett was composed but friendly. Her daughter seemed overwhelmed by the sheer number of people in the room, but she warmed to the children eventually.

As for his charges, they were polite but wary. While there were no strong bonds forged during the meeting, it was a start.

* * *

Eileen watched the ease with which Mrs. Leggett interacted with the children. It was as if they instinctively recognized her maternal qualities, something Eileen knew she lacked.

She tried to ignore the sharp jab of jealousy that thought produced, especially when Molly introduced Flossie to the woman. She'd thought she had adjusted to the fact that she would never have children of her own, but it seemed she hadn't.

Later, when she was alone, she turned to silent prayer.

Heavenly Father, I know I've been so blessed in my life and that I've done things that have let You down. Help me to focus on the good and not wallow in self-pity when I see others who have the things I want.

"Mrs. Pierce?"

Eileen looked down to see Molly standing there, looking up at her with liquid-filled, pleading eyes.

Alarmed that something might have happened to her, Eileen stooped down and mentally made note of where Simon was in case she needed him. "Yes, sweetheart? What is it?"

The little girl held out her doll and Eileen saw a tiny tear in one of her cloth arms. "Flossie has a boo-boo. Can you fix it for me like Gee-Gee used to?"

Relieved that is wasn't anything more serious, Eileen was nevertheless startled that Molly had come to her for help rather than Doyie or Mrs. Leggett. Then she smiled at the girl. "Poor Flossie. But I think I can fix her up. Do you want to help?"

Molly's expression immediately blossomed into a toothy smile, and she nodded vigorously.

Eileen straightened and held out her hand for the doll. "Then come along. Let's go fetch my sewing basket."

Rather than handing over the doll, Molly took Eileen's hand herself.

As they left the room, Eileen sent up a silent prayer of thanksgiving. Never had she had a prayer answered so quickly.

Chapter Fifteen

Tuesday morning, Simon went down to the train station to meet the Fredrickses. Though he'd never met them in person before, he recognized Wilbur Fredrick as soon as the man stepped from the train. There was a surface resemblance to his sister, but where she always wore a smile, this man looked dour. Of course, that could be the way he expressed grief, but there was something about the way the man carried himself that reminded Simon of his uncle Corbitt.

But it wasn't for him, of all people, to judge. He pasted a respectful expression on his face as he stepped up to greet them. "Mr. and Mrs. Fredrick?"

"Yes?"

He held his hand out. "I'm Simon Tucker. I'm sorry for your loss, sir. I admired your sister greatly."

"Ah, Mr. Tucker, thank you for contacting me." He gave Simon's hand a quick shake, then dropped it. "Is everything set for the funeral?"

"Yes, sir. Reverend Harper will perform a short service at the cemetery at two o'clock this afternoon."

"Excellent. Thank you again for attending to those details." He tugged on the cuff of his jacket. "I suppose there are some bills to be settled."

"Everything has been taken care of, except for the undertaker."

Mr. Fredrick nodded without comment, then changed the subject. "If you don't mind directing us to the local hotel, my wife and I would like to rest up from our trip before the funeral."

"Of course." Simon had expected him to at least inquire about the children. But perhaps the oversight was just due to travel fatigue and grief over his sister. He reached for the bag the porter deposited beside the couple. "It's just a few blocks. Allow me to escort you there."

Mr. Fredrick made arrangements to have their other bags delivered to the hotel, and then Simon led the way away from the station. In deference to Mrs. Fredrick, who seemed rather frail, he set a slow pace.

Mr. Fredrick broke the silence first. "May I ask just what your relationship was to my sister?"

"I regret that I didn't know her well. My sister Sally was her housekeeper for a number of years. Sally passed away a few months ago and your sister took in her two children—my niece and nephew—since I was not equipped to do so myself. In return I offered to help her where I could."

"And you were traveling with them to provide escort?"

"In part. It was also my intention to move to Hatcherville myself so I could be close by, both for the sake of my sister's children and my promise to your sister."

"I see. I don't understand what Georgina was thinking, embarking on such a trip. That's very likely what did her in. That and the strain of caring for so many cast-off children over the years."

Simon did his best not to react to that statement. "I know you're tired from your travels and are still in mourning, but I need to ask—do you wish to have any involvement with any of the children who were formerly in your sister's care? I understand the three older girls are relations of yours."

The man stiffened, as if Simon had insulted him. "*Distant* relations, I assure you." He gave the ends of his vest a sharp tug. "And no, Mrs. Fredrick and I will *not* be taking them in."

That resemblance to his uncle seemed even stronger now. "I see." Obviously this man was nothing like his sister.

Mr. Fredrick cleared his throat. "I'm sure The Kirst Sisters' Orphan Asylum in St. Louis will be happy to take them in. It is one of the charities my wife and I support."

Not if he could help it. "That won't be necessary. I gave your sister my word that I'd see them safely and comfortably settled into the home in Hatcherville, and I intend to follow through with that. I'm certain I can find a good person willing to serve as caretaker for them."

Simon saw the couple exchange a look, but neither responded. Instead, Mr. Fredrick changed the subject. "Have you gathered up my sister's things?"

"The things she had with her. But many of her possessions were sent ahead to Hatcherville. I'll have those sent to you as soon as I arrive."

"Did she have any of her important papers with her?"

"I didn't go through her things. She did mention she had the deed to the property with her, along with her other important documents, but other than that I don't know."

"And where are her things at the moment?"

"Mrs. Pierce, a widow who lives here in town, has provided lodging for me and the kids. Your sister's things are there, as well."

"I would appreciate it if you would have it all sent to me at the hotel as soon as possible."

"Of course." What exactly was the man expecting to find in his sister's things? Some kind of family heirloom perhaps? But they had arrived at their destination. "Here we are, The Rose Palace Hotel."

Mr. Fredrick seemed unimpressed with the exterior of the building, but he merely held out his hand to offer Simon a handshake. "Thank you for escorting us. I will see you at the funeral, I presume."

"Yes, sir. Would you like me to swing by here on my way so I can show you the way?"

"Thank you, but that won't be necessary. I'm sure we can get directions from someone here."

There was an obvious note of dismissal in the man's tone. Simon took his cue and accepted the handshake with a promise to send over Miss Fredrick's things right away. Then he headed back to Mrs. Pierce's home.

The only word he could come up with to describe Mr. Fredrick was *officious*. He was relieved the man had no intention of getting involved in the children's lives—that wouldn't have gone well at all. He just hoped the man had enough common decency to keep his feelings about the children to himself for the short time he would be in their company.

But he'd given the self-righteous popinjay enough consideration. He needed to turn his thoughts to getting everyone ready to move on to Hatcherville. Mrs. Pierce would be glad to get her home back to herself.

As he turned in the gate he realized he was going to miss this place. In the short time they'd been here it had begun to feel like home.

Truth to tell, he was going to miss the lady of the house even more.

Would she miss him, even if just a little?

The scene at the graveyard was solemn. Mr. Fredrick and his wife stood apart from the others in town. Mrs. Fredrick was dressed entirely in black, including a black veil that covered her face and a lacy black handkerchief that she occasionally dabbed beneath her veil. Neither made any move to introduce themselves to the children or speak to Simon.

There were a surprisingly large number of townsfolk in attendance. Dr. and Mrs. Pratt, Regina Barr, the Parkers and a number of others he only knew by sight. Even Miss Ortolon, the woman who had seemed so opposed to Mrs. Pierce taking them in that first day, was present.

The children were sober, several of them tearful. Dovie and Eileen had done their best to find appropriate mourning clothes for them. Since Mrs. Pierce was herself a widow, she had a few pieces she'd adapted and Dovie had items, as well. Fern wore a skirt that had been made over to fit her. A black cape was found for both Lily and Rose. Dovie found or made black bonnets for each of the girls. For the boys, they each had a black armband to wear.

Simon felt a touch of pride in them. Though there were more than a few sniffles and tearstained cheeks, the children were, on the whole, well behaved. Mrs. Leggett and her daughter stood with them, and the three adults arranged themselves so that each of the children had an adult close at hand.

Reverend Harper performed the service with as much solemnity and thoughtfulness as if Miss Fredrick had been a longtime member of his congregation. Simon was sure the woman would have been pleased.

Once the service was over and the crowd began to disperse, Mr. Fredrick approached him.

"There is a matter I need to discuss with you." The man didn't spare so much as a glance for the children.

"Of course." Had he changed his mind about the children?

"Perhaps you would accompany me and my wife to the hotel."

Wondering what this was all about, and more than a little concerned that he wouldn't like whatever it was, Simon turned to Mrs. Pierce. "Would you and Mrs. Leggett escort the children back to your home. Perhaps help them gather and pack their things for our departure tomorrow."

At her nod, he turned back to Mr. Fredrick and indicated the man should lead the way.

They strolled to the hotel without a word. When they arrived, Mrs. Fredrick excused herself and went upstairs to her room. Mr. Fredrick waved toward a pair of chairs in a quiet corner of the lobby.

Impatient to be done with this, Simon leaned forward as soon as he took his seat. "What can I do for you?"

"I've gone through all of my sister's things that you sent over earlier."

He certainly hadn't wasted any time. Whatever he was looking for must be pretty important.

"It was just as I figured. Unless it is among the things she sent ahead, which I very much doubt, Georgina didn't leave a will."

Simon held his tongue. *That's* what this was about? His sister's possessions?

"What that means," the man continued, "is that as her brother, I inherit all of her material possessions."

Simon hoped the man was not counting on a large inheritance. Miss Fredrick had spent most of her funds on the Hatcherville property. "I believe she had the majority of her funds transferred to the bank in Hatcherville. If you need my help in securing them for you, let me know." Not having any of Miss Fredrick's funds would make things a little tougher, but Simon wasn't particularly worried— he'd find a way to make it work.

The man dismissed Simon's offer with a wave of his hand. "I have a solicitor to handle those sorts of matters. What I wanted to make certain you understood is that the Hatcherville property now belongs to me."

Simon straightened. That was definitely something he hadn't considered. "Does that mean you'll be requiring rent money when we move in?"

"Actually, I plan to sell the property."

"Sell it?" Simon's heart sank further. Having negotiated Miss Fredrick's purchase of that same property a few short weeks ago he knew there was no way he could afford to buy it himself. "But where will the children go?"

"As I said, the good people at The Kirst Sisters' Orphan Asylum will be happy to take them in. In fact I've already discussed the matter with the Misses Kirst personally and they have said as much."

So the man had been planning this from the outset. "Surely you know this isn't what your sister would want."

The man drew himself up. "Mr. Tucker, as you've said yourself, you only knew my sister for a short time. And even if what you said was true, Georgina often let her soft heart get in the way of common sense. A failing we did not share." Mr. Fredrick tugged on his lapels and stood. "Now, if you will excuse me, I need to check on my wife. We'll be departing on tomorrow's train. Good day to you."

Simon watched him leave, his mind reeling from this new setback. Without the house in Hatcherville, he had nowhere to take the children. And sending them to that orphanage Mr. Fredrick was so fond of was completely unacceptable. What now?

Eileen was working in the front flower bed when Mr. Tucker returned to the house. Truth to tell, that had just been an excuse to keep a watch out for his return. And she was glad she had. One look at his face told her something was terribly wrong.

"What's happened?"

He raked a hand through his hair, not answering her.

She needed to pull him aside before the children saw him. She waved toward the bench. "Let's sit here a minute, shall we?"

With a nod, Simon followed her up the porch steps.

She took a seat on the bench, folding her hands in her lap, but he remained standing. "Now, what happened?"

"Mr. Fredrick is claiming that, as his sister's heir, he has ownership of her property, including the Hatcherville house."

"I see." That certainly explained his agitation. "I assume he's refusing to let the children live there."

"He plans to sell the place." Simon waved a hand indignantly. "As for the children, it seems he's already talked to the owner of an orphan asylum about taking them in."

Eileen stiffened. The idea of Molly—or any of the children—relegated to a group home was unthinkable. "But that goes against everything his sister stood for."

"I agree. But that doesn't seem to bother the man." He paced the porch like a caged animal. "He believes his sister's mission was beneath her, and he has no intention of sullying his own hands with it."

"Beneath her? What could possibly make him think

the care of children was beneath her? Is it because they are orphans?"

Simon shifted uncomfortably, then gave her a searching look. "I'm going to trust you with some information. But I need your word that you will treat it as confidential."

Eileen's throat tightened. From the look on his face, she wasn't certain she wanted to hear this. But she was oddly touched that he felt he could trust her. "You have my word."

"These children aren't just orphans—they are social outcasts."

"Outcasts?" She understood why that had happened to her, but— "They're only children. What could they have—"

"Not because of anything they've done," he said quickly, "but because of who their parents are."

Eileen sat back. *This* she understood.

"Fern, Rose and Lily's father died in prison. Their mother insisted he was falsely accused, but that didn't erase the stigma."

Eileen thought of Fern's attitude, and felt she understood the girl a little better now.

"Russell, Harry and Tessa's father turned to drink after their mother died. He got killed in a bar fight." He raked a hand through his hair. "As for Molly and Joey…"

There was a long pause, and Eileen braced herself, not wanting to hear about any ugliness that might be associated with the littlest ones.

He finally continued, "There are those who think they were left on Miss Fredrick's doorstep by women who were, well, to put it delicately, less than reputable."

Eileen knew exactly what he meant. "That leaves Audrey and Andrew. Surely they are not touched by any ugliness."

Mr. Tucker winced. "My sister Sally wasn't always the best judge of character. The man she married was abusive. There were rumors that his death was not accidental but there were never any charges brought against her."

Eileen didn't say anything. She was still trying to take it all in. She definitely understood why Simon had kept this information to himself. Appearances were important, after all, and one's pedigree was a big part of that. The stains these children bore on their individual pedigrees would be difficult to overcome.

She'd grown up around people who would have shunned these children just as Mr. Fredrick had. Her stepfather had had a difficult enough time accepting her, and her only sin was having a father who came from a family of unsophisticated merchants.

But these children were already carrying the burden of being orphaned or abandoned. It wasn't fair for them to have these additional blots on their names to weigh them down. And they were innocents, after all. Just as she had been. At least in childhood.

"I hope this won't taint the way you view them."

She glanced up at his words and noticed the doubt in his expression. How long had she sat there without saying anything?

She lifted her chin and met his gaze levelly. "Who their parents are is not their fault. They should not be held responsible."

He relaxed and then grimaced. "You'd be surprised how many people feel differently."

Actually, she wouldn't be surprised at all. "Including Miss Fredrick's brother?"

"Apparently." He leaned against the railing. "Whether for that reason or mere greed, he intends to see that the children do not take up residence in that house."

"Are you certain he has the power to do that?"

"Unless I find a will among her things in Hatcherville, which I very much doubt will happen, he is her heir by default."

"Why do you think it would be so unlikely to find a will in the things she sent ahead?"

"Because she had all her important papers with her. She was quite definite about not trusting them to the freight company."

Her mind immediately began looking ahead. "What do you see as your next move?"

"We definitely can't head to Hatcherville tomorrow as planned. I suppose I should let Mrs. Leggett know I no longer require her services—at least for the moment. And I should let the kids know, as well."

"What will you say to them?" She certainly didn't envy him that conversation.

"Just the bare facts, I suppose—that we're postponing our trip until some issues about the house are resolved."

"So you think there's a chance Mr. Fredrick will change his mind?"

"No. The only chance we have is if there is indeed a will amongst her things in Hatcherville, and that she worded it in a way to protect the children's interests."

"Which you don't believe will prove true."

A muscle in his jaw jumped. "I don't."

"Then what?" she pressed.

"I haven't had a chance to work that out yet." His voice fairly vibrated with his frustration, but she knew it wasn't really aimed at her.

Would he welcome a suggestion from her? "Perhaps you should talk to Adam Barr about this."

That brought a furrow to his brow. "Adam Barr?"

"You met him at church Sunday. He is Regina's husband and the manager of our local bank. He also has experience as a lawyer."

Simon stroked his chin. "I'm not sure what he could do, but I don't suppose it could hurt to talk to him. I'm willing to try anything at this point."

"He should be at his office in the bank. I'll take you there."

"You mean now?"

"Don't you think this requires immediate attention?" Considering the question moot, she added, "As soon as I speak to Dovie, we'll go."

He nodded slowly. "You're right. If nothing else, it'll help to know if I have any options I haven't figured out yet."

Eileen had to admit she wasn't exactly disappointed that Mr. Tucker and his charges wouldn't be leaving tomorrow after all. She'd gotten used to having her house filled with people. And to having Mr. Tucker to talk to.

Perhaps she could help the children deal with their grief. It had been many years since she'd lost her father, but she still remembered the overwhelming sense of loss she'd experienced. She hadn't had anyone to talk to back then.

Perhaps she could be that someone for these children.

Chapter Sixteen

Simon immediately liked Adam Barr. The man seemed to have a level head on his shoulders. He heard Simon through without interruption, then leaned back in his chair and steepled his fingers. "Do you know if Miss Fredrick formally adopted any of the children?"

"Not to my knowledge."

"And you're absolutely sure she didn't leave behind a will?"

"It's possible, but I didn't see one among the papers she had with her."

"Nevertheless we should carefully check what was sent ahead to Hatcherville. And I suggest you be the one to do the searching."

Simon had every intention of doing so. "And if a will isn't found?"

Adam spread his hands. "Then I'm afraid by default her brother inherits her entire estate. I'm sorry, but legally he is within his rights to take possession of the property and to do with it however he wishes."

Mrs. Pierce, who'd taken a seat behind him after making the introductions, leaned forward now. "Is there nothing Mr. Tucker can do?"

Simon heard the cool confidence in her tone, but this time attributed it not to a sense of superiority but to concern.

"He can contest the claim," Adam replied, "but there's not much chance he would win."

"But would that delay Mr. Fredrick's ability to sell the house?" Mrs. Pierce pressed.

"It would. But only for as long as the case was unresolved."

Simon frowned, wondering if this was a waste of time after all. "What good will that do if he's going to eventually win the case anyway?"

"It will give you extra time to try to convince him to do the right thing," she responded calmly.

Simon dismissed that as a futile effort. "My sister put every bit of money she'd saved into that property, and now Audrey and Albert have nothing to fall back on."

Adam's gaze sharpened. "Your sister invested in this property?"

Surprised by Adam's reaction, Simon nodded his head. "Yes, and I did, too. After all, Miss Fredrick agreed to provide a home for Albert and Audrey."

"Do you have any kind of proof of that?"

Simon tried not to get his hopes up. "I have some letters from Sally that mention her investment. And I have a receipt Miss Fredrick insisted on giving me for the bit I gave her." He sat up straighter. "Why? Does that make a difference?"

"It could." Adam's demeanor had changed to that of a hound on the scent. "If we can show that you and your sister have a partial claim to the place, no matter how small, then that might be the leverage we need. It could at least give you some say into the property's disposition. It's a long shot but one worth looking into—that is if you'd like me to?"

"Absolutely. What do you need from me?"

"Do you have these letters with you? And the receipt from Miss Fredrick?"

"Yes on both counts."

"Good. Get those to me as soon as you can." Then he gave Simon a direct look. "You do understand that it may take some time to get this resolved."

"How much time?"

"Difficult to say for certain. But I'd count on anywhere from two to six weeks."

"I see." Drawing this out would make things more difficult for the children, but he didn't appear to have much choice. The one bright side was that he'd be spending more time in Mrs. Pierce's company.

"I suggest you allow me to speak to Mr. Fredrick on your behalf before he leaves town. That will put him on notice not to act too hastily in disposing of the property."

"By all means. Do you want me to go with you?"

"Yes, but just to perform the introductions. I recommend you let me do the talking." He glanced at the clock on the wall behind Simon. "Let's say five o'clock. That will give me time to look over the paperwork you have and frame my arguments."

Simon stood and extended his hand. "Thank you for your help."

"Don't thank me yet. We still have a long way to go, and in the end nothing may come of it."

Simon escorted Mrs. Pierce from the bank, feeling more optimistic than when he'd entered. And he had Mrs. Pierce to thank for prodding him to take this step.

"It appears you and the children won't be leaving so

Get 2 Books FREE!

arlequin Reader Service,
**a leading publisher of
nspirational romance fiction,
presents**

Love Inspired HISTORICAL

**A series of historical love stories that will
lift your spirits and warm your soul!**

REE BOOKS!
et two free books
y acclaimed,
spirational authors!

REE GIFTS!
et two exciting surprise
ifts absolutely free!

Love Inspired HISTORICAL

2 FREE BOOKS

▲ To get your
2 free books and
2 free gifts, affix
this peel-off sticker
to the reply card
and mail it today!

W

e'd like to send you two free like the one you are enjoying now. Your two free books have a combined price of over $10, but they are yours to keep absolutely FREE! We'll even send you two wonderful surprise gifts. You can't lose!

Each of your **FREE** books is filled with storical periods from biblical times to World War II.

GET 2 FREE BOOKS!

HURRY!
Return this card today to get **2 FREE Books** and **2 FREE Bonus Gifts!**

Love Inspired **HISTORICAL**

YES! Please send me the 2 FREE Love Inspired® Historical books and 2 free gifts for which I qualify. I understand that I am under no obligation to purchase anything further, as explained on the back of this card.

affix free books sticker here

102/302 IDL GGF9

Please Print

FIRST NAME

LAST NAME

ADDRESS

APT.#   CITY

STATE/PROV.   ZIP/POSTAL CODE

◄ DETACH AND MAIL CARD TODAY! ▼

© 2014 HARLEQUIN ENTERPRISES LIMITED
Printed in the U.S.A.

LIH-N14-LA-13

soon after all," she said now. "In fact, it sounds like you may be stuck here until the end of the year."

He'd already given this some thought. "Don't worry. I promised I wouldn't impose on you for more than a few days, and I aim to stand by that. I'll start looking for other accommodations—"

But she raised a hand to interrupt him. "Nonsense. Of course you should stay at my place. The children are already settled in, and besides, there is nowhere else in town able to accommodate all of you comfortably. Unless you want to take over the hotel."

He felt as if a great weight had been lifted from him. "That's generous of you." Then he turned serious. "Of course some things will need to change."

"Such as?"

"We can't expect the townsfolk to supply our meals indefinitely. And we need to stop acting like visitors and begin to behave like residents."

She didn't seem as happy to hear that as he'd thought she would be. "I appreciate your intentions, but that's not necessary. The people of this town *want* to help."

"But I wouldn't feel right continuing to accept their charity." He raised a hand to halt any objections from her. "And don't worry—that doesn't mean I expect you to provide for all our meals. As I mentioned, I'm a handyman and cabinetmaker. I'll see if I can pick up some odd jobs here in town, then pay you what I can in room and board from that."

Was handyman work as far as his ambitions took him? "Perhaps Adam could find you a job at the bank."

He shrugged off her suggestion—he'd been down that road before. "Working with my hands is what I'm good at. It's how I make my living." Then he changed the subject.

"I have to thank you for suggesting I speak to Adam. He seems to be a good man to have in my corner."

"If anyone can get a good outcome from this, it's Mr. Barr." She glanced sideways at him. "What will you do if you don't win your case against Mr. Fredrick?"

The woman was always trying to look ahead. "I suppose I'll have to find another place for them to live. Even if I have to build it myself."

"So you don't consider sending them to an orphanage to be an option?"

"Not as long as I have a breath in my body."

Eileen found the passion in his tone reassuring. Just the thought of the children being handed over to strangers who might not treat them kindly, or perhaps even try to split them up, squeezed something in her chest.

"Supposing you do win your case," she said. "What then? I mean, how will you go about finding someone to take Miss Fredrick's place?" She'd already decided he couldn't hire just anybody. It had to be someone who would love the children and treat them like family.

"First off, I hope when the time comes that Mrs. Leggett is still willing to help us get settled in, wherever we end up. Then I'll take out an advertisement for a permanent caretaker."

"But how will you make your selection?"

He gave her a raised-brow look, as if surprised by her tone. "Trust me, I'll interview the applicants thoroughly. And check references carefully. It'll take a special sort of person to fill Miss Fredrick's shoes."

"You are taking a lot on yourself."

"They don't have anyone else."

"And once this paragon is found and they are settled in, do you still plan to settle nearby?"

"Of course."

Despite the fact that she would miss them, she continued to be impressed by his sense of responsibility to the children. Was it because his niece and nephew were among their number? Or would he have been this determined regardless?

She spotted Miss Whitman up ahead, stepping out of the apothecary shop. "Perhaps, since you will be extending your stay, you should get the children enrolled in school." She waved a hand to bring the schoolteacher to Mr. Tucker's attention.

Mr. Tucker nodded and stepped forward to let Miss Whitman know his intentions.

That done, they continued on their way.

"What do you plan to tell the children?" Eileen asked.

"That we've run into a bit of a snag on moving into the Hatcherville house, but that they needn't worry—I'm sticking around until we get everything worked out. And in the meantime, you have agreed to let us stay right where they are."

"It's going to be difficult for them to hear another bit of bad news."

"I think, for some of them, it might be a relief not to have to move just yet. After all, the place in Hatcherville is an unknown to them." He stopped. "There's something else I need to discuss with you before we reach your house."

"Of course." His tone had been diffident, as if he didn't think she would like what he had to say. Was there even more bad news?

"What Adam said, about my looking for a will amongst Miss Fredrick's things in Hatcherville—I think it best I take care of that right away, just so we have that question answered before this goes much further."

"I see." He was about to go off and leave her with the children. Thank goodness Dovie would be in the house to help her. "How soon do you plan to leave?"

He gave her a surprised look. Had he expected her to protest?

"Tomorrow."

Eileen tried not to wince. He *had* said as soon as possible.

"I need to collect the children's things, as well," he continued. "They can't continue with just the things they had with them on the train."

How thoughtful of him. "I'm sure they will be happy to have their belongings with them."

He gave her a relieved smile. "I truly do appreciate how generous you've been to me and the children. And I'm sure they feel the same."

His words, and the sincere tone in his voice, warmed her from the inside out.

As soon as they walked into the house the children gathered around, full of questions.

"Why did you tell us to stop packing?"

"When are we leaving for Hatcherville?"

"Where did you go?"

"Is Gee-Gee's brother still here?"

Eileen clapped her hands for attention. "Children, it's rude to all speak at one time. Quiet now, and give your uncle Simon a chance to let you know what has happened."

They quieted immediately, though they stared from her to Mr. Tucker expectantly.

With a look for her that she couldn't quite read, Mr. Tucker turned to address the children. "I'm going to explain everything and answer all your questions. But first, let's go into the parlor where we can all be comfortable."

She caught his gaze, wondering if she should join them or let him handle it alone. Apparently he understood her silent question.

"Mrs. Pierce and Dovie, if you don't mind joining us, this affects you, as well."

The children filed into the parlor and Eileen saw the apprehension in their faces. She couldn't blame them, given what news had been delivered in their last group meeting.

Mr. Tucker didn't draw things out. As soon as everyone was seated he spoke up. "I'm afraid there's been a hitch in our plans to go to Hatcherville tomorrow."

"What's a hitch?" Joey asked, wrinkling his nose.

"A delay," Simon explained. "It means we won't be heading there tomorrow as we'd planned."

"Well, I'm glad," Molly stated. "I like it here and don't want to leave."

"Well, I do," Joey said.

Eileen was taken aback by his declaration. She had expected something like that from Fern, but she'd thought Joey liked it here.

"Why is that?" Simon asked.

"Because I can't get my dog until we get to our new place."

Eileen relaxed when she heard the boy's reason. It had nothing to do with him liking or disliking being here.

"Besides, this isn't our home," Fern said firmly. "Our home is waiting for us in Hatcherville." She turned to Simon, her eyes narrowing. "Why can't we leave tomorrow?"

Eileen noted that the rest of the children wore expressions varying from worry to mere curiosity. Fern was the only one who appeared suspicious.

"Miss Fredrick's brother wants to check into the situation before we move in," Mr. Tucker explained. "It turns out the property might belong to him now."

Russell leaned forward. "But he hates us. If he owns that house, he'll never let us move in."

"I doubt he hates you, Russell," Eileen offered. "He doesn't even know you."

But Russell shook his head. "I know he does. I once heard him tell Gee-Gee that it was beneath her to take in such riffraff."

"What's riffraff?" Joey asked.

"It means he thinks we're rubbish," Fern said stiffly.

Eileen felt that insult as deeply as if it had been said of her. "Surely you misunderstood," she said quickly. "And if he *did* say such a thing, he would be quite mistaken. As your Miss Fredrick obviously believed, as well." How could anyone say such a thing in a child's hearing?

Simon wanted to do a whole lot more than give Mr. Fredrick a piece of his mind. Such pomposity and self-righteousness was inexcusable. But when it was aimed at a small child it was beyond mean-spirited. It was wounding, on par with inflicting disfiguring physical scars.

He took a deep breath, hoping to keep his tone even. "Mrs. Pierce has the right of it. Just remember how Miss Fredrick felt about you and ignore her brother's words."

"But that don't change the fact that Mr. Fredrick is gonna try to take our place from us," Russell said.

"Moving to Hatcherville is what Miss Fredrick wanted for us," Fern reiterated. "It's not right for her brother to try to keep us away."

Simon leaned forward, trying to get through to the girl. "I know, but Mr. Fredrick *is* her brother and her things belong to him now."

"Even our house?"

"That remains to be seen. But until we can untangle this mess, we'll have to stay put."

"What about all our things that were sent ahead to Hatcherville?" The girl's expression remained hard. "Does he own those, too?"

"No, of course he doesn't." Simon glanced around at each child. "Those things belong to you. It's just the ownership of the house and furnishings that we need to straighten out."

Then he smiled. "The good news is, while we're getting things all worked out, Mrs. Pierce has generously agreed to let us continue to stay right here with her."

"You mean we get to stay here?" Molly perked up at that.

Apparently the girl had formed an attachment for the place. Simon wasn't sure if that was a good thing or bad thing. "For a while. But not forever." He looked around. "But while we're here, I'm going to enroll you in Turnabout's school so your studies don't suffer."

"Does that mean we can go to a real school just like the other kids?" Lily seemed excited by the prospect.

Predictably, Fern was not. "Gee-Gee always taught us our lessons at home."

"And I'm sure she did a fine job." Simon was careful to keep his tone conversational. "But I know she planned to send you to the town school when we moved to Hatcherville. So I think she would approve of you going to school here."

"Me, too?" Molly asked.

"No, sweet pea, you and Joey are too young to attend the town school. You'll stay here and keep the grownups company."

"Okay. And Flossie can keep you company, too."

"When do we start?" Harry asked.

"Tomorrow."

That got everyone's attention. There were lots of exchanged looks and shifting in seats. "I suggest you each go up to your room and make certain you have presentable clothes."

"But most of our things were sent ahead to Hatcherville," Rose said.

"About that. After you kids go off to school in the morning, I'll be heading to Hatcherville to make certain there aren't any important papers amongst Miss Fredrick's things. I'll gather up your belongings while I'm there and bring them back with me."

"You're leaving us? With her?" Fern's tone made it clear what she thought of *that* idea.

"You are coming back though, aren't you, Uncle Simon?" Audrey's expression looked on the verge of crumbling. Too many people she loved had disappeared from her life lately.

"Of course I'm coming back." He held his arms out and she rushed forward. "Didn't I promise I would be around whenever you need me?"

Audrey nodded as he settled her on his knee.

"And I always keep my word." That statement gave him a twinge of guilt. A more honest statement would have been he always *tried* to keep his word. "So you see, I have to come back." He tapped her nose. "And when I get back I'll have all of your clothes and other things with me."

"Like my wooden horse?"

"Exactly."

That seemed to placate her, and he let her slide from his lap and return to her seat next to Albert.

There was an immediate clamor as the children began asking him to make certain he got specific personal items for each of them.

After a moment Simon raised his hands for silence. "I

promise I will get everyone's things. But I want to make something clear. I'll only be gone overnight. And while I'm gone, I expect you to treat Mrs. Pierce and Nana Dovie as if they were in charge—because they are. Is that understood?"

There was a chorus of "yes sirs" backed up by various levels of enthusiasm.

Simon stood. "Now, these two ladies and I have some things to talk over before I leave town tomorrow. Why don't you all go out in the backyard for a while? Fern and Russell, you two keep an eye on the younger ones, please."

Chapter Seventeen

Eileen had been impressed with the way Mr. Tucker handled delivering the news to the children. He'd managed to inform and reassure them at the same time.

As soon as the children obediently trooped outside, though, he'd excused himself from the room to look for the papers Adam had asked him for, leaving her and Dovie to discuss what was in store for them over the coming days.

"He's a good man."

Eileen glanced over at Dovie, surprised by the woman's out-of-the-blue statement. "He is." She was careful to keep all inflection from her voice.

"There's not many as would so easily accept responsibility for ten young'uns that weren't his own."

Eileen agreed, but rather than saying so this time, she changed the subject. "I hope you don't mind that I told Mr. Tucker the two of us would watch over the children while he's gone."

"Glad to do it."

"I think the first thing we need to decide is what is the minimum we need to do to get the eight older children ready for school in the morning. I want to prepare a routine that takes everything into account. It wouldn't do for them to be late on their very first day." She certainly hoped Dovie was more enlightened than she on that subject.

Dovie smiled, seeming undaunted by the task before them. "There are two main things we need to focus on, and neither one of them is difficult. First is making sure they all get up on time."

"Of course." Eileen had actually already thought of that one. "With so many to get ready, I think it best to set up shifts—by bedrooms perhaps." She raised a brow. "What is the second thing?"

"Getting eight lunches prepared and packed up." Dovie waved a hand as she continued. "We don't have lunch pails, so we'll need to fix something simple that they can carry in small sacks."

Meals. Of course. She should have thought of that without having Dovie tell her. Just another indication that she was sadly lacking in motherly instincts.

But she *was* a good planner. "Then we need to come up with eight lunch sacks as well as the meals. I have some fabric scraps we can use, but I'm not sure it will be enough to make all eight." She didn't relish the idea of cutting up another of her dresses, but if that was—

"I have a few old flour sacks I been saving for next time I got a mind to make a quilt. We can use those, too," Dovie offered.

"Good. As for what we'll fill them with…" She paused, distracted by Mr. Tucker's return, then turned back to Dovie. "As you said, we should start with something simple but filling." She mentally went through the items she had on hand. "A boiled egg. Some bread. A chunk of cheese. And I believe we still have a nice-size piece of summer sausage that we can divide up among them."

Dovie nodded. "And I can make some pecan and mo-lasses cookies tonight that we can add as a special treat."

Mr. Tucker groaned. "You ladies are making me hun-gry with all this talk of food."

Dovie grinned. "Don't you worry, Mr. Tucker. I'll bake a couple of extras so you can take some on the train with you."

He gave her a boyish grin. "Thank you, ma'am." Then he sobered. "But I'd take it as a great favor if you'd call me Simon. After all, you insisted I call you Dovie. And it looks like I'm going to be here for a while."

Dovie blushed like a schoolgirl. "How can I refuse such a request from a handsome young man like yourself?"

"Good." Then he turned to Eileen. "And I'd like to extend the same offer to you, if it's not too impertinent."

Eileen froze. The use of first names between an adult man and woman was an intimate thing and not to be taken lightly. Dovie was old enough to be Mr. Tucker's mother so that was a different matter. But for her…

The last thing she needed was to be the subject of more gossip, especially now when she was starting to see signs of acceptance again. She knew from experience that one could only get away with flaunting the conventions when one's place in society was beyond reproach.

His smile faded as he shifted on his feet, and she real-ized she'd let the silence draw out too long.

"My apologies," he said with a smile that had a self-conscious edge. "I didn't mean—"

She cut him off before he could withdraw the offer. "Please don't take this the wrong way."

"No, of course. It was presumptuous of me to ask."

Feeling she owed him an explanation of sorts, she lifted her chin, trying to say this before her courage failed her. "My standing in the community is not the strongest." It took every bit of control she had to say that matter-of-factly, as if it was of no consequence. "So I'm sure you understand that I would want to avoid anything that would lead to fresh gossip."

Then she managed a more genuine smile. "But that said, I would be pleased to take you up on that offer when we are here at home, just among family."

The flash of surprise in his expression gave way to a look that turned her insides to warm honey. Then he gave a short bow. "I'm honored by your trust."

She felt a tremendous rush of relief when she realized he wasn't going to press her on her confession or appear to think the less of her for it.

Of course, he didn't know the details, didn't know of her culpability in her husband's death. Would he still be as friendly if he did?

Simon excused himself a few moments later to deliver his papers to Adam.

As he headed down the sidewalk, he thought about that little speech Eileen had made. She'd delivered it in her best dry-as-a-kiln manner, but he'd sensed that it had cost her dearly, not only in emotion but also in pride. Yet she had done it anyway, and for that he couldn't help but admire her.

Perhaps she was warming to him after all. That thought put a little extra bounce in his step.

He couldn't help but wonder, though, what it was that had ostracized her from her neighbors. He considered asking Adam, but immediately dismissed the notion. If she wanted him to know, she'd tell him herself.

Then he grinned, remembering how, when she made that small concession to use first names, if only in a limited capacity, she'd spoken of the house as *their* home, and she'd spoken of the group as *family*. Was that how she'd really come to think of them?

Had she even realized she'd said it?

Not that it mattered, because she *had* said it. Which meant, whether she cared to admit it or not, they were getting through to her.

Perhaps soon the ice queen would be thawed for good.

As soon as Eileen heard Simon return, she stepped out into the hallway, closing the parlor door behind her. She couldn't tell from his expression how things had gone with Mr. Fredrick, so she asked outright.

He grimaced. "Adam presented the case very convincingly, but Mr. Fredrick didn't take the news well. He intends to get his own solicitor involved and fight our claim."

Not good news, but not surprising, either.

Simon held his hat in front of him and he fidgeted with the brim as he talked. "He also wasn't happy about me going to Hatcherville tomorrow without either him or his solicitor present. But he agreed that the sooner we settle the matter of whether or not a will actually exists, the better."

"Does that mean he will accompany you to Hatcherville tomorrow?"

"No. Adam suggested a compromise—that we have the sheriff in Hatcherville accompany me as I go through all of the items. That seemed to appease the man."

Eileen was surprised that he was taking the implied lack of trust so well. "So what is the next step?"

"Adam will contact the circuit judge to schedule a date for a hearing on the matter. And Mr. Fredrick said his solicitor would be in touch."

Eileen tried to find a silver lining. "Perhaps, once Mr.

Fredrick discusses this with his solicitor and sees what proof you have, he will be more willing to sit down and work out some kind of arrangement with you."

"Perhaps." His tone lacked any assurance. "But at least he won't try to sell the property before we settle this matter." He glanced around. "It's mighty quiet around here. Where is everyone?"

Eileen waved toward the parlor. "Working on lunch sacks for tomorrow."

He raised a brow. "They know how to make lunch sacks?"

She smiled, trying not to show how smug she felt. "Children can be taught almost anything if it is presented in the right way. Dovie made a simple pattern and the boys are cutting them out and then, once they are sewn together, they work on inserting the tie strings. The girls are embroidering each child's initials on their individual bags."

Which reminded her of something. "I have a question about the children."

He gave her a cautious look. "I'll be glad to answer it, if I can."

"I understand why the older children have different last names—those come from their birth families." She'd just learned their surnames when she was helping them trace the initials onto the cloth. "But why do Joey and Molly have Darling as their last names, especially if they are not siblings?"

He smiled. "It just so happens I know the answer to this one. Sally was working for Miss Fredrick when both Joey and Molly were left on her doorstep. Joey was first, and Sally said that Miss Fredrick thought long and hard about what name to give him. The first name was easy— her own father's name was Joseph, hence Joey. For the surname, though, that was trickier. She didn't want to give him her own, mainly so it wouldn't make the others feel he was more dear to her. But she did want to give him a special name so that later in life it might in some way ease the sting of knowing he'd been abandoned. She settled on Darling because every time anyone called him by his full name, he would be Joey Darling. When Molly came along, she used the same surname, for the same reason, and also so the two of them might feel the closer connection the other natural-born siblings in the house had."

"What a very thoughtful thing to have done."

Eileen's admiration for Miss Fredrick grew another notch. She would like to believe she would have been as thoughtful in selecting a name, but she doubted it. She would have been much more likely to select something practical.

And, sad to say, she wouldn't have been in that position in the first place because she very likely wouldn't have taken in such a foundling herself.

Hearing the children's laughter from the parlor, she felt embarrassed by that self-knowledge. Whose life had been the richer these past ten years—hers or Miss Fredrick's?

She knew what those in the world of her mother would say.

And she also knew they'd be quite wrong.

Simon wasn't at all surprised when Wednesday morning rolled around and all eight of the school-bound children were lined up at the front door on time to head out. They each held one of the brand-new lunch sacks filled with the items Eileen and Dovie had planned out the evening before.

There was something to be said for Eileen's insistence

that schedules and routines be devised and followed. He just wished she wasn't so rigid in *everything*.

Dovie stood at the bottom of the stairs with Molly and Joey. Eileen stood at the front of the line and Simon moved in place at the end of the line, nodding at her that he was ready.

As they marched through town, their little parade elicited smiles and greetings from everyone they passed.

When they arrived in the school yard the children were still milling around waiting for the call to go inside.

Fern and Russell declared themselves old enough to fend for themselves, so Simon accompanied Eileen as she escorted the six younger children into Miss Whitman's classroom.

The introductions were quickly made and then it was time for them to leave. Simon could tell Eileen had something on her mind as they made their exit, but he decided to wait her out.

Before she'd made it to the bottom of the schoolhouse steps, she paused and glanced over her shoulder.

"Do you think this is too soon? After the funeral, I mean?"

Simon smiled, pleased to see that she was concerned about their feelings. Had this softer side of her always been there, hidden away inside, or had the children instilled it in her?

"No, I don't." He placed a hand at her elbow, gently urging her forward. The unexpected warmth that caressed his fingers through her sleeve caught him off guard, but he did his best to ignore it. "In fact, having something new to focus on, and being around other kids their age, will keep them from dwelling too much on what they've lost."

She nodded. "Of course, you're right. But I wonder,

should I check in on them at lunchtime to see how they are faring?"

Now that the steps were behind them, he really should remove his hand from her arm, but she didn't seem to mind…

"I'm sure Miss Whitman and Mr. Parker are both excellent teachers and they'll keep a close eye on the children. You should take advantage of having fewer kids underfoot to relax." He raised a hand to forestall her comment. "And before you ask, no, you don't need to be here to escort them home after school. They have strict instructions to return to your house as soon as school lets out, and Fern and Russell will see that no one takes a wrong turn. Don't worry, they're reliable."

He could tell from the momentary flash of sheepishness in her eyes that that was exactly what she'd been about to ask.

Her expression quickly resumed its customary aloof appearance. "Are you packed and ready for your trip?" She was obviously ready to change the subject.

"There's not much to pack—I'll only be gone for one night."

"The weather has been turning cooler. I hope the children have coats among their belongings that you'll be bringing back."

"I'm sure they do. St. Louis has colder winters than you do here."

The rest of the walk back to her house was spent in the same meaningless chitchat. But when they stepped up on the porch, he placed a hand lightly on her arm. "Eileen."

She turned to him, her expression wary.

"I want to thank you."

He saw surprise and relief flit across her face before she closed off again. "For what?"

"For caring about the children so much."

She seemed to soften right there in front of his eyes. Not just her expression, but all of her, as if she'd had a hard outer shell covering her that had suddenly sloughed off.

"You're quite welcome," she replied, and even her voice was softer.

The image was so real he wanted to reach out and touch her cheek. But he blinked and as quickly as it had happened, the illusion was gone and she was back to normal.

"Now, you have a train to catch and I have matters of my own to attend to," she said briskly. "If you'll get the door…"

After Simon left for the train station, Eileen looked down at Molly and Joey. She needed to find some sort of educational or enlightening activity for these two. Something that would present a challenge to their minds or social skills yet be appropriate to their ages.

Perhaps she should start with something every child loved, such as art. Learning to draw simple shapes and to color within the lines would be a good first step.

She stepped into the parlor to fetch her pencils that were stored in the small writing desk. Dovie was there, darning a pair of stockings.

When she answered the older woman's question about what she was doing, Dovie looked at her thoughtfully. "You do know that it isn't good for kids to be cooped up in the house all day, don't you?"

Eileen frowned. That wasn't the way she'd been raised. In fact the headmistress at her boarding school had taken great pains to let her young ladies know how unseemly it was to get too much sun.

Then again, she wouldn't necessarily call her upbringing ideal. And she trusted Dovie.

"But I can't just let them go outside without supervision."

"Of course not. But I believe there are a few late carrots still in the ground and some turnip tops that are ready to harvest."

Eileen nodded. Gardening could be educational. And if she could instill her love of the activity into one or both of these children, it would be something altogether satisfying.

Smiling, she set the pencils back in the desk and went to tell the children about the change of plans, already anticipating the things she could teach them.

Later, Eileen sat in the kitchen watching Dovie teach Joey and Molly how to shell pecans for the pie she intended to make. The carrots and turnip greens they had harvested had been washed and were ready to go into the soup for tonight's supper.

Their gardening session had met with mixed success. Joey had been more interested in trying to get a look at the dog he could hear barking from another house down the block. He'd ended up pulling up an entire turnip plant rather than just the top and then had accidentally stomped on another.

Molly, on the other hand, had listened closely and asked the kind of questions that told Eileen she was truly interested in getting it right.

The current lesson on shelling pecans seemed more like playtime as Dovie showed them different techniques, made silly faces when shells went flying and pretended not to notice when they sneaked a few bites every now and then.

Eileen envied the older woman's ease around the children. She knew she would never be able to duplicate it.

The sound of the door chime brought her back to the

present, and she stood. "I'll get that. The three of you look like you have your hands full."

It was probably one of the members of the Ladies Auxiliary with something for their supper meal. Simon hadn't followed through on his decision not to accept more food from the community yet.

The buzzer sounded again before she got to the door, and she frowned at the unseemly show of impatience.

When she opened the door, a breathless youth—Leo Dawson, she thought—stood there. Before she could ask him his business he blurted out, "Harry fell off a swing in the school yard and hurt himself. Miss Whitman asked me to come and tell you she sent for Doc Pratt."

Chapter Eighteen

Eileen's heart fluttered painfully for a moment as she stepped out on the porch. "You'll find Miss Jacobs in the kitchen straight down that hall." Eileen was already halfway down the stairs. "Tell her I've gone to the school and will be back as soon as I can."

With that she was off, not even bothering to fetch a hat. How badly was he hurt? Simon had trusted her to look after his charges. He hadn't been gone two hours yet, and already one of the children was hurt. Please God, let the boy be okay.

She didn't stop to exchange greetings, didn't see anyone—the streets and sidewalks could have been empty for all she knew. When she at last reached the school yard it was to see a group of children standing outside peeking in the windows and doorway.

They parted for her, and she rushed inside to find Miss Whitman and Dr. Pratt bent over a white-faced Harry.

"What's wrong? Is he going to be okay?"

"I hear he was testing the limits of the swing when he fell off," Dr. Pratt said drily. "But he'll be just fine."

Eileen's pulse slowed slightly. "Where is he hurt?"

"He bumped his forehead and sprained his wrist. We'll

need to keep a brace on his wrist for the next week, but it should heal without any permanent damage."

"He's been very brave," Miss Whitman said solemnly. "He hasn't cried a bit."

Harry's chest puffed out at the praise. "I'm no crybaby." But she could tell he was in pain.

Eileen nodded, careful not to let him see how shaken she'd been. "I can see that. But I think it best if you also try to be a little less of a daredevil."

Harry's grin made no promise on that score.

Dr. Pratt closed his medical bag and looked down at his patient. "There will be no more roughhousing for you, young man, at least for the next couple of weeks. Understand?"

"Yes, sir."

"Good." Then the physician turned to Eileen. "Can I speak to you for a moment?"

Her worry returned. Was Henry more seriously injured than he appeared? She followed Dr. Pratt across the room while Miss Whitman fussed over Henry.

"I think it would be best if he goes on home now and gets some rest," Dr. Pratt said, "but he should be fine to return to school tomorrow."

"So he really is going to be okay?"

"Of course. Most boys get scrapes and sprains from time to time—it's all part of them wanting to test their own limits. Just keep an eye on him today, and keep him awake until suppertime if you can. If he appears dizzy, queasy or overly confused, send for me. Otherwise just make sure he doesn't do anything strenuous or use that left hand of his and he should recover in no time."

He gave her a searching look. "How are you doing? It can't be easy having all these children thrust on you so suddenly."

Eileen, realizing she'd been wringing her hands, straightened and gathered herself together. "I'm managing just fine, thank you, Doctor. Is there anything else I should look out for?"

"If his hand or head start hurting too much you can give him a cup of willow bark tea. You can get the powder at the apothecary shop if you don't have any yourself."

"Very well. If you'll put the fee for your services on my tab I'll settle up with you at the end of the month."

Dr. Pratt nodded, and, with another warning for Harry to take it easy, he took his leave.

Eileen escorted Harry out of the schoolroom. As soon as they stepped outside, the other children tried to press closer to get details.

Miss Whitman clapped her hands loudly. "Give them some room, children. Harry is going to be just fine, but we don't want to jostle him, now, do we."

Most of the children obeyed and parted for them to pass. But Fern stepped forward, blocking their way. "Are you okay, Harry?"

"I'm fine," Harry boasted. "It'll take more than a little fall like that to keep me down."

Eileen placed her hand on his back. "I am taking him home now so he can get some rest. You can check in on him after school."

Fern held her ground. "Maybe I should come, too, so I can help take care of him. You're not used to taking care of hurt kids."

"I think I can handle this and you need to focus on your studies."

Fern didn't seem at all happy with that response. She lifted her head with an expression that bordered on a challenge. "I suppose with Nana Dovie there, Harry will be okay."

They stared at each other for a few minutes, but Miss Whitman and Mr. Parker called the children back to their studies so Fern finally turned and headed back to the schoolhouse.

Eileen's walk back to the house was much more dignified than her earlier rush to get to the schoolhouse had been. Not only did she adjust her steps to match Harry's, but she kept her back straight and her head high. But her thoughts were less dignified. Why did Fern dislike her so? Now that she knew a little of the girl's story, it was easier to understand why she felt she had something to prove. And as the oldest of the children, it was only natural that she would feel protective of the others.

But understanding the girl didn't make her belligerence any easier to deal with. She had to find a way to show Fern that she would not try to take her place in this family, or even that of her beloved Gee-Gee.

But that was something to ponder later. Right now she had more immediate problems. Like making sure Harry was properly cared for.

And figuring out how she would face Simon tomorrow with the news that she'd failed so spectacularly in meeting his trust to keep the children safe in his absence.

When the children returned home from school, it was as if a swarm of frisky puppies had descended on the place again. They were full of talk about the new friends they'd made, what sort of lessons they'd worked on and the games they played at recess. Eileen found herself actually enjoying the ruckus. It was too bad Simon wasn't here to see how much they'd enjoyed their first day of school.

The others made a big fuss over Harry, who was not above milking the attention for whatever he could get out of it.

At supper that night, once everyone had been served and the blessing had been said, Audrey started the conversation. "I heard some of the other kids talking about a Thanksgiving Festival. What's that?"

Eileen paused a heartbeat before responding. "Every year on Thanksgiving Day, everyone gets together to celebrate the day as a community." She used to look forward to the event, taking great pleasure in the festivities. Right up until everything changed two years ago.

"You mean like a big party?" Audrey asked.

Eileen smiled. "In a way. But it's an outdoor party."

"What all do you do there?" Harry asked. "Is there stuff to eat?"

"More food than you'd believe the schoolhouse could hold." Eileen saw she had everyone's attention and set her fork down. "Everyone brings lots of food—meats, vegetables, desserts—and it's all shared. Reverend Harper starts us off with an outdoor prayer service. Then we all eat our noon meal together. There are games and competitions for the children and some for the grown-ups, too. Lots of visiting with each other, of course. And in the afternoon there's a dance."

"Ooooh, that sounds like fun." Rose had a faraway look as if trying to picture it. "Can we go, even if we don't really live here?"

"Yes, can we?" echoed across the room.

"Everyone is welcome. Besides, you live here now, even if it's only temporary."

"I can't hardly wait," Audrey said. "When is Thanksgiving?"

"A week from tomorrow."

That brought more chatter and grins.

But not from Fern. "Do you really think it's proper

for us to be thinking about going to a party when we just buried Gee-Gee yesterday?" the girl asked.

The room grew quiet as each of the other children cast guilty looks Fern's way.

"Gee-Gee was like a mother to us and we should show some respect by mourning her proper." The older girl's expression had the tight look of someone who thought they were right and everyone else was wrong.

Dovie reached over and placed a hand lightly on Fern's arm. "It's very understandable that you would think of your Gee-Gee that way, Fern. But just because we lose someone we love, doesn't mean we can't ever allow ourselves to be happy again. I'm sure your Gee-Gee wouldn't want you to miss a chance to celebrate God's blessings amongst friends and neighbors just because you miss her."

"She did encourage us to always find ways to show we were thankful," Russell said.

"I suppose." Fern stirred her soup listlessly. "But we should think about her while we're celebrating," she said defensively.

The other children nodded solemn agreement and then the talk turned to other topics.

What sort of food would she bring to the gathering this year? Back when Thomas had still been alive and she'd been an admired member of the community, she'd taken great pride in furnishing exotic and elegantly prepared dishes. That first Thanksgiving after Thomas's death, she'd made do with a couple of pies made from pumpkins harvested from her own garden and a ham that had cost her more than she could afford, but her reception had been lukewarm. Last year, coward that she was, she hadn't even attempted to go.

But that wouldn't do for this year. There would be twelve members of her household present and that called for a much larger contribution to the meal. Could she make her funds stretch to purchase something from the butcher?

The children obviously wanted to go, and she wouldn't let her cowardice stand in their way. Besides, she knew that the folks in Turnabout would make them welcome, regardless of how they felt about her.

That evening, when she rocked the younger children on the porch swing, she missed having Simon's quiet presence nearby. How was he faring in Hatcherville? Had he found a will? If so, given how much the woman had cared for the children, surely she would have left her estate in a manner to benefit the children. Having the Hatcherville property available for the children to move into would solve most of Simon's problems.

And it would mean they would move on from here fairly quickly.

Well, she would insist they remain here through Thanksgiving at the very least. After all, the children were so excited about the upcoming community festival that it would be a shame to make them miss it.

How empty this large house would feel once they left was something she refused to contemplate.

Simon stepped off the train at the Turnabout station and felt as if he'd returned home. Strange how attached he'd gotten to the place in just a few days' time.

Though not so strange, he supposed, given how much drama had occurred since their arrival.

He made arrangements to have the trunks he'd brought back with him delivered to Mrs. Pierce's home, then headed off at a brisk walk. He was anxious to see how Eileen had fared with the children since he'd been gone. She was a capable woman, of course, and goodness knows she was up to the task of planning for just about any contingency. Still, when one had ten youngsters under one roof, it was hard to anticipate *everything* that could go wrong.

The older kids would still be at school so he'd be able to speak to her without having them all underfoot.

When he passed by the bank, he hesitated a moment. He ought to stop in and let Adam know that his search for a will had been fruitless. But he decided that could wait a little longer. The urge to check in with Eileen was too strong to ignore.

When he arrived at her house, he climbed the porch steps two at a time and entered the house without knocking.

The first person he saw was Molly.

"Hi, Uncle Simon. Did you bring our things back with you?"

"That I did, sweet pea. The man at the train depot is going to send them over just as soon as they get unloaded from the train."

"Good, 'cause I want to wear my blue dress to the Thanksgiving Festival."

"Thanksgiving Festival?" What was she talking about?

"Yes. It's like a great big party that the whoooole town goes to. And they even have dancing. And Mrs. Pierce is gonna teach me how to dance so I can dance, too."

He pictured Eileen gliding across a dance floor with his arms around her and found it a very pleasing image indeed. "Well, now, I'll bet you'll be the prettiest little sweet pea on the dance floor."

Molly giggled. Then she grabbed Flossie and began twirling about to her own humming.

Still in search of Eileen, Simon checked in the parlor and found her there with her sewing basket. It looked like one of the boys' shirts in her lap.

She glanced up and he was pleased to see a smile blossom on her pretty face. "Hello."

A heartbeat later, though, the smile was replaced by an expression he couldn't quite read. What was wrong?

"Did you have any luck?" she asked him.

"If you're asking if I found a will, I'm afraid not. I did get the children's things collected and shipped back with me, though. They'll be delivered here shortly."

The smile she gave him this time was her old reserved smile. "I know the children will be glad to have the rest of their clothing and their other belongings."

"So how did things go with the children while I was gone?" he asked, still fishing for what had put that uneasiness in her manner. "They behaved themselves, I trust."

Her hesitation told him he'd hit on the source of her discomfort. Had one of the children done something to make her uncomfortable?

"I'm afraid there was a little accident yesterday."

He stiffened, suddenly shifting his focus from worry about her to concern for the children. "What happened? Is everyone okay?"

"Harry fell off of a swing in the school yard." Her words were rushed, her expression full of self-recrimination. "He has a cut on his forehead and a sprained wrist. Dr. Pratt says he should be fine as long as he doesn't try to do too much with that hand for the next week or so."

Was that all? "So it's nothing serious."

"Nothing serious." There was a touch of outrage in her voice. "Didn't you hear me say he had a sprained wrist?"

She obviously didn't have much experience with active boys. "It'll mend."

"But you left him in my care and I didn't keep him safe."

Her feeling of responsibility was both sweet and misplaced. He crossed the room and sat on the sofa beside her, glad of the excuse to take her hand. "Eileen, this would have happened even if I had still been in town. You can't watch them all the time. Kids will take spills and have accidents. That's all part of growing up."

But her lips were set in a stubborn line. "Nevertheless, you shouldn't leave them in my care like that again."

He gave her hand a squeeze and was pleased to see a touch of pink grace her cheeks. "Come now, you're being much too hard on yourself."

Before he could say more on the subject, the door chimes sounded. No doubt it was Lionel with the trunks.

He rose to take care of the delivery, but not before he gave her hand another squeeze. "We'll speak more about this later, but know this—I would trust you with these children at any time, under any circumstances, without any reservation whatsoever."

Eileen blinked as she watched him leave the room. Had he meant that? But he didn't know—

She felt her chest constrict. It was getting harder and harder to maintain her distance. Soon, she'd have to tell him of her past failings. And she was dreading what that would do to his trust in her.

Chapter Nineteen

When the children got home from school, Simon made a big show of asking Harry about his injured hand. Just as he suspected, though, he didn't doubt the injury was still painful, the boy was much more concerned with making certain his bravado was acknowledged than with any pain it might have caused him.

"Did you find what you were looking for?" Fern asked.

"I'm afraid not."

Rose tugged on his pant leg. "Did you bring our things back with you?"

"I did. I've put the trunk with the girls' things on the second floor and the one with the boys' things on the third. You can go upstairs and unpack in a moment. But first, I have something else for all of you."

He led them into the dining room, where a small trunk sat on a chair. The lid was open, and from what Eileen could see, it appeared to contain Miss Fredrick's things.

"That's Gee-Gee's trunk," Fern said. She glanced Eileen's way as if suspicious that Eileen had been rummaging through the contents.

"I know." Simon walked over to the trunk and placed a hand on the lid. "Miss Fredrick's brother went through these things while he was here and took the items that were important to him. He wanted you children to have the rest. So you could each have something to remember her by."

Eileen knew Mr. Fredrick would not have put it so generously. It was more likely Simon had requested the items on the children's behalf. She found the fact that he'd even thought to ask for such a thing oddly endearing.

"Fern, would you like to help me lay out her things?"

With a nod the girl stepped forward. When she was done she gave Simon a dismayed look. "Gee-Gee's silver hairbrush and comb aren't here. And neither is her broach that she kept for special occasions."

"Those were probably things her brother wanted as his own mementos," Simon said calmly.

Other than a few articles of clothing, there wasn't much to be had. A carved wooden box that held sewing implements; a hat that was decorated with two silk flowers, a feather and a hatpin; a couple of lace handkerchiefs and some other odds and ends. One by one the children stepped up and selected an item.

Fern took the hatpin from the hat.

Rose, Molly and Tessa each searched through the contents of the sewing box. Rose took a small decorative pair of scissors, Tessa a brass-handled darning egg and Molly took a silver thimble.

Audrey took a lace fan that had seen better days.

And Lily took a lace handkerchief.

Harry found a magnifying glass in the sewing box and Russell took the box itself. Joey took the feather from the hat and Albert took her wire-rimmed spectacles.

When they were finished Simon returned the few remaining items to the trunk and shut it. "Now, those things you selected are yours, to use however you like. Consider them early Christmas gifts from Miss Fredrick."

Each of the children nodded silently.

"So, upstairs with you and unpack those trunks I brought back from Hatcherville."

Once they were alone, Eileen turned to Simon. "I hadn't realized you were such a sentimental man."

He shrugged, seeming uncomfortable with that label. "I just figured they needed something of hers to hold on to."

"I would say you figured correctly." She thought of the small wooden cigar box the housekeeper had retrieved for her from her father's study after his funeral. It was the only thing she still had of his, and she wouldn't trade it for anything in the world.

Yes, Simon had done a very good thing for those children.

The next morning, as soon as the children left for school, Simon headed out to find some work. Eileen had her doubts, but when he came back at lunchtime he already had a new job well underway.

"Eldon Dempsey hired me to do some work around his farm." Simon's voice indicated he was pleased. "His roof needs some work and he's putting in some new fences. The job should take me a couple of days."

Eileen didn't know Mr. Dempsey, other than to greet him in church. He was an older man who owned a small farm outside of town. But the job sounded like simple manual labor. Didn't Simon know that he was capable of so much more?

"I met Hank Chandler over at the lumber mill when I went to pick up some supplies we needed," Simon continued. "Hank's going to let me work there part-time when I get through at the Dempsey place."

"Have you worked in a lumber mill before?" She'd only seen inside the place one time. It seemed a loud, dusty, dirty place.

"Yes. It's hard work but not as difficult as some other things I've done."

"Are you sure you wouldn't rather talk to Adam about getting a job at the bank? It would be easier work." And cleaner.

Simon grimaced. "I wouldn't be much use sitting at a desk or behind a teller window all day—I'm much happier working with my hands. Besides, I already shook hands with Hank on taking the job."

He snatched one of the biscuits Dovie had baked to go with their lunch. "I'm going to barter with Hank for some scrap lumber so I can set up a place in the carriage house for the chickens to roost."

That brought her up short. "What chickens?"

"The chickens Mr. Dempsey is going to give me in exchange for the work I'm doing for him." He pinched off a piece of the biscuit, his expression turning thoughtful. "I suppose they can just roost on the rafters until I build something more suitable, but it would be helpful to have some nesting boxes for them as soon as possible."

Eileen brought the conversation back to what she considered the salient point. "He's paying you in *chickens?*"

Simon nodded, a boyishly proud grin on his face. "It was my idea."

"But what in the world am I going to do with a flock of chickens after you are gone?"

He frowned as if she'd said something nonsensical. "You'll still want eggs to eat after we're gone, won't you? And you can sell any extra they produce to the mercantile for pin money."

That gave Eileen pause. Another source of income,

however small, would be welcome. And how difficult could it be to care for chickens? "I suppose, if you want to take responsibility for getting it all set up, I won't stand in your way."

Then she had another thought. "Do you know anything about raising chickens?"

"Of course. I spent the first eleven years of my life on a farm."

Interesting. It made her want to ask him what had happened to change that, but she held her tongue.

"And I'll teach you so you can continue after we leave," he added. Then he gave her another grin. "And don't worry. When I go to work at the lumber mill, most of my pay will be in the form of cash. I'll have money to contribute to our expenses."

"Mr. Tucker, I have never asked you for payment, nor do I intend to. You and the children are my guests, not my boarders."

"I appreciate that distinction. And I gratefully accept your offer of a roof over our head. But if we're going to be here long-term, and it looks like we probably will be, I insist on contributing to the grocery bill. It's the only fair thing to do."

"Very well. But I will only take food money—nothing else."

"By the way, I've asked around about this Thanksgiving Festival the kids mentioned. It seems like that is a big deal around here."

"It's the biggest community-wide event we have. Except perhaps for the picnic and fireworks display we have on Independence Day."

"Well, we'll be long gone before July gets here, but since we'll still be around for Thanksgiving, and you just accepted my help with the food bill, you can count on me to contribute a ham or goose to the menu."

"But—"

"You and Dovie can provide the dessert." Simon was obviously not going to take no for an answer. "I'm partial to pumpkin pie, by the way, if anyone's interested."

She decided to accept his offer graciously, "Very well." Then she raised a brow. "But I make no promises as to what kind of pie we'll be bringing. I'm rather partial to buttermilk myself."

Simon watched her walk away, appreciating the added bounce in her step. No doubt about it, she was warming to him.

The next day was Saturday, which meant no school. It also meant it was laundry day. With so many people in her house, Eileen had moved laundry day to a day when there were all hands available to assist. The only person excused was Simon, who headed out for work as soon as breakfast was over.

Simon had built her some additional lines in the backyard to handle the increased volume of laundry, and he'd also come up with the idea of lining the wheelbarrow with an old sheet and using it to transport the heavy loads of laundry from the washtubs to the lines.

Eileen was very glad she had a wringer machine, but still it took all morning to get the washing done. The clothing was washed first and then beds were stripped and dirty towels and napkins collected.

She made it clear everyone was to pitch in, boys included. Those not actively working on the laundry were put to work dragging the rugs from the various rooms in the house outside and beating them to get the dirt out.

By lunchtime everything was finally hung on the line

to dry. Her helpers all looked worn-out. She figured she wasn't going to hear any objections today when it came to sending them to their rooms for quiet time after lunch.

And she was right.

Later that afternoon, when she was taking the now-dry laundry from the lines, Simon arrived riding in a small horse-drawn wagon. The children immediately abandoned their chores to crowd around him.

"Where'd you get the horse and wagon?" Russell asked.

"Can we keep it?" Albert asked.

"Hank over at the mill loaned it to me so I could get my lumber here. I'm bringing it back to him as soon as I get it all unloaded." Simon singled out the two boys who'd just spoken up. "You two want to lend me a hand with this?"

The boys enthusiastically complied, while Eileen called the others back to help her finish collecting the laundry.

A chicken coop in her carriage house. What in the world could she look forward to next?

But she was smiling as she contemplated the possibilities.

Chapter Twenty

Before the church service on Sunday morning, Simon asked permission to address the congregation.

"First off, I want to say thank you again to you folks. All of you have been extraordinarily kind to a group of strangers who landed in your midst. Most of you have probably heard that we're going to be sticking around a bit longer than we expected. Thanks to Mrs. Pierce, we have a place to stay, but I don't want to continue to trespass on your generosity, so thank you for all you've done this past week, but starting right now, you no longer need to provide us with the food for our meals."

He nodded toward a man sitting in the third pew. "Thanks to Hank Chandler there, I have a job, so I should be able to purchase food for our table myself." He spread his hands, hoping to strike a neighborly tone. "The mill is not taking up all my time, though. So if any of you have a need for a handyman, I'm available and more than happy to accept the chance to do an honest day's work."

Then, with a thank-you to Reverend Harper, he headed back down the aisle.

He received several smiles and friendly nods as he made his way to his pew. Hopefully that would lead to a job or two. But his gaze was focused on Eileen. Seeing the light of approval there was quite gratifying.

Eileen watched him walk back to his seat and saw the positive impact his little speech had made with the folks in the congregation. Not that she'd had any doubts on that score. He was a personable man with a forthright, honest air. Who wouldn't respond to that?

And his assurance that he was ready to take responsibility for his and the kids' meals was admirable. There was no getting around it, Simon Tucker was a good man.

And perhaps, just maybe, some of his likableness was splashing over on her. Folks were actually smiling her way again. Would it last beyond his stay here?

After the service, Eileen noticed that Simon received several offers of work. Most of it was of the manual labor variety, but that didn't seem to bother him at all.

Still, if she could just steer him to something of the office or even shopkeeper variety, surely he'd be happier. After all, didn't all men have aspirations to better their lots in life?

Later that day she decided to broach the subject again.

"I know you said working with your hands is what you're good at, but I think you're selling yourself short."

His expression hardened. "I've tried working in an office before. It didn't work out."

His tone made it clear he wouldn't welcome further discussion. Had he had a bad experience? How could she convince him to give it another chance?

Monday morning dawned overcast and chilly.

Simon took inventory of what rainy day protection the children had and found they were woefully lacking. Audrey and Albert each had a heavy wool cape that would repel a light rain. Russell had an oiled canvas coat that had belonged to his father. Other than Simon's own slicker, that was it.

Dovie appeared a moment later with a heavy wool cape. "Here. This is old but it'll keep the wearer dry."

"Thank you." Simon handed his own slicker to Rose and Dovie's cape to Fern. "Let's hope it doesn't rain before school lets out," he told the children, "but if you do have to walk home in the rain, you all share as best you can to help Harry, Tessa and Lily stay dry, too."

The rain held off the first part of the morning, but by ten-thirty there was a light mist in the air.

Joey had spent much of the morning on the back porch playing with his tin soldiers. But when Eileen stepped out the back door to make certain he was staying dry, he wasn't there. His toy soldiers lay in a forlorn pile, but Joey himself was nowhere to be seen. Puzzled, she stepped back into the kitchen, where Dovie was cooking and Molly was playing house with Flossie under the table.

"Did Joey come back inside?" she asked them.

"I haven't seen him." Dovie gave her a puzzled frown but didn't seem particularly worried.

"Me and Flossie didn't see him, neither," Molly called out.

"Either," Eileen corrected absently. The memory of Harry's accident was still fresh enough to make her nervous. "I certainly hope he hasn't gone out in this weather. He could get a chill."

She stepped back out on the porch and went to the top of the steps. She called his name a couple of times, but he didn't answer. Then she noticed the door to the carriage house was open. Had he decided to play in there?

Worried about all the sharp-edged tools that were

stored inside, she lifted her shawl to protect her head from the drizzle and headed for the outbuilding at a trot.

When she reached the door she pulled her shawl back to her shoulders as she waited for her eyes to adjust to the shadowy interior. But her ears were working just fine and she could hear Joey talking to someone.

"Joey, are you okay?"

"Yes ma'am. But you're scaring him."

Scaring who? She heard some scrabbling sounds and was finally able to make out the shadowy form of Joey, kneeling on the floor and bent over an animal of some sort.

Her protective instincts kicked in and she rushed to the boy's side. "What is that? Move away."

She put her hands on his shoulders, trying to urge him to move away.

But Joey didn't budge. "It's a puppy and it's hurt. We need to help him."

Eileen wasn't so sure about that. But now that her eyes had fully adjusted she could see that it was indeed a small dog. The animal was wet, dirty, and there seemed to be something wrong with its right front paw.

She'd heard once that injured animals were the most dangerous, which meant her first priority had to be to make certain Joey was safe. "Move aside," she said more firmly. "I'll take a look at him."

Joey looked at her doubtfully, then slid over to let her take his place. The animal lifted its head from the ground to stare at her, but it appeared weak and after a moment set its head back down again. The animal's gaze remained on her, though, as if waiting for her to do something.

Her heart went out to the poor thing. Joey was right— they had to help it. But how?

"I think he's hungry," Joey said. "Do you think we can

give him something to eat?" He looked at Eileen earnestly. "He can have my lunch."

Eileen smiled at the boy's sincerity. "I think we can find something else for him to eat without you giving up your meal." They would need to clean the animal up, too, if they were going to see what was wrong with his paw.

She wished Simon were here; he'd know what to do. Should they keep the dog shut inside here until Simon returned?

No, if she did that Joey would insist on staying with the creature and she couldn't have that.

With a sigh, she made the only sensible decision. Slipping off her shawl, she turned to Joey. "Go on inside and ask Dovie to find our friend here something to eat and then put the big kettle of water on the stove."

"What are you going to do?" Joey's tone held an edge of suspicion.

Eileen began to gently wrap the dog in her shawl. "Something I'll very likely regret."

At his worried look, she smiled reassuringly. "Don't worry. I will take good care of him."

With a nod, Joey jumped up and raced to the house to do as she asked. Eileen slowly finished wrapping the animal, careful not to touch its injured paw, then stood with him tucked securely in her arms. The poor thing was shivering, but it looked at her trustingly.

With another sigh, Eileen pulled the animal against her chest and headed for the door. Naturally the rain chose that moment to go from a drizzle to a full-blown shower.

Simon took off his wet boots on the back porch and shook the water from his hat before entering the kitchen. He was definitely ready for a nice hot bowl of the soup Dovie had been preparing when he'd left this morning.

He stepped inside the kitchen and then halted on the threshold. What in the world—

Joey and Molly sat on the floor, and Joey had a dog on his lap that he was feeding what looked to be biscuits soaked in broth.

But more remarkable than that, Eileen sat on a chair nearby, her dress damp and covered in muddy smears, and she was attempting to dry her hair with a towel.

It was the first time he'd seen her with her hair down and she looked so completely different it left him speechless. Always before, her hair had been pinned up in a perfectly smooth, tidily arranged bun. What he saw now was a gloriously wild full mane, long wavy tresses that danced and twisted with a mind of their own. And oh, my, was that a set of bare toes peeking at him from the hem of her dress?

For a moment he couldn't even breathe.

"Uncle Simon! Look, I have my puppy!"

Joey's exuberant exclamations brought Simon's thoughts back down to earth and allowed him to collect himself before Eileen could catch him staring.

"I named him Buddy," Joey added proudly.

"That's a fine name for a dog." Simon crossed the room and crouched down in front of the dog. "And just where did Buddy come from?"

"Joey founded him in the carriage house," Molly answered. "And Mrs. Pierce brought him inside so we could feed him and doctor him up."

Simon cut a quick look Eileen's way. *She'd* brought the animal inside? That explained the smears on her damp dress. But what could explain her change of heart?

Her cheeks warmed guiltily under his stare, and he found himself totally enchanted by this more vulnerable and feminine Eileen.

But Molly's words got through to him and he turned back to the kids. "Doctor him? What's wrong?"

"Buddy has a boo-boo on his paw," Molly said.

"We gave him a bath so we could see it better," Joey added. "But he won't let us touch it."

"I figured we'd let the poor thing eat before we give it another try," Eileen said. "He seemed practically starved to death."

"Let me have a look." Simon bent closer to study the animal's paw without touching it. There seemed to be something stuck inside the sensitive pad of his foot. Knowing what he had to do, Simon stood and looked at Eileen, trying to gauge if she was up for this.

Telling himself she would have to be, he turned to Joey. "Hand Buddy over to Mrs. Pierce, please."

Apparently recognizing the seriousness in Simon's tone, Joey stood and gave the animal to Eileen, who'd already set aside her towel.

"What are you going to do?" Joey asked.

"I'm going to remove whatever is jammed in his paw. But I'm afraid he's not going to like it."

"Will it hurt him?" Molly asked, hugging Flossie against her chest.

"Yes it will, sweet pea. But it's the only way to help him heal and get better."

He looked at the two children, who both seemed ready to cry. "Why don't you both go in the parlor until we're done here?"

Dovie stepped forward. "I think that's a good idea. And I'll go with you. Buddy probably doesn't want you to see him cry."

When they had left the room, Simon turned back to Eileen. "I need you to hold him as still as possible. From what I can see, whatever is stuck in his foot has a barb on the tip and this is not going to be very pleasant for him."

Her eyes widened. "I don't know. Perhaps Dovie would be better—"

"You're perfectly capable of doing this." Then he gave her a smile. "Besides, not only does it seem you're the one who brought Buddy into the house, but it seems you're already dressed for the part."

She glanced down at the dirt on her dress and grimaced. Then she looked up, apprehension drawing her brows down. "But what if I can't hold him still?"

"Just do the best you can." He picked up her discarded towel. "I'm going to wrap him snugly in this to make him easier to contain." He quickly put his words to action and in no time at all Buddy was securely wrapped with only his injured leg free.

Simon took a deep breath then met Eileen's gaze. "Ready?"

Her eyes were huge and apprehension fairly thrummed from her, but she tightened her hold on the dog and gave him a nod.

Admiring her strength, he took firm hold of the animal's paw. Praying he wouldn't have to resort to his pocketknife to dig the offending item out, Simon went to work.

Buddy's yelps and howls were painful to hear, and Simon could imagine how the children in the parlor were reacting. At one point he looked up to check on Eileen and saw how white her face had turned, but she gamely held on and uttered not a word.

At last it was done, and Simon leaned back, the ugly-looking thorn in his hand. As he'd suspected, the thing had a barb on the tip and it hadn't come out without inflicting a great deal of pain on the poor dog.

Simon rubbed the animal's head, softly. "I'm sorry, Buddy. But I promise it was for your own good."

"Will his foot get better now?"

Simon looked up, surprised by the raw concern in Eileen's voice. He unwrapped Buddy and set him on the floor without taking his gaze from Eileen's. Then he gently brushed a stray tendril of that glorious hair from her cheek. "You did good. Assuming an infection doesn't set in, Buddy should be much better in a week or so."

The kitchen door opened and Joey and Molly peeked inside, with Dovie standing behind them. "Is he better now?" Joey asked fearfully.

"The thorn is out, but his paw is still going to be very tender for a while."

"Poor Buddy," Molly said as she came closer. "We're going to take real good care o' you so you can get all the way better."

"I'll get some gauze to bandage it up," Dovie said. "And I know how to make up a poultice for drawing out infection. If it works on people, I dare say it'll work on dogs, too."

Joey squatted down next to Buddy again. The boy looked up at Simon. "I can keep him, can't I?"

"Assuming he doesn't already belong to someone else, I'm okay with it. But this is Mrs. Pierce's place. She's the one you really need to ask."

Joey turned his pleading eyes on Eileen, and she gave a big sigh. "I don't suppose I could say no after we've gone to so much trouble to fix him up."

Joey let out a triumphant whoop.

But Eileen held up a hand. "However, Buddy is an outside dog, not an inside dog. You can make a place for him in the carriage house if you like."

"Yes, ma'am."

She reached over and scratched the dog behind the ears. "I suppose, though, while his foot is bandaged we really ought to keep a close eye on him. So, just until he's better, he can sleep here in the kitchen."

Joey's face lit up at that. "Yes, ma'am!"

"But just the kitchen, mind you—he's not to run loose in the rest of the house. And that's just until his paw is better."

Joey nodded.

"And you are responsible for cleaning up any messes he makes, without any fussing or foot-dragging," Simon added.

"I will. I promise," Joey said.

"Very well then," Eileen said, "I guess Buddy is part of the family now."

Simon caught her eye and didn't try to hide his amusement.

She tilted up her chin, then reached for the soiled shawl and towel. "Now I need to go clean up. You two get your uncle Simon to help you fix up a bed for Buddy over there in the corner. Then get yourselves cleaned up for lunch."

And with that she marched out of the kitchen without a backward glance.

Simon's grin widened. Who would have guessed she'd have such a soft spot for animals? It made him curious as to what other vulnerabilities she was hiding. Perhaps, now that he was going to be spending more time here, he'd have the opportunity to find out.

Then he turned to the kids. "You heard Mrs. Pierce. Let's hop to it."

Eileen twisted her hair back up in a smooth chignon, still unable to believe she'd let herself be won over by the scruffy little dog. But when he'd looked at her so trustingly, and borne his affliction so resignedly, she hadn't been able to abandon him to his fate.

So now Joey had his longed-for dog, and she had an animal invading her home. Well, she'd just have to see that Joey followed her instructions and kept the animal contained.

Of course, she was honest enough with herself to admit that the real source of her discomfort was the look Simon had given her when he first walked in. She really should have left the room to dry her hair before Simon arrived, but she hadn't wanted to leave Joey and Molly alone with the animal.

What had he thought of her disarray—hair down and messy, clothing damp and smeared with mud, and feet bare? She'd looked a complete hoyden, she was sure.

Yet disapproval was not what she'd read in his glances. There was a warm appreciation there that had set a little pinwheel spinning crazily in her chest.

Perhaps it was best she not try to interpret just what it *had* been.

Chapter Twenty-One

Unlike the day before, Tuesday promised a day of sunshine and mild temperatures. Eileen could hear Joey and Buddy playing on the back porch and smiled at the way the boy talked to the dog as if the animal could understand him.

The other kids in the household had accepted Buddy as part of the family immediately. It hadn't mattered to any of them that he was a scruffy mutt or that he had an injury; they were all ready to make a fuss over him and claim him as their own.

And she hadn't been unaware that several scraps had been slipped to the animal as the kitchen was being cleaned up after supper. Buddy had definitely found himself a loving home.

Just as Eileen was putting the last of the breakfast dishes away, she heard the door chimes. Reflecting that she'd had more visitors in the short time since she'd taken in her houseguests than she'd had in the past two years, she hurried to see who it might be.

When she opened the door, a middle-aged man with a receding hairline stood there with his hat crushed in his beefy hands. "Good morning, ma'am. I'm Eldon Dempsey."

"Good morning, Mr. Dempsey. If you're looking for Mr. Tucker, I'm afraid he's not here. You can catch him down at the lumber mill."

"I have his chickens."

The chickens—she'd forgotten all about that. "As I said, Mr. Tucker is not in right now. Perhaps you should come back—"

"Oh, that's okay. He told me if he wasn't around, I should just put the cages in the carriage house. I only wanted to let you know I brung 'em." And with a friendly wave, he turned and moved back before she could think of something else to say.

Feeling at a loss as to what she was expected to do, Eileen tracked down Dovie in the parlor.

"Mr. Dempsey has brought the chickens."

Dovie looked up with a smile. "That's nice. It'll be good to have fresh-laid eggs again."

"What should I do?"

"I don't reckon you need to do anything until Simon comes home."

Molly popped up from the sofa where she'd been playing with Flossie. "Can I go see the chickens?"

Eileen hesitated. "Perhaps we should wait until your uncle Simon comes home."

"But—"

Dovie spoke up. "While those birds are still in their cages is a good time for you to get acquainted with them. Come along. Let's go have a look." She turned to Eileen. "You, too. You need to get used to being around them."

Eileen started to object that she had no intention of getting acquainted with farm animals. But the protest died in her throat when she saw the determined look in Dovie's eye. Instead she meekly nodded. Perhaps she should at least look in on the fowl.

By the time they headed out the back door, they found Joey already on Mr. Dempsey's heels, asking him questions about the birds in the cages, and Mr. Dempsey was patiently answering each one.

The man dropped off four cages containing two chickens each. When he was done he tipped his hat Eileen's way. "Just tell Mr. Tucker to drop off those cages back at my place when he's done with them."

Eileen assured him she would and then he was gone.

She looked at the squawking birds and decided she didn't care to get any closer than she was now, regardless of the security of the cages. The other three, however, had no such compunction.

"Are we really going to get our very own eggs from these birds?" Joey asked.

"Sure will," Dovie answered. "Probably get the first few bright an' early tomorrow."

"Can I come get 'em?"

"I tell you what. Until you get the hang of it, why don't we come collect them together."

"Okay." Joey turned to Molly and puffed out his chest. "I'm gonna be a chicken farmer."

"I want to be a chicken farmer, too," Molly said quickly. "And so does Flossie."

"Well, now, there's a lot more to taking care of chickens than collecting their eggs."

"Like what?" Joey asked.

"Well, for the first few days I reckon your uncle Simon is going to want to keep them penned up in here so they get used to this being their new home. That means they'll have to have feed and clean water. It'll also mean everyone will have to be real careful when going into and out of the carriage house so one of the birds doesn't escape."

"I can do that," Joey said.

"Me, too," Molly echoed.

"Then, once he's ready to set them loose, someone will need to make certain they get shut up tight in the carriage house at night so owls and other critters won't get them." She gave Joey a stern look. "And that includes your dog. Buddy's going to have to be trained to protect them, not chase after them."

"Don't you worry. Buddy is going to be the best chicken watchdog there ever was."

Eileen let them continue their discussion about the chickens while she quietly slipped back inside the house.

She had given in on the matter of the dog simply because Buddy's plight had touched her heart.

The chickens, on the other hand, were not nearly so endearing. She was perfectly happy to stay away from them as long as she was able.

Wednesday morning dawned cold and overcast, and Eileen guessed they wouldn't have many more days to wait until the first frost arrived. School was out until the following Monday and the lumber mill was shut down for the same period, so everyone was home. The children were nearly vibrating with anticipation for the festival the next day and Eileen sincerely hoped it lived up to their expectations.

Simon slipped out right after breakfast to run a mysterious errand of some sort.

Eileen, Dovie and some of the girls were still working on cleaning the kitchen when he returned.

"Here you go," he said, setting a very large ham on the table with a proud expression on his face. "I told you I'd provide the main course for our contribution to the town's Thanksgiving meal."

Dovie bustled over to examine his purchase. "Now, this is a very fine ham indeed. I'll spread some molasses on it and let it bake nice and slow today. It'll be juicy and tender for tomorrow."

"You should let me do that," Eileen said. "It hardly seems fair for you to do all this work since you won't get to come with us."

"Oh, I forgot." Tessa looked suddenly stricken. "You can't leave the yard or your heart will hurt."

Eileen had noticed the seven-year-old seemed to have formed a special attachment to Dovie.

The child walked over and took Dovie's hand. "Do you want me to stay with you so you don't have to spend Thanksgiving alone?"

Dovie looked down at the little girl with an aching tenderness. "Thank you, Tessa. I think that's just about the sweetest thing anyone's ever said to me. But you need to go on to the festival with the others so you can come back and tell me all about it. Okay?"

Tessa nodded tentatively, obviously still worried about Dovie.

"Besides," Dovie added, "I won't be alone the whole time. Ivy promised to fill up a plate of all that good eatin' and bring it over so she and Mitch can take their meal with me." She winked at Tessa. "You make sure she puts a big old slice of peach cobbler on there for me."

Tessa nodded more enthusiastically this time.

"Good. I know I can count on you." Dovie straightened. "Now, you girls finish with the dishes while I find a pan big enough to bake this ham in. And you two—" she turned to Eileen and Simon "—you get to work shelling pecans for me. I plan to bake an apple pecan pie to go with this ham."

By midmorning a soft rain had started falling. That, combined with the dropping temperatures, drove everyone indoors except Joey, Audrey and Albert, who were in the carriage house playing with Buddy. Simon made certain there was a roaring fire in the parlor fireplace and most of the other children drifted in there to enjoy its warmth.

Eileen sought out Simon and found him on the front porch, carving on a flat piece of board. "What are you working on?"

He held it out to her. "What does it look like?"

It was square and had lines carved into it going both vertically and horizontally. "A chessboard?"

He smiled. "Close. A checkerboard. I thought it would be good for the kids to have something to do. I actually plan to make two of these so they won't have to wait so long for a turn."

"Perhaps you can try chess pieces for the second one?"

"I can make playing pieces to go with a checkerboard without much trouble. Chess pieces would be more difficult."

She swallowed her disappointment. "Of course."

He went back to work. "So you're a chess player?"

She drew her shawl more tightly around her. "I know the basic moves, but I haven't played much."

"How are you at checkers?" He blew the wood dust from the board.

"I've never played, but it's a child's game, isn't it?"

He gave her a sideways look before eyeing his board again. "It *is* simple enough for a child to learn, but for the serious player, there's a whole different level of complexity and strategy to be learned, as well."

She settled for a noncommittal *Hmm*.

He leaned back and gave her a look that she assumed was meant to be stern but somehow failed.

"I can see you don't believe me," he said. "I guess I'll just have to prove it to you."

Her pulse quickened in response to that look of challenge he gave her. "And how do you plan to go about doing that?"

"By teaching you to play."

"Whenever you have the game ready, I am at your disposal."

"Just give me about twenty minutes."

She glanced at the board and frowned. "But it's not even painted yet. And we can't use it while the paint is still wet."

"I don't plan to use paint."

"Then how—"

"Watch." He used his knife to start carving shallow diagonal stripes into one of the squares. When he had that one done to his satisfaction, he moved over to another, leaving an untouched square between them.

Eileen studied the affect and smiled appreciatively. The alternating grooved and smooth squares were as distinctive as the inlaid board her stepfather had had in his study. "Will you be marking the playing pieces the same way?"

"No. I'm using something much simpler." He nodded toward a pile of round discs on the porch beside his chair and she stooped down to study them.

They were surprisingly uniform in size and thickness. But they were made from two different woods, one light and one dark. A simple but effective means of differentiating the opposing pieces. And there appeared to be enough of them to use with the two boards Simon planned to make. "Clever."

He grinned. "You don't have to sound so surprised."

She smiled back at him and realized that her current position put their faces nearly level. When she inhaled, she caught the scent of sawdust and soap and outdoors—of him. The sounds of the rain and the wind and voices from the house were drowned out by her own heartbeat. Could he hear it, too?

Simon saw Eileen's eyes widen and heard the little hitch in her breathing. There was a tiny smudge just below the corner of her lush lips. She would no doubt be mortified if she knew it was there, but he found it endearing. He tightened his hold on his knife, forcing his fingers to ignore the overwhelming urge to reach over and stroke that sassy little smudge away for her. Even stronger was the urge to kiss it away.

Would she slap him if he tried?

She swayed forward slightly, and he decided it might be worth finding out....

The door opened behind them, and Eileen blinked, then stood up as if something had propelled her.

"Whatcha doing?" Lily asked.

Eileen brushed at her skirt, not making eye contact. "Your uncle Simon was just showing me the game he's making."

"What kind of game?"

"Checkers."

"Oh, can I play?"

Simon finally looked away from Eileen and toward the little girl. He smiled at her eager expression. "I promised Mrs. Pierce I'd teach her first. But you can play afterward."

Lily looked at Eileen. "Don't you know how to play checkers already?"

Eileen shook her head.

"But even Joey knows how to play." The confused look on Lily's face was almost comical.

"Don't worry," Simon said, keeping his expression appropriately solemn. "I'm a good teacher. I'm sure she'll pick it up in no time."

Simon felt Eileen's glare without even looking at her and knew she'd definitely be playing to win when the time came. He was looking forward to it.

By the time they sat down at the dining room table with the handcrafted checkerboard between them, all of the children had heard about this being Eileen's first game of checkers. Not only were they gathered to watch, but sides were being taken, mostly along gender lines.

Simon won the first game handily and tried not to let his amusement show when Eileen's lips pinched in irritation.

She recovered quickly, though, and gave him an arch look. "I believe I have the hang of it now. Shall we try again?"

"If you insist." And he set up the board again.

He won the second game, but this time he had to make more of an effort.

"I think I really have the hang of it now." There was definitely a glint of determination in her eyes. "Shall we try once more?"

And to his surprise, she did indeed manage to win that third game.

Delighted by the flush of triumph on her face, he stood and made a short bow. "Well done. Congratulations."

She smiled graciously. "I did, after all, have a good teacher."

Before he could explore this playful side of her further, several of the children began clamoring for a turn at the game, and Eileen gave up her seat with a smile and excused herself to help Dovie in the kitchen.

As Simon moved back to the porch to begin work on a second checkerboard, he found himself whistling. Someday soon he was going to kiss that woman.

And the sooner, the better.

Chapter Twenty-Two

As they all gathered back in the parlor after lunch, Dovie turned to Eileen. "Did I hear you say there's going to be dancing at this festival tomorrow?"

Eileen nodded. "There is."

"Who provides the music?"

"There are two fiddlers in town, as well as a banjo player and a couple of harmonica players. They play in shifts or in pairs to keep the music going most of the afternoon and evening. It's not the same as having an orchestra, but it keeps the dancers twirling."

"It sounds mighty festive." Dovie turned to the children. "How many of you know how to dance?"

Her question was greeted with silence. "None of you? Well we can't have that. I'll hazard a guess that Mrs. Pierce is a fine dancer. Perhaps we can talk her into teaching some of you."

Eileen felt suddenly shy. She refused to allow herself to glance Simon's way, but she was very aware of his presence. "There's no music."

"We can sing for you," Audrey offered.

"I can do better than that." Dovie quickly left the room and shortly returned carrying a lap harp.

"What a beautiful instrument." Eileen moved closer to examine it. "How come I haven't seen it before?"

Dovie shrugged. "Haven't had a reason to pull it out until now. But I reckon I can still play us a lively tune." She settled in her chair and plucked a few notes, fiddled with the knobs, then plucked at the strings again. Finally she looked up with a grin. "Now, claim your partner, and let's see what you can do."

Eileen supposed there was no getting out of it so she stood and looked around with a smile. "Who wants to go first?"

No one stepped up.

"Perhaps they'd like to see a demonstration first." Dovie waved toward Simon. "You know how to dance, don't you? Come over here and partner with Eileen and show them how it's done."

Dovie began playing her harp and the strains of a lively jig soon filled the room. It wasn't exactly what Eileen was used to, but Simon stepped up and bowed gallantly. She curtsied and away they went with him leading her through the paces of a vigorous country dance. By the time the music died, Eileen was breathless and smiling.

Simon was a surprisingly good dancer. Not ballroom caliber perhaps, but his movements were confident and smooth. And she'd had no trouble whatsoever matching her steps to his.

"Now let's try something different," Dovie said. "Why don't you demonstrate a waltz for our young students?"

A waltz. Eileen's gaze quickly flew to Simon's, and she found him holding out his hand, a slight challenge in his smile. Telling herself this was just a demonstration, she placed her hand in his and allowed him to step closer and place his other hand at her back. When the soft strains of the music began she followed him effortlessly, as if they'd danced together like this many times. Her gaze never left his, and the pleasure and admiration she saw reflected there was intoxicating, as if the music flowed not just around her, but through her.

Everything else fell away, and she gave herself up entirely to the music, to the feel of his hands, to the look in his eyes. Like a bit of dandelion fluff, she was floating on the wind that was the music.

When the music stopped it was as if she'd been rudely awakened from the sweetest of dreams.

She looked around, blinking as reality blanketed her again. She found Dovie watching them with a knowing grin. Merciful heavens, how much had she revealed?

Immediately she stepped away from Simon and tried to regain her mental equilibrium.

"Now," Dovie said briskly, "Eileen, why don't you work with the boys and, Simon, you can work with the girls to try to teach them a few simple steps."

Grateful for the change of focus, Eileen immediately took both of Joey's hands and tugged him to the middle of the room. They practiced for the next hour or so, meeting with mixed success. Some of the children took to it quickly, some barely managed the basics and a few dived into it enthusiastically, dancing to their own tune and quite happy to do so.

Finally Simon collapsed on the sofa, declaring himself too exhausted to continue. The rest of them took that as a cue to take a break as well, and everyone found a seat to plop down on.

Once Dovie stopped playing and the children were still, Eileen could hear the rain. If anything, it seemed to have intensified. She rose and went to one of the windows to take a look. Sure enough it was coming down in sheets, and didn't show any signs of letting up. This didn't look good for tomorrow's festival.

She felt someone come up to stand behind her and knew even before she saw his reflection in the glass that it was Simon. Their gazes met in the windowpane, and she wondered if he was remembering that lovely waltz with the same tingly, unsettled feeling she was.

Rose joined them, breaking the spell, and she edged her way between Eileen and the window. "What happens if it doesn't stop raining?" she asked glumly.

"The ground will keep getting wetter."

"Uncle Simon! You know what I mean. What happens with the festival?"

"I'm afraid the festival will be canceled," Eileen said regretfully. "There's no place in town big enough to seat everyone for the meal, and the games and the dance would all get bogged down in the mud even if we attempt to hold them."

"Maybe it'll stop before morning," Harry said hopefully.

"I hope so." Molly twirled around the room holding Flossie's hands. "I want to show everyone how I can dance."

Eileen glanced out at the downpour. The first Thanksgiving after her marriage to Thomas had been like this, and the festival had been canceled. She had partially salvaged the day by inviting two dozen of Thomas's closest friends to spend the day with them. Thomas had been so proud of her hostessing abilities and the event had cemented her place as a social arbiter in the town.

She couldn't hope to duplicate that success, but surely there was something she could do to mitigate the disappointment the children were feeling. They'd had enough setbacks to face over the past few weeks—it was time to find something to celebrate.

She looked around, noting the grumbling and moping that was already spreading through the room. This wouldn't do at all.

"Children." She used her best authoritative tone and it captured everyone's attention. "I am disappointed in you. There are going to be troubles you have to face in this life—everyone has them. If you want to be respected rather than pitied, you must learn to handle them with grace and dignity—not whining and complaining."

From the corner of her eye she saw Simon's frown. Did he think she was being too harsh? Surely he knew these were lessons the children needed to learn.

But she wasn't without sympathy for them. "Besides, just because we can't celebrate with the whole town, that doesn't mean we can't celebrate at all."

That earned her a few hopeful glances.

"What do you mean?" Harry asked.

"Well, we still have all the food Dovie is cooking, and all of this room, and even some music—why can't we have our own festival right here? I imagine your uncle Simon could even come up with a few friendly competitions for you to take part in."

"You mean inside?" Russell didn't sound overly impressed.

"Yes, inside," Eileen answered calmly.

"But it won't be the same," Rose said.

"No, it won't." Simon sent Eileen a supportive look. "But that doesn't mean we can't make it fun."

"That's right." Dovie threw in her support for the idea. "We can have an indoor picnic."

"What's so special about eating on the floor of the parlor?"

Eileen could see their efforts were not meeting with total success, and she searched her mind for a way to get the children excited.

There was one thing that might do it…

She hesitated. The hideaway, as she called it, had once been her favorite room in the house, and Thomas had given it over to her for her private use. But she'd closed it off when she'd been forced to sell off all the lovely furnishings it had housed. Looking at it as it was now only served to remind her of all she'd lost.

But there was really no good reason, other than her pride, for her to keep it closed off and hidden. And if it would cheer up this gloomy-looking crew of kids, it might be worth opening up to serve a new purpose.

"Who said it has to be in the parlor?" she asked, arching her eyebrows.

Simon gave her a "what are you up to" look, but didn't say anything.

"Where else would we have it?" Harry asked.

"Well, there's always the *secret* room."

That immediately captured everyone's attention.

"Your castle has a secret room?" Molly asked, her voice almost a whisper and her eyes wide. "How come we never seen it before?"

"Never *saw* it," Eileen corrected. Then she put her hands behind her back and rocked back on her heels. "Because then it wouldn't be much of a secret, would it?"

Joey, who was standing next to Dovie, turned to her. "Do *you* know about her secret room?"

Dovie shook her head, but there was a decided twinkle in her eyes. "No, but I sure am curious to find out more. What about you?"

Joey nodded vigorously.

"Will you tell us the secret?" Harry asked.

Eileen looked around, meeting each set of eyes solemnly, enjoying the sense of anticipation and excitement in the room. "I would have to know that I could trust you to keep my secret," she said, making her tone doubtful.

There were vigorous nods and choruses of "yes."

"Very well." She straightened. "The entrance to the secret room is actually right here in the parlor."

Immediately everyone began scanning the room, looking for where that entrance might be.

"Surely you've noticed the turret attached to this house when you're outside." She stepped away from the window. "Haven't you wondered where the inside of that tower is? I mean, such a room would have round walls, wouldn't it?"

"Oh." Impossibly, Molly's eyes widened more. "Please can we see it?"

Some of the quicker-witted children were focusing on the far wall, the wall that was closest to the turret. Eileen headed across the parlor in that same direction. She smiled when she heard them following close behind.

"Where is it?" asked Molly. "Do you have to say a special word for the door to appear?"

Eileen laughed. "No. You just have to look very, very carefully." She stepped up to a chair positioned in front of what to the casual observer appeared to be an ornate panel, identical to all the other ornate panels that were evenly spaced on the walls throughout the room. A closer look, however, showed that this particular panel had unobtrusive hinges on one side, and that the edges of the panel were actually seams in the wall, in fact, they were the outline of a door. She reached for one of the carved flowers and tugged. It easily pulled out to form a decorative doorknob.

And with a flick of her wrist she twisted the knob and dramatically flung open the door.

It was shadowy inside and the musty smell of disuse tickled her nose before she even entered.

Eileen stepped all the way inside and the children crowded in behind her. She crossed the room and pulled open the drapes. And turned to see the children looking around the room with expressions of awe and delight. What on earth did they see in this sadly empty space to warrant such a reaction?

She turned and studied the room herself. And for the first time, didn't see the ghosts of the beautiful furnishings that were no longer there. Instead she saw the flowered paper on the walls, the gilt work on the ceilings, the ornate scrollwork that capped the built-in shelves, the beauty of the stone hearth, the grandeur of the tall curved windows that gave the room its rounded shape. The fact that the lower half of the view from the windows was screened by holly bushes only enhanced the air of mystery.

"It's like a princess's room."

Eileen raised an amused brow at Molly's words. "A princess's very *dusty* room."

"Once we get it cleaned up, this will make a very nice place to hold our very own Thanksgiving Festival," Dovie said.

"And a wonderful bonus of having our Thanksgiving at home is that Nana Dovie can join us," Simon added.

"That's right." Tessa took Dovie's hand. "The whole family can be together."

Eileen saw the emotion in Dovie's eyes at the little girl's simple gesture and words, and felt a lump in her own throat for just a moment. She turned away and her gaze snagged on Simon's. They stared at each other for several heartbeats, and though he was across the room, the warm understanding in his gaze was like a gentle caress to her cheek.

"This room will definitely need a good cleaning before we're able to serve a meal in here."

Dovie's words brought her back to her senses and she dropped her gaze.

"We can do that," Lily said.

"I agree." Dovie put her hands on her hips. "And now is as good a time to get to it as any."

"After we clean it, can we decorate?" Tessa asked.

"I think that's a marvelous idea."

Dovie organized the cleaning, assigning the various tasks to the children according to their abilities. Before long the room was a hive of activity. Even Simon and Eileen had tasks assigned to them.

What the younger children lacked in skill and reach, they more than made up for in enthusiasm.

Eileen gave in when Joey asked if Buddy could join them "for a little while" and the animal seemed to sense the festive atmosphere.

Molly brought Flossie into the room to "help," of course, and held a running conversation with her doll about what a wonderful room it was and how the two of them could have tea parties and picnics in here over the coming days.

At one point the little girl looked over at Eileen. "You can come to our tea party, too, if you like. You can be the queen, and I shall be the princess and Flossie will be our very dear friend."

"That sounds quite lovely," Eileen responded, touched that the little girl wanted to make her a part of her make-believe adventures.

When they were finished cleaning, it was time to decorate. Dovie asked each of them to go through their things and find at least one item that they would be willing to share with everyone for the one day of Thanksgiving, and that would be their decorations.

Eileen went up to her room and looked around. At one time she had owned so *many* beautiful things. Thomas had showered her with clothing and jewelry and gewgaws. All of it was gone now. She'd had to part with everything, just to pay off the debts Thomas had left her with—not to mention purchase the simple necessities for herself.

She glanced at her trunk. No, not quite everything. There was one item, her most prized possession, the one thing she'd held on to through all those hard times.

She moved to the trunk and pulled out a tissue-wrapped package from the very bottom. She laid the package on the bed and carefully unwrapped it. The fabric spilled out, still as vibrant and beautiful as it had been the day Thomas gave it to her. The iridescent fabric of the shawl shifted between the rich blues and greens of a hummingbird's feathers with every movement. There were tiny beads sewn throughout the shawl with metallic threads, giving it even more shimmer. The fabric was supple and unbelievably soft. She could picture it hanging on the wall in the "secret" room, next to the fireplace where a tapestry had once hung.

But what if she let Dovie use it for decoration and something happened to it? Children were always having accidents and spills. She could always bring the brass candlestick by her bedside to set on the mantel, and no one would be the wiser.

But she'd know.

Eileen carefully refolded the shawl, grabbed the candlestick and headed downstairs with both items.

Chapter Twenty-Three

"Just a little higher on the left." Eileen ignored the rolling of Simon's eyes as he towered above her on the ladder. "You want it to be straight, don't you?"

"At this point, I just want it to be done." But he obligingly lifted the cord-wrapped nail a tiny bit higher.

"Stop! That's perfect."

"At last." Simon quickly hammered in the nail, as if afraid Eileen would change her mind.

As soon as she'd told him what she had in mind for the placement of her shawl, he'd gone to work rigging up a cord to hang it from using clothespins.

She turned to take the shawl from Fern, who'd offered to hold it for her. The girl was stroking it with an almost-reverent awe.

"I've never seen anything so beautiful in my life," the girl said as she reluctantly handed it over. "And you actually wore this."

Eileen smiled. "A few times—not often. My late husband and I used to throw wonderful parties for all of his friends. The house would be filled with people and lots of food. Everyone would dress up in their finest clothes and sometimes we'd even have musicians come in."

"That sounds lovely."

Eileen studied the thirteen-year-old. She was of an age where romantic notions could take over her daydreams. She hoped whoever Simon eventually found to care for the children would know how to keep the girl grounded without totally destroying her dreams.

Fern seemed to remember suddenly that she and Eileen weren't on good terms and with a short nod turned and moved to help Rose with a project she was working on.

Sighing, Eileen turned and handed the shawl up to Simon.

He gave her a sympathetic look, obviously having caught the exchange. "Give her a little more time. I think she's thawing toward you."

Hoping he was right, Eileen gave a short nod.

Then they turned their attention to hanging the shawl, and in short order it was done.

Eileen stepped back to study their handiwork and declared herself satisfied.

She looked around at the rest of the room and smiled at what a hodgepodge the group had brought into the space to decorate it.

Two other candlesticks in addition to hers stood on one end of the mantel. On the other was a large yellow-and-white stoneware vase. Who had donated that—Dovie?

Hanging from the very center of the mantel was the tired little black hat with the two red silk flowers that had been in Miss Fredrick's valise. She cast a quick glance Simon's way. How typical of him to want to include the memory of the children's foster mother in their celebration tomorrow. Then she studied the rest of the room. Scattered here and there were colorful toys, hair ribbons and pretty glass jars.

It was a far cry from the expensive furniture pieces

and gilt-framed pictures and mirrors that had once graced this room. But she couldn't say that she liked it any less for all that.

"You all have done an amazing job," she said to the room in general. "The secret room has come alive again."

"It does look mighty nice," Dovie agreed. "And Simon and I came to a decision while you were upstairs."

"Oh?"

"Right after breakfast tomorrow," Simon said, "me and the boys are going to bring the dining room table in here."

Eileen wrinkled her brow. "But why?"

"Because a few of us don't think our old bones can take all the getting up and down that's involved in eating on a picnic blanket," Dovie answered.

"Then why don't we just eat in the dining room and then come in here after."

"What?" Simon put his hand to his heart, as if shocked by her suggestion. "Not have our Thanksgiving meal in the secret room? That would be tragic."

Eileen rolled her eyes, then looked around to see several of the children nodding in solemn agreement. "Very well. If you want to go to all that trouble I won't stand in your way."

"I knew you'd see reason. All right, kids, we're eating at the table in here tomorrow."

A cheer went up and then Dovie clapped her hands for attention. "It's been a long day, and we've got lots of things planned for tomorrow. Time to get cleaned up and ready for bed."

Eileen nodded. "After you're cleaned up, we'll do our story as usual—"

"Can we do it in here?" Molly asked.

"I suppose so. I'll ask your uncle Simon to help me drag in a few chairs while you're getting ready for bed." She waited for his nod before continuing. "As I was saying, we'll do our story as usual—I have a really good one for you tonight. But I'm afraid it's much too cold and wet to go out on the swing tonight. I thought perhaps instead, I could come to each of your rooms and sing a song while I tuck you in."

That plan seemed to meet with general approval, and in a few minutes they had all trooped out of the room to take care of their nightly routines.

Simon quickly brought four chairs inside the room, then stood staring at them while he stroked his chin thoughtfully. After a minute he glanced her way. "I think I'll construct three or four long benches to set along the walls in here. They won't be fancy but they'll be easy to make and it'll save having to move chairs in and out of here every time you want to use the room."

"How thoughtful. But don't feel like you have to be doing such things for me."

He smiled. "I don't mind. And it's the least I can do."

What did he mean by that?

He leaned a shoulder against the wall. "Don't think I don't know what you did this evening. It was more than generous of you to open up this room to the children. You must have had it closed off for a reason, yet when you saw how disappointed they were at the thought of missing out on the festival, you did this for them. And not only that, you're sharing your shawl, which apparently is very special to you, with the children, as well."

There was that warm-honey-in-her-veins feeling again. What this man could do to her with just a look and that crooked smile of his. "Neither the room nor the shawl was doing any good to me or anyone else locked away the way they were. It was time they saw the light of day and the joy of use again." As she said the words she realized how very true they were. Were there other things in her life, in *her,* that had been locked away for too long?

"That may be true—" he took her hands "—but there's not many as would have chosen ten orphans and their unprepared guardian to share them with."

She liked the way her hands felt in his, liked the rough calloused strength of them, the feeling that those hands would never let any harm come to her, and that, despite the work-roughened state of them, those hands knew how to be gentle, as well.

Wanting to convey her emotions, she gave his hands just the tiniest of squeezes. Immediately his gaze sharpened and she saw his focus shift to her lips. Was he going to kiss her?

Suddenly, with every fiber of her being, she wanted him to do just that. She leaned forward slightly, her gaze never leaving his face. His own gaze flew back up to her eyes and then they were searching, as if uncertain.

She gently disengaged her right hand and brazenly moved it to his cheek. What would he think of her?

He smiled then, a warm, triumphant, top-of-the-world smile. He turned his head without looking away and kissed her palm, all the while keeping his gaze locked to hers.

Eileen had never felt so shameless and so cherished at the same time. Every nerve in her body screamed at her to do something, but she didn't know what.

Finally he nudged her hand away and she didn't know whether she was glad or sad.

"Eileen."

The way he said her name set her pulse racing. "Yes."

"I'm going to kiss you proper now, if that's okay?"

Chapter Twenty-Four

Simon pulled Eileen to him, gratified when she slipped her arms around his neck to hold him close. Then he kissed her, and those enticing, full lips of hers were every bit as sweet and warm as he'd imagined. He could hold her like this forever, for as long as he could feel her heart pounding in rhythm to his.

But finally she pulled away. The reluctance with which she did it, however, was quite edifying.

"Dovie or the children…" she said, her voice shaky.

Of course. This house was too full of people. He shouldn't have put her in a position to have been embarrassed or shamed. "I'm sorry—"

She halted his words with a finger to his lips. "I'm not."

Simon smiled then and gave her shoulder a quick squeeze before putting a little distance between them. He couldn't believe he'd ever thought this woman an ice queen. She was warm and vibrant and altogether irresistible.

When she'd reached up and touched his face, it had been the sweetest and the most unbelievably sensual gesture he'd ever experienced.

And that kiss just now, that had been absolutely amazing.

They needed to talk, to figure out what this meant. He wanted to make certain she knew how he felt, how he wanted to protect her and cherish her and be by her side always. Surely, after that kiss, she felt the same?

He led her to one of the chairs and had her sit. "Eileen, I—"

Molly padded into the room just then, cuddling Flossie and yawning widely. "Am I first?" she asked sleepily.

Simon gave Eileen's hand a squeeze, then stepped back. They would have to wait until the children were in bed to have their talk.

"You most certainly are, sweet pea," he said in answer to Molly's question. "Why don't you and Flossie come sit over here by the fire where it's warm while we wait for the others."

But later, when the children had all been tucked in and Dovie had disappeared into her own room, Eileen professed to be tired and wished him a good-night.

Simon watched her climb the stairs, confused. Surely he hadn't misread how she felt.

Was she confused by her own feelings? But she was a widow, not a blushing maiden, so he assumed it wasn't the first time she'd been kissed in such a fashion.

There had to be something else holding her back. But what?

Eileen stared at the ceiling of her bedroom calling herself a coward and a fool. She should never have let their relationship get this far. Simon wasn't the man for her, perhaps no man was.

She knew he had wanted to talk tonight, to discuss

what had happened between them, but she hadn't been ready.

Because she knew, no matter how she felt about him, she couldn't let this go any further until she told him the truth about herself. And she wasn't strong enough to do that yet. Because once he knew the truth, the way he looked at her, the way he felt about her, would all change.

And she truly did not think she could bear that.

The next morning there was no opportunity for her and Simon to speak privately—she made sure of that. There was breakfast to be tended to and morning chores to be done. Buddy, who was obviously on the mend, seemed to be underfoot constantly. Twice he escaped the kitchen to wander other parts of the house and had to be tracked down.

Since it was a special day, Eileen limited the chores to what absolutely had to be done along with special preparations to be made for their own version of the Thanksgiving Festival.

As soon as breakfast was over, Simon and the older children removed the leaves from the table and carried it across the hall, through the parlor and into the secret room. There the leaves were reinstalled and then all the chairs were transported there, as well.

Simon threw himself into the preparations as enthusiastically as the children, but from time to time she caught him watching her with a seriousness that was unnerving.

Once their chores were completed, the children were allowed to play. Simon had finished his work on the second checkerboard so two games could go on at one time. Fern was overseeing the memory game Dovie had taught them with some of the younger children.

About an hour before lunch, the door chimes sounded.

Wondering who would have ventured out in such nasty weather, Eileen went to the door. She opened it to see Ivy and Mitch standing there, a large hamper in hand.

"I hope we're not intruding," Ivy said as Eileen ushered them inside. "I spent the day cooking yesterday, hoping against hope the festival would be held today. I didn't want it all to go to waste, and since we'd already planned to have our meal with Nana Dovie—"

"You are more than welcome to join us," Eileen assured her. "Assuming you're willing to put up with a bit of a rambunctious celebration. We're holding our own festival."

"Oh, what fun!" Ivy loosened the ties of her shawl. "As long as you're certain we're not intruding."

Simon had joined them by this time. "Of course not. The more the merrier."

Molly tugged on Eileen's skirt. "Are they allowed to see the secret room?"

"Secret room?" Ivy's smile broadened. "How intriguing."

"I think we can trust them to keep our secret," Eileen replied solemnly. "Don't you?"

Molly nodded. "Can I show them?"

"Of course. You show them while I let Nana Dovie know they're here."

Before they could move, Buddy came scurrying by as fast as his three good legs could carry him. He was closely followed by Joey, who was scrambling to catch him. When he saw Eileen he skidded to a halt. "He moves pretty fast for a dog only using three legs," he said proudly. Then he started off again. "Don't worry," he called over his shoulder, "I'll have him back in the kitchen in no time."

Ivy stared at Eileen, an amused expression on her face.

"I see your feelings about allowing dogs in your house have undergone a change since I boarded here."

Eileen shrugged. "One must learn to adjust."

Ivy laughed outright at that, then followed Molly into the parlor.

By Eileen's estimation, the first annual Pierce household Thanksgiving Festival turned out to be a great success. By midday she'd stopped trying to keep Buddy penned in the kitchen, only warning Joey to keep a close eye on him.

There was plenty of food to go around, the games Simon devised for them to play kept everyone entertained and they even enjoyed a bit of dancing.

Eileen made certain she and Simon did not share another waltz, of course. But she did accept his hand for a reel and she even danced a round with Mitch.

All in all she decided she'd had as much fun as if they had been able to attend the community-wide event. Perhaps even more.

Before Ivy and Mitch left, Mitch helped Simon move the table and chairs back into the dining room, and Ivy helped with the dishes.

By the time the couple said goodbye it was time to get the children ready for bed. Once the last child was tucked in bed, Eileen slowly descended the stairs to where Simon waited for her, knowing this couldn't be put off any longer.

He met her at the foot of the stairs, and she could see the questions in his expression.

"Shall we sit in the parlor?" she asked.

With a nod, he followed her into the room and waited quietly while she took a seat on the sofa. He remained standing.

"There's something I have to tell you," she said without preamble.

"I'm listening."

"I suppose you've noticed that I am not the most popular of persons in this town."

"I *have* noticed that there are some folks here who treat you rather rudely."

"There is a reason for it."

He made a sharp gesture of disagreement. "There's never a good reason to be rude to a lady."

She smiled at his quick defense. "Thank you for that. But perhaps you should reserve judgment until you hear the story."

He finally moved to sit beside her. "Don't feel as if you owe me an explanation."

"But I do owe you one. And you're going to hear me out."

His brows drew down at that. But he gave a short nod and leaned back.

She took a deep breath. This wasn't going to be easy.

Simon waited, not sure he really wanted to hear whatever it was she had to say.

"I'm not originally from Turnabout. I was born and raised in Charleston, South Carolina."

So that accounted for the slight accent he heard in her voice. "Not being from around here is not a crime."

"No, that wasn't my crime. Please hear me out. I met Thomas Pierce when he made a business trip to Charleston. He became quite smitten with me, and I did nothing to dissuade him. It was something of a whirlwind courtship—we were married a mere month after we met."

He noticed she said nothing about her being smitten with Thomas. Had she cared for her husband?

"When Thomas and I moved back here, he was quite eager to spoil me. He indulged my every whim and I let him, even encouraged him."

He couldn't really picture her in that role. She was so controlled, so refined.

"What I didn't know was that eventually Thomas over-extended himself. He was a partner in the town's bank and he began dipping into funds he had no right to touch in order to pay his bills—bills that he incurred to indulge me in my frivolity. And then, when it became clear the truth would be discovered, he took his own life."

Shocked, he reached over and took her hand. "I'm sorry. That must have been very difficult for you."

Her eyes registered surprise at his reaction. She gently disengaged her hands from his and resumed her story. "In the eyes of the town, I had been responsible for Thomas's ruin and his downfall. Thomas was one of their own. I was not. I was like Delilah, preying on the weakness of a good man."

His anger over what her neighbors had put her through rose yet another notch. "It seems to me," he said firmly, "that a man should be held accountable for his own actions. Your husband could have simply told you no. He could have also told you the state of his finances so that you could adjust your behavior, which I believe you would have, had you known. Instead he chose to play the indulgent benefactor and then was too cowardly to face the consequences of that choice." The blackguard had taken his own means of escape and left Eileen to face not only his debtors but also her judgmental neighbors.

Eileen studied him with something akin to wonder in her eyes. "I don't believe I've ever met another man like you." Then her expression closed off again. "But there's nothing that says I won't turn into that woman again should I ever have the opportunity. In fact there is every indication that I would."

"You're wrong. Besides, if you picked the right man to marry, he wouldn't let you."

That won him a smile. But she sobered quickly. "There's another thing."

He waited for her to continue, certain it was of as little consequence to his feelings for her as the first had been.

"More than anything else Thomas wanted a big family." She waved a hand. "If nothing else, this house is a testament to that. And I wanted to give him one. But I failed at that, as well. It appears I can't have children."

Simon felt a pang at that. He'd always wanted to have children. But then the irony of that hit him. "Look around you. I don't think having a big family will be a problem."

She drew herself up in obvious affront. "This isn't funny."

"Of course it isn't. And I'm sorry that you can't have children of your own, if that's what you want. But there are ten wonderful children right here who need you very much."

"They have you, and they have Mrs. Leggett."

"But neither of us is *you*." What was it she was so afraid of?

Her expression closed off, and she stood, drawing herself up to her full, shoulders-back height.

He got to his feet as well, bracing himself for whatever other objection she was prepared to make.

"If you must know," she said stiffly, "while I like and even admire you, I don't think we would suit well together, not as husband and wife. Our lives and our backgrounds are much too different."

Backgrounds? Did that mean what he thought it did?

But she wasn't quite done. "This doesn't change anything regarding your stay here. You and the children are more than welcome to remain for as long as you need to. And I hope we can remain friends while you are here. I merely thought it important that you understand exactly where my feelings lie."

"Oh, I think you've made that crystal clear. And don't worry, I won't be bothering you again with anything other than business concerning the children. Now if you'll excuse me, I think I'll go out on the porch for a breath of fresh air."

He couldn't believe this had happened—it was like being back in Uncle Corbitt's home once more. He'd thought she understood who he was, but apparently not. Or rather, who he was didn't measure up to her standards. He should have realized her feelings on the matter when she'd kept pressing for him to ask Adam for a job at the bank.

She wanted to remain friends—he wasn't sure that was possible. Civil was about the best he'd be able to manage.

He'd made a fool of himself. It was time he pressed for a resolution to this matter of the Hatcherville property.

He couldn't move out of here soon enough.

Eileen's shoulders slumped as she watched him leave the room. That hadn't been easy or pleasant, but it had been necessary. Much as she'd like it to be otherwise, she knew that she would end up making him unhappy if she agreed to marry him. She had only to look at the marriage between her own parents to know the truth of that. Marrying her father had ruined her mother's life and turned her into a bitter, unhappy woman. She couldn't stand the thought of doing that to Simon.

Eileen trudged up the stairs to her room. Yes, she'd absolutely done the right thing.

So why did she feel as if her heart was breaking?

Chapter Twenty-Five

To Eileen's relief, at breakfast the next morning, the kids provided most of the conversation with their rehashing of their favorite parts of yesterday's celebration. Hopefully no one noticed the lack of any interaction between her and Simon.

Just before they finished the meal, Dovie spoke up.

"I've been thinking. Being as all of you will be here for Christmas, I thought it might be a good idea for each of us to select one person from the group to give a gift to. We can pull names out of a hat to make it fair."

This sparked a little buzz of excitement around the table and everyone generally seemed to think it was a good idea.

"To make it even more special," Dovie said, "why don't we make something handcrafted for whoever's name we get rather than going out and buying something?"

"That sounds like a lovely idea," Eileen agreed. It would keep anyone from feeling inadequate due to not having money.

"But what if we don't know how to make anything?" Albert asked.

"Oh, I don't think that will be a problem." Eileen

gave the boy an encouraging smile. "Use your imagination. You can draw a picture, or build something, or sew something—it'll be fun."

"What might make it even more fun is if we keep it secret from the person whose name we draw," Dovie suggested.

"Secrets are fun," Molly said. "Like the secret room. "

Fern, naturally, had misgivings. "What if the matter of the Hatcherville property gets settled faster than Uncle Simon thought and we get to leave here before Christmas?"

Eileen winced at the girl's telling use of the words *get to.* "Then we will exchange gifts a little early," she said. "But I'm hoping you'll plan to be here for Christmas, regardless." She cast a quick look toward Simon, but he wasn't looking her way.

"If we're here for Christmas, can we have a tree?" Rose asked.

"I think we can work something out. You'll just need to talk your uncle Simon into cutting one down for us."

Simon did look up at that, but his gaze slid right past hers and landed on Rose with a smile. "We'll go out a couple of days before Christmas and find us a nice, full one."

Molly clapped her hands. "We can put it in the secret room and decorate it with lots of pretty things. It'll be the most beautiful Christmas room *ever.*"

Eileen thought about the elegant decorations she'd had before her fall from grace. Molly would have been enchanted by them. "I'm afraid I don't have any decorations."

"That's okay." Dovie waved a hand, as if waving a baton. "We can make those, too. That'll be more fun anyway."

Thirty minutes later Eileen looked at the name she had

drawn and felt her heart sink. Fern. The girl would never welcome any gift from her.

Of course, since it was supposed to be secret, no one would know if she swapped names with someone. And she was certain Fern would prefer a gift from just about anyone else over her.

She followed Dovie into the kitchen, relieved to find they were alone for the moment. "I have a favor to ask."

Dovie crossed her arms over her chest. "What can I do for you?

"Would you mind trading names with me?"

Dovie gave her a surprised look. "Now, why would you want to do that? You don't even know who I have."

"It doesn't matter. I drew Fern's name. The girl doesn't care for me, and I think perhaps she would appreciate anything you would give her much more than something from me."

"Nonsense." Dovie patted her hand. "Perhaps this is your opportunity to make friends with Fern. She doesn't really dislike you, you know. She's just hurt and confused by the blows life's landed on her, and she needs someone to lash out at. Be patient with her."

Eileen tried again. "I'm being patient. It's just not bearing any fruit yet."

Dovie raised a brow. "Tell me this. If one of the children came to you with a request to swap names because they didn't get along with the person whose name they had, what would you tell them?"

Eileen winced at that, then sighed. "I would tell them that they should try to work things out." She gave in. "Very well, I'll see what I can come up with."

Eileen slowly exited the kitchen, trying to decide what kind of gift she could come up with that Fern would like. Perhaps she could take one of the delicate lace handkerchiefs she still had and embroider Fern's initials on it for her.

She went to her trunk and threw open the lid.

There, right on top where she'd placed it last night, was that beautiful iridescent shawl.

She remembered the way Fern had looked at it, the almost-reverent way she'd stroked it.

Eileen stroked it much the same way now. It was still the most beautiful thing she'd ever owned.

Making up her mind, she shut the lid of the trunk and took the shawl to her bedside where her sewing box was stored.

Simon threw the board fresh from the saw onto the proper stack. It had been six days since Eileen had told him of her true feelings, and the sting still hadn't gone away.

So far they'd managed to remain civil, friendly even, but the tension was there, just below the surface, and he wasn't sure how much longer he could keep up the charade.

The worst part about it was he found himself still attracted to her, more fool him. He still enjoyed listening to the emotion in her voice when she recounted her nightly fairy tales to the children. Still found the little selfless things she did for the children admirable. Still found his heart touched when she did something that revealed her vulnerability.

Still ached to hold her in his arms again.

Fool! Why couldn't he just focus more on the snobbish reason she'd pushed him away?

He looked up to see Adam standing across the way watching him. When their gazes met, Adam waved him over.

Simon walked over to meet him, tugging off his work gloves as he went. What was up? Did they have some kind of decision on the case?

It was hard to tell from the expression on Adam's face if it was good news or bad.

The two men shook hands and then Adam got right to business. "Mr. Fredrick has made an offer."

This was it. "What kind of offer?"

"He's willing to refund the amount you and your sister contributed to the purchase of the property in Hatcherville. Period. He is not willing to give you any partial ownership in or access to the property itself."

A not entirely unexpected offer. If Eileen had taught him nothing else, she'd taught him to plan ahead for every contingency. "Do you think this is a fair offer?"

Adam spread his hands. "*Fair* is a relative term. I do think, however, it's the best you can hope for from Mr. Fredrick unless you want to take your chances in court."

Simon rubbed his chin while he thought about it. The kids associated the place in Hatcherville with Miss Fredrick. How would they feel about settling somewhere else?

On the other hand, there was no guarantee how it would go if they took the case to court—he could end up with nothing. And it was unfair to the kids and to Mrs. Pierce if he let this business continue to draw out when he could put an end to it now.

With the money Mr. Fredrick was offering, he could find them another place. It wouldn't be as big as the Hatcherville property, but as long as he found something sound and with enough land for them to have a proper garden and some farm animals, he could take care of adding on to the house over time.

He met Adam's gaze. "I accept his offer."

Adam nodded, not making any sort of judgment on

the decision. "I'll have the papers on my desk tomorrow morning for you to sign. The money should be wired to the bank by the end of the week."

Thanking Adam for his help, Simon went back to work feeling lighter of spirit. At last he was free to move forward again. To move out of Eileen's house.

To move out of her life.

That afternoon, when the kids got home from school, he gathered everyone together and explained the latest development.

"So there you have it," he said when he'd finished. "I'm sorry we won't be able to move into the place in Hatcherville, but this will give us the opportunity to find a new place to call home."

"Maybe we could just stay here," Molly suggested. "There's plenty of room. And Mrs. Pierce could be our mommy. And Nana Dovie can be our grandma."

Simon avoided looking Eileen's way. "But this isn't our home, sweet pea. We promised Mrs. Pierce we'd be gone right after Christmas." Perhaps even sooner.

Not satisfied with his answer, Molly turned to Eileen. "You'd like for us to stay, wouldn't you?"

Before Eileen could answer, Dovie spoke up. "There's nothing to keep you from looking for a place right here in Turnabout, is there?"

The kids perked up at that.

"Really?" Harry said. "You mean we could keep going to school here with our new friends?"

"And keep Miss Whitman for our teacher?" Rose added.

"I suppose that's one option," Simon said slowly, not sure he wanted to go that way. But the more he thought about it, the more it appealed to him. It would actually have a lot of benefits. He wouldn't need to uproot the children again, at least not entirely. Mrs. Leggett might be willing to become the permanent caretaker for the children if she didn't have to move away from Turnabout. Hank had indicated Simon could go to work at the mill permanently if he wanted. And since he wouldn't be living in this house, he really didn't have to see much of Eileen at all.

"But we wouldn't live in this house anymore," Molly lamented.

"No, but you could come visit whenever you want," Eileen said quickly. "And the secret room would always be available for you and Flossie to have tea parties in."

That cheered Molly up considerably. Simon supposed it would be up to Mrs. Leggett as to how often Molly visited here.

Assuming he found a place in Turnabout.

And assuming Mrs. Leggett would accept the job offer.

Two days later, Eileen sat in the parlor patching a pair of Albert's pants and felt ready to scream. This stiff formality between her and Simon was driving her crazy. She longed for them to go back to the friendly relationship they'd had before she'd made the horrible mistake of flirting with him and encouraging that kiss. That sweet, tender, glorious kiss.

She pricked her finger with her needle and lifted the digit to her mouth, tasting the metallic tang of blood. Feeling distracted and restless, Eileen put away her sewing and fetched her winter cape. She let Dovie know she was going for a walk, then headed out the door.

She pushed open the front gate, then hesitated. Deciding she wasn't in the mood for people, she turned away from town and headed toward the open countryside.

After five minutes of vigorous walking in the blustery air, she felt better. Perhaps, if she was persistent, she could convince Simon to at least call a truce. They didn't have to be best friends, but perhaps they could at least be honestly cordial.

How serious was he about looking for a place in Turnabout? And how did she feel about it?

The sound of an approaching wagon caught her attention and she quickly moved to the roadside. Hopefully whoever was driving would take care not to spatter mud on her.

She was pleased when she heard the vehicle slow down, then surprised when it seemed to be stopping altogether. She looked up to see Simon in a buggy.

He sat there silently watching her, and she finally couldn't stand it so she broke the silence first. "Hello. Were you out looking for me?"

"No. I'm actually going to take a look at a place down the road that's for sale."

"Oh." She moved closer to the side of the buggy. A week ago she would have invited herself to go with him. A week ago, he would likely have invited her himself.

As if coming to some sort of decision, he gave a short nod. "Would you care to come with me? I'd value having your opinion."

Pleased by the invitation, she nodded and grabbed the side of the buggy to pull herself up. He reached for one of her hands and assisted her in. Was he finally ready to forgive her?

When she was settled he clicked his tongue and flicked the reins to set the buggy in motion. They rode along in silence for a while. She couldn't sense any softening in his attitude toward her.

She finally gathered her courage and spoke up. "I'm very sorry for causing all of this awkwardness between us."

He cut her a surprised look, but then turned back to face the road without saying anything.

She tried again. "I know this is all on my shoulders, but if there is anything I can do to fix it, I wish you'd just tell me."

Still he remained silent, his jaw tight.

"I truly value the friendship we had." Unbidden, a little sigh escaped her. "I don't have many friends," she added quietly.

He maintained his stiff demeanor for a heartbeat longer, then his shoulders relaxed. "I value our friendship, too." He gave her hand a quick squeeze. "But you have to know it can't be like it was before."

"I know." She told herself this was a start and that she should be happy to have this second chance.

"So how far is this place we're going to look at?" she asked, ready to change the subject.

"Not far. I want something that will put the kids close to school." He slowed the wagon to a stop. "In fact, I think this is it."

They were sitting in front of a ramshackle farmhouse that looked as if it would blow over with the first strong wind to come along. "Are you sure this is the right place?"

Simon gave her that familiar crooked grin that she'd missed so much these past few days. "Don't let appearances fool you. I want to check how solid the frame and foundation are. Everything else can be fixed with paint, lumber, nails and good old-fashioned sweat."

She couldn't picture any amount of work, other than tearing the whole thing down and starting from scratch, that would make this place livable.

He came around the buggy to hand her down, then started toward the house. Was he planning to go inside?

"Mr. Stringman told me there are three bedrooms upstairs and a small office downstairs that can be converted to a bedroom if I need it."

"You plan to get all of the kids into four bedrooms?"

"Three. I figure the downstairs one will be Mrs. Leggett's." He began walking around the exterior, peering closely at the walls and windows, tapping on the wood here and there. "I know it'll mean they'll have to share more than they are now," he said absently, "but it'll still be as roomy, if not a little roomier, than what they had back in St. Louis."

Smaller than this? How had they managed?

She peered through a large window into what was probably the dining room. "It will be difficult to seat everyone in there at one time for their meals."

"We can squeeze in by using benches instead of chairs until I can expand on the house. Come on, let's look inside."

She followed him inside and tried to find some positive things to say. "The big windows in the dining room are nice."

He nodded and moved toward the back of the house.

"The kitchen is a good size."

Again he merely nodded absently as he checked walls and floors.

She gave up and simply followed him from room to room. At last they headed back outside.

"It's not ideal, but it'll work," he said. "And there's plenty of room for the children to play and for us to have some animals—chickens, a milk cow, maybe even some goats or pigs. There's room for a nice garden, too."

"And what about you? Do you intend to live here with them?"

"Of course, at first anyway. I can stay in the lean-to—it's not ideal but I've slept in worse places. My priority will be to take care of the major repairs first and then to expand on some of the downstairs rooms. It won't ever be as big or fancy as your place, but it'll suit our needs just fine."

Eileen decided too ignore the *fancy* comment. He probably really hadn't meant anything by it. If this was what he truly wanted for himself and the children, than she would support his choice.

"Of course, I wouldn't want to live in that lean-to forever. I was thinking, eventually, I might build myself a little cabin on one corner of the property—far enough away to give me some breathing room, but close enough so they can easily call on me if they need anything."

It began to sink in that they would all be moving out soon. She would see them at church, of course, and maybe occasionally in the mercantile or some of the other shops around town. But it wouldn't be like now. It would be Mrs. Leggett the children would be looking for to doctor their hurts, cheer on their accomplishments and to shape their world.

"How soon do you plan to move in? Surely you don't intend to move the children here until you've made it weather-tight. We are heading into the coldest, wettest time of year, after all."

"They're a hardy group, and I'll make certain we have lots of firewood and blankets."

"But you will stay at my place at least through Christmas as we'd planned?"

"Of course." Then he smiled. "But we're getting a little ahead of ourselves, aren't we? I haven't purchased the property yet."

But he intended to. And she had no doubt at all that he would make it happen.

And then what would she do?

Chapter Twenty-Six

At supper that evening, after the blessing had been said and all the plates served, Fern cleared her throat. "Uncle Simon?"

"Yes?"

"Dora Sanders is having a party at her home to celebrate her birthday on Saturday afternoon, and she's invited me."

"And who is Dora Sanders?"

"She's Mayor Sanders's daughter," Eileen answered. "I believe she is about the same age as you are, Fern, isn't she?"

"Yes, ma'am." Fern turned back to Simon. "May I go, please?"

"When is this party?"

"Saturday at one o'clock."

"That's laundry day, isn't it?"

Eileen couldn't believe he was teasing the girl like this. "I believe, if Fern helps in the morning, the rest of us can take care of things without her in the afternoon."

He pointed his spoon Fern's way. "Does that sound like a good plan to you?"

"Yes, sir."

"Well, in that case, I don't see any reason for you not to go."

"Thank you." She turned to Eileen. "I promise to work hard as can be Saturday morning."

"I know you will." Eileen gave the girl an encouraging smile. Fern had changed over the past few days. She seemed more content, more like a schoolgirl rather than a mother hen.

Perhaps the two of them could become friends after all.

"I know why Fern wants to go to this party," Russell said.

Fern glared at him across the table. "Russell Lyles, you just hush your mouth."

But Russell only grinned wider. "It's because Kevin Grayson is gonna be there and she's sweet on him. You should see how twitterpated she acts when he's around."

Fern's face turned beet-red, and she looked ready to sink through her chair.

"Russell, that's enough." Eileen knew girls Fern's age were easily mortified, and it was too bad of her brother to take advantage of that. "You shouldn't be teasing your sister that way."

Hoping to take the focus off Fern, Eileen then turned to Dovie. "This chicken stew you cooked is delicious. Is that rosemary I taste in there?"

"It is." Dovie took Eileen's cue and turned to Joey. "I do believe Buddy is starting to put some weight on his hurt foot. He must be feeling better."

"Yes, ma'am." Joey launched into a story about the latest trick he'd taught the dog, and before long conversation around the table returned to normal.

Later that night, for the first time since Thanksgiving, Eileen joined Simon on the porch after the children had gone to bed.

"You seem unusually pensive tonight."

Simon shaved another curl of wood from the piece he was whittling. "I'm just thinking about Fern."

"Don't worry. She'll get over Russell's teasing in no time."

"It's not that."

"Then what?"

He was silent for a moment as he sliced away another curl. "Do you think Russell's right about her being interested in this Kevin Grayson kid?"

Her lips quirked up as understanding dawned. "Most likely."

"That's what I was afraid of." He sounded downright forlorn. "How do I handle things when she starts getting really serious about boys? Or worse yet, when they start getting serious about her?"

Eileen smiled. "I have a feeling you'll do just fine. And you'll have Mrs. Leggett to help you."

His only response to that was a muttered "Six girls. Six!"

A change of subject was definitely in order. "Have you decided about the Stringman place?" Eileen asked.

"Stringman is out of town, but I'll be putting in an offer when he returns on Monday."

"I see."

He must have heard something in her tone because he cut her a quick, speculative look.

She turned to look out into the night, feeling suddenly hollow inside. "When are you going to tell the children?"

"Not until I'm certain the deal will go through."

She nodded. "That's probably wise."

Then, on a totally unrelated note, she said, "We need to make this a Christmas for the kids to remember." And for her to remember, as well.

* * *

Fern was very excited about going to the party. She'd picked out a set of pretty hair ribbons as a gift for her friend and carefully wrapped it in tissue that Eileen had on hand.

Eileen had also taken the delicate lace collar from one of her own dresses and sewn it onto Fern's Sunday best. On Saturday, Fern pulled her hair back with a silver hair bow that had been her mother's, then stood back for Eileen to check her out.

"You look absolutely beautiful," Eileen declared. She wished she still had the cheval glass mirror that had once stood in her bedroom so Fern could get the full effect.

Fern looked down at her dress doubtfully. "The other girls' Sunday dresses are nicer."

Eileen pinched her lips in disapproval. "Someone will always have nicer things than you. And someone will always have things that are less nice than yours." She gave the girl's hands a squeeze. "But there's not many as will have greener eyes or rosier cheeks."

Fern did smile at that.

"Now, are you sure you don't want me to accompany you just to the front gate?"

Fern shook her head. "I know the way."

"All right. Just make sure you come straight home when the party's over."

"Yes, ma'am."

Eileen watched her go. Yes, Simon would have his hands full with his new family.

And she ached to be the one by his side to help him through every bit of it.

Chapter Twenty-Seven

Eileen walked out to the carriage house, where Simon was feeding the chickens. She rubbed her arms to ward off a sudden chill.

He glanced up at her, then immediately frowned in concern. "What's wrong?"

How could he read her so well? "It might be nothing. But I was expecting Fern to be home by now."

"You mean she's not back from that party yet?"

"No."

He set the pan of feed down. "I tell you what. You're probably right that it's nothing. But just to set your mind at ease, I'll go down to the Sanders's house and check on her." He started toward the house. "Chances are they just got to having so much fun they lost track of time."

"But Mayor Sanders and his wife wouldn't have."

"Just tell me how to get to the Sanders's home and I'll be on my way."

She decided she wasn't in the mood to sit back and wait. "I'm going with you."

He looked prepared to argue, then seemed to think better of it and nodded. She quickly stuck her head in the back door to let Dovie know where they were going, then led the way around to the front of the house. All the way to the Sanders's home she kept getting a nagging feeling that something was wrong.

Please God, let it just be my overly active imagination. But if it's not, hold her tightly in Your hands until we can find her.

They reached the Sanders's home without her having much memory of having made the walk.

Mrs. Sanders answered her knock and appeared surprised to see them. "Eileen, Mr. Tucker, what can I do for you?"

"We're looking for Fern. Is she still here?"

"Why, no. The party broke up an hour ago. But I believe Fern left before that."

Dora appeared at her mother's side. "That's right. She got real upset when she caught that fancy shawl of hers on a nail. She said she had to leave."

Fancy shawl? Fern had been wearing her black wool shawl when she left the house. "What did the shawl look like?"

"It was all shimmery-like and had lots of beading on it."

Mrs. Sanders shared a look with Eileen. "It's that fancy one you used to wear on special occasions. I just assumed you'd loaned it to her."

"Of course. Fern knows she can wear it whenever she likes. I just didn't realize she'd worn it today."

Fern had taken the shawl. Without permission.

Why hadn't the girl just asked her?

More importantly, where would she have gone?

As soon as they were out of earshot, Simon gave her a worried look. "That was the shawl you pulled out on Thanksgiving, wasn't it?"

Eileen nodded. "Fern has run away. We have to find her."

* * *

Two hours later Fern still hadn't been found, and it would be dark soon. Eileen stood at the kitchen window, staring at nothing in particular, racking her brain for the hundredth time on where the girl might have gotten off to. Wherever it was, she prayed that it was sheltered, because it was going to be a very cold night.

Simon had been out there searching all this time. And a number of men from the town had volunteered to help. Surely Fern would be found soon.

Dovie was keeping an eye on the other children in the parlor. Ivy was there, too. Eileen hadn't been able to sit still, and she hadn't wanted her own anxiety to convey itself to the children.

Fern was an intelligent girl, she kept telling herself, full of curiosity and quick wit when she wasn't being sullen. Once she had decided to let go of some of her belligerence she'd made surprisingly good company. Just a few days ago she'd asked Eileen questions ranging from how to bake a pumpkin pie, her favorite, to where the tower rooms were on the other two floors.

Eileen stilled. Could she really be that close?

She quickly headed for the stairs, then paused with her foot on the bottom tread.

She turned and stuck her head in the parlor. All eyes immediately turned to her.

"Sorry, no news," she said. "I just need to speak to Ivy for a moment."

Ivy immediately joined her out in the hallway, her eyes wide with worry. "What is it? Has something happened?"

Eileen shook her head, then signaled for Ivy to follow her up the stairs. "There's a possibility that she's hiding right here in the house. If I'm right, I'm going to need to go in and talk to her, but I thought someone should see that the signal is sounded so the searchers can return home."

"Of course. Do you really think she's here?"

"I'm praying really hard right now that I am right."

A moment later they were on the third floor and Eileen went straight to the little door set in the far wall. Taking a deep breath, she eased the door open. At first she didn't see anyone, and her spirits sank low enough to walk on. But then she heard a rustling noise. "Fern, sweetheart, is that you?"

Her only answer was a hiccuping sob.

Relief flooded through her as she realized that Fern was indeed here. With an unapologetically tearful smile and nod to Ivy, she ducked inside and closed the door behind her.

She slowly made her way across the low-roofed room, guided more by sound than sight as her eyes slowly adjusted to the gloom.

"Are you okay?" she asked.

A muffled "yes" drifted back to her.

"Everyone's been out looking for you. We were all very worried."

"I've done something awful."

Eileen was finally able to see the girl, and she plopped down on the floor beside her. "I doubt it's as awful as you think."

"But you don't know what I've done." The girl's voice was almost a wail.

Eileen put an arm around her shoulder and drew her close. "It doesn't matter what you've done, sweetheart. Nothing could be bad enough to make us want you out of our lives. Please don't ever run away like this again."

"I took your beautiful shawl."

"I know."

"And I ruined it."

"I doubt that it's ruined," Eileen said calmly.

Fern carefully unfolded the fabric and showed Eileen the rip. "See."

"Rips can be mended."

"But it will never look the same."

"No, I don't suppose it will."

"Aren't you even the least bit angry with me?"

"Not at all. In fact, if you don't mind, I don't know why I should."

The girl looked thoroughly confused. "What do you mean? Why should I mind?"

"I hate to spoil the surprise, but I pulled your name from the hat for Christmas. This was going to be your present."

"You're just saying that to make me feel better."

"Are you calling me a liar?"

"No. I mean—"

Eileen turned the shawl and held up a corner. "Look here, right in the very corner."

Fern studied the place Eileen indicated. Embroidered there in Eileen's most elegant script, were the words *To Fern from Eileen.*

Fern looked from the shawl to Eileen, her expression one of confusion. "But this is so beautiful. And it is special to you. Why would you give it to me? Especially after I've been so mean."

"Because it was something you wanted much more than I did. And because I know you've only been pushing me away because you're afraid I'll hurt you like others have." She stroked the girl's hair. "But I won't Fern. I promise, nothing you do can make me not like you. Anyway, you didn't ruin anything of mine. You tore a shawl that was your very own."

"But when I took it, I didn't know it was going to be mine."

"True, and that was wrong of you."

"It makes me a thief." Fern's tone was full of self-loathing.

Eileen winced, suddenly realizing what this was really about. "Perhaps. But a penitent one."

"A thief is a thief."

"Fern, look at me. You are not like your father."

The girl's head shot up in surprise. "You know about my father?"

"Yes, I've known for a while now."

"But, doesn't that make me riffraff?"

"Don't you dare ever say such a thing again. What your father did or didn't do doesn't dictate the kind of person you are. You are responsible for your own actions only, not the actions of your parents."

"But those women who visited Miss Fredrick, they quoted the Bible, saying something about the sins of the fathers being visited on their children. Doesn't that mean God is going to punish me for what my father did?"

Eileen chose her words very carefully. "First of all, the Bible also tells us not to judge others, so those women should have kept their noses out of your business unless they had something charitable to offer. And second of all, I don't claim to understand all of God's ways, but I think those verses the women were referring to have more to do with the consequences of a man's sin on his family's happiness than with how God views that man's children."

She smiled at the girl, trying to let her see the sincerity of her words. "God loves you very much and so do I. I don't want to hear any more talk of you being anything less than a beautiful child of God."

"Oh." She looked at Eileen, hope stirring in her eyes. "I'm sorry I treated you so mean before."

"I know, sweetheart."

She heard the sudden ringing of the church bells. Ivy had gotten the word out.

"But for right now, why don't we go downstairs and let all those very worried people see that you're all right. We can work out our apologies later."

With a nod, Fern got shakily to her feet. "Do you think Uncle Simon's going to be mad at me?"

Eileen smiled. "Very likely. But he's also going to be very, very glad to see that you're all safe and sound."

It just might take him a few minutes to remember that part.

Chapter Twenty-Eight

As predicted, Simon was by turns angry and relieved at Fern's safe return to the family. The girl's punishment for her actions was an extra load of chores and having to make an in-person apology to every man who'd given up his time to help in the search for her.

But Fern wasn't the only one who'd learned some hard lessons up in that turret room. Eileen had had some difficult truths driven home to her, as well. She'd tossed and turned all of Saturday night and had taken a long walk on Sunday afternoon to try to sort things out in her mind. But now she thought she had the straight of it.

And she knew what she had to do.

She only hoped she hadn't waited too long to see what had been right in front of her all along.

After the children had gone to bed, she stepped out on the porch and marched right up to Simon.

"Don't buy the Stringman place."

He looked understandably startled. "I beg your pardon."

"Don't make an offer on that house. I want the children to stay right here with me."

"With you?"

"Yes. I love them. All ten of them. I can't imagine my life without them in it now."

"Are you sure this isn't just some kind of reaction to the scare we had yesterday?"

"Absolutely, positively. I wanted them before Fern disappeared. I just didn't know it."

"You didn't—" He took a deep breath. "Do you know what you'd be letting yourself in for?"

"Not everything." She grinned at his confused expression. "I'm sure there'll be surprises every day. Things I hadn't planned for. Emergencies that will turn all my routines upside down. But I'm not afraid of that anymore. In fact, it's what I want in my life."

"Are you sure? Absolutely sure? Because these are the children's lives we're talking about. You can't say you'll do this and then renege in two months or a year. That would be unbelievably cruel."

"I'd *never* even consider doing that to them. And yes, I'm sure. And you can find yourself a place close by, so you can be near them to keep a close eye, just like you always planned."

He leaned back and studied her. "Something's changed. I can't quite put my finger on it, but you're not the same person you were before."

She smiled, happy he'd realized that. Because that would make this next part a whole lot easier. "I *have* changed. And it's because of something I realized when I was talking to Fern yesterday."

"And what was that?"

She took a deep breath. "First, there's something else I need to tell you."

"What kind of something?"

She supposed she couldn't blame him for being suspicious.

"Things about me, about how I am, and more importantly, why I am that way."

His expression flattened. "Eileen, we've been through—"

"No. Please hear me out. This is different. This is something I just learned about myself." If she had to get on her knees and beg him to listen, she would. It might be too late, but if she had to lose him she couldn't let it be because she didn't tell him this.

He was silent for a long, nerve-racking moment. But finally he scrubbed his hand across his face and gave her a weary nod. "Say your piece."

"My mother came from a very prominent, old money family," she said without further preamble. "When she was just eighteen she met a young man and fell in love with him. This young man, however, wasn't from her same social circle. He wasn't poor, but he came from a family of merchants. This didn't matter to my mother at the time. Despite my grandfather's threats to disown her, she had romantic notions and thought love would conquer all. And truth to tell I don't think she thought her father would follow through on his threats.

"So she married Arnold Beamus and moved into a comfortable home in a vastly different part of town from the area she'd grown up in. Not only did her father cut her off, but it turns out her in-laws weren't very happy with the match their son had made either, thinking she was too snobbish. She lost most of the friends she had in her old circle and had trouble making any new ones in her husband's circle. This made her very unhappy and bitter."

Simon was watching her with more interest now, and her hopes fluttered to life.

"What I remember most from those early years was how very loved I felt by my father and how very unhappy my mother was. Poppa passed away when I was five, and

I missed him terribly. But my mother moved back in with her parents and seemed to want nothing more than to wipe his memory from her life. I was sent to boarding school, and eventually Mother remarried, to a man who was part of that social circle she had missed so very, very much."

She chose her next words carefully, not wanting to sound maudlin. "My stepfather didn't care for me much. On one of the rare occasions when I was home, I heard him tell my mother that breeding would out. Mother kept telling me how lucky I was to be so pretty, that it was my one saving grace. She said if I tried very hard to be just as perfect as I could, that I *might* make a successful match."

She saw the muscle in his jaw jump and wondered what he was thinking.

"Mother also told me that love was never a reason to marry—that all it had ever brought her was disappointment."

She definitely had Simon's attention now. "My dowry was not large. All the money my father had left me had been spent on those awful boarding schools I was relegated to. So I did my best to do as Mother said, to play up my looks, to make certain I was as close to perfect in every social grace I could manage, and to never, ever let myself fall in love."

She stared directly into his gaze, hoping he could read what she was feeling. "Until you kissed me."

There were tears inside her screaming to get out, but she ruthlessly held them back, not wanting to have him merely feel sympathy for her. She wanted so much more from him. "I've believed most of my life that, though I loved my father deeply, because of who he was, it made me unlovable. That my worth was based solely on outward things rather than on who I am inside."

She felt her smile waver. "And the strange thing is I

didn't even realize it until I heard Fern confess those very same thoughts about herself."

Eileen took a deep breath, ready to get through this, wondering if she was making a difference in how he felt about her. "I'm sorry, Simon. I guess what I wanted to say to you is that I'm this terribly confused and mixed-up person, but I want to change. I want to be the kind of woman who can trust in the power of love. Because I do love you. And when I realized it, it scared me so badly I pushed you away. And it still scares me."

She had to fist her hands to keep from touching him. "But I no longer want to push you away."

She was done. She stood there, waiting for whatever he would do or say next.

And she didn't have long to wait.

Simon stood abruptly, nearly toppling his chair. He closed the gap between them, put a hand on either side of her face and proceeded to kiss her quite thoroughly.

Some time later, Simon released her lips, but not his hold on her. There was quite a bit of what she'd just told him that he hadn't grasped entirely yet, but that could wait for later. All that mattered right now was that she'd said she loved him.

He brushed the hair from her face, entranced by the shimmery quality of her eyes. "And you don't mind that I enjoy working with my hands and will probably make my living that way for as long as I'm able."

She turned her head to kiss the palm of his right hand. "I love these hands," she said. "I love every scar and every callus. Because these hands make you the man you are, the man I love."

He didn't think he'd ever tire of hearing her say she

loved him. "In that case, Eileen, will you do me the very great honor of consenting to marry me?"

With a blush that he found altogether irresistible, she gave him a resounding "yes," which he followed up with another kiss.

Epilogue

"Aunt Eileen, come onnnn." Molly had her hands on her hips in a pose that would have made the strictest of schoolmarms proud. "Everyone's waiting."

Eileen laughed. But then she seemed to be doing a lot of that these days. And why wouldn't she? There were so many things bringing joy into her life.

She loved that it was Christmas morning and the house was filled with children. She loved that the children now called her Aunt Eileen. She loved that she and Fern had grown so much closer.

But most of all, she loved that six days ago she had become Mrs. Simon Tucker.

"I'm coming, sweetheart. I just need to get the last cookie on this platter."

"But it's taking for*ever*."

Eileen hid her smile this time. She supposed when a group of eager children was gathered in front of the Christmas tree ready to open gifts, a few minutes *did* seem like forever.

"There." She lifted the platter with both hands and spun around. "Lead the way."

Molly did an immediate about-face and trotted from the

room. As they proceeded she turned back occasionally as if checking that Eileen was keeping up. They crossed the parlor, and Eileen reflected that they'd have to rename the secret room. The recessed door was rarely closed these days, and it had become the favorite place for the family to gather.

Family. Another word that made her smile.

"Here she is," Molly announced as they stepped through the door. "At last," she added melodramatically.

"And well worth waiting for." Simon stepped forward and kissed her on the cheek. Then whispered in her ear. "Have I told you lately how much I love you, Mrs. Tucker?"

Eileen felt the warm tingle of those words all the way down to her toes. "I don't mind hearing it again," she said archly.

"Can we start *now?*"

At Joey's question, Simon let out an amused huff in her ear, then stepped back and relieved her of the platter. The look he gave her promised they would continue the discussion later.

"Since you've all been *so* patient," he said as he escorted her to one of the new benches he'd installed in the room, "I suppose we're ready."

Fern scooted over to allow Eileen to sit between herself and Molly. It gave her a good view of the large tree Simon and the children had selected two days ago. The homemade decorations were scattered on it with gloriously imperfect abandon, and she decided she'd never seen a lovelier tree.

Near the top of the tree Simon had placed Miss Fredrick's hat. Gee-Gee was a part of these children's lives, and it was only right that her spirit should be represented in their celebration.

While they waited for Simon to retrieve his Bible from the mantel, she allowed the excited chatter in the room to wash over her. Even Buddy, who had somehow become an indoor dog when she wasn't looking, was adding an occasional yip to the babble.

Simon moved to stand in the front, between them and the tree, then opened the Bible to the Christmas story. Everyone quieted as he began to read. She listened to his strong, confident voice reading of that long-ago miracle that spoke of an unfathomable grace and love, and the message resonated with her as it never had before.

When Simon finished and closed the book, he asked Russell to lead them in prayer. That was another thing she found to admire and love about her new husband, the way he was training up the children. He might not believe in routines and discipline in the same way she did, but he would do his best to see that they had a proper upbringing. And that they knew they were loved.

When Russell had finished and the amens were said, Simon gave them all a broad smile. "Shall we exchange the gifts?"

The children all scrambled to fetch the gifts they'd placed under the tree last night, and to hand them to their recipients.

There were exclamations as the children discovered who had pulled their names and then more excitement as they unwrapped the packages.

Eileen handed a small package to Fern. "Merry Christmas."

"But…" The girl looked up at her in confusion. "I thought the shawl—"

"It's not much, but I couldn't leave you with nothing to open on Christmas morning."

Fern gave her a watery smile, then very carefully unwrapped the tissue paper. Inside was a lace handkerchief with Fern's initials stitched in one corner. She stood and gave Eileen a hug. "Thank you."

"You're welcome."

Eileen felt a presence at her shoulder and turned to see Simon. He slipped an arm around her waist and led her away from the knot of children.

"I've got something for you," he said, pulling a package from his coat pocket.

"Did you pull my name?" she asked suspiciously.

He drew himself up in mock affront. "Can't a gent get a gift for his wife without pulling her name from some hat?"

She laughed at his teasing. "Forgive my indecorous question."

"As it happens, I did end up with your name, but I had to trade Dovie for it."

"You cheated! I don't know whether to be upset or flattered."

"Definitely flattered." He handed her the gift. "Now, are you going to open this?"

She accepted the package and felt a fluttering excitement, similar to what the children must have felt. When she lifted the lid on the box, she found a delicate wood carving of a star and a quarter moon.

She lifted them out and placed them in the palm of her hand, admiring the craftsmanship that had gone into their creation.

She looked up. "You made these?"

He nodded. "I know it's not anything fancy. But it's a reminder of what you mean to me, that if I could, I would give you the moon and the stars from the heavens for your very own."

What had she ever done to deserve such a love, such a man?

"So you like it?"

Ignoring the fact that they weren't alone, Eileen wrapped her arms around his neck and gave him a quick but very satisfying kiss. "I like it very much," she said when she stepped back. "It's the finest Christmas gift I've ever received." She put a hand to his cheek. "From the finest man I've ever known."

The sudden heat in his expression brought an answering warmth to her cheeks.

Then Joey called Simon over to admire the rawhide strips that had mysteriously appeared under the tree for Buddy. With a light squeeze and wink, Simon left her side.

She watched him go, then looked at the room full of people who were enjoying this Christmas together. Her family, all of them, including Dovie and even Buddy. For a moment she stood apart, remembering how far she'd come in a few short weeks.

She'd gone from knowing she could never have children to now having ten wonderful children to love and raise as her own. From having a mother who made her feel as if she'd been a regrettable mistake, to having an older woman in her life who offered her friendship and wisdom. And she'd gone from being the widow of a husband who treated her as little more than a pretty poppet, to being the wife of one who truly loved and respected her.

She offered up a silent prayer of thanksgiving for this blessing of a new family—one she hoped to surround herself with for a very long time.

Then Simon turned, gave her that crooked smile that always made her heart do a flip and held out his arm. With a light step and a full heart, she moved to his side and joined her forever family.

* * * * *

Dear Reader,

Thanks for picking up *Her Holiday Family.* This was a book I've been wanting to write ever since I finished the first Texas Grooms book, *Handpicked Husband.* Eileen Pierce, who appeared to have everything, seemed so selfish and unhappy under the surface in this story that I kept trying to figure out what had made her that way. I hope you were happy with how her story unfolded. And that you'll agree Simon Tucker was the perfect hero to heal her wounded heart.

This book also marks the next stage in my Turnabout, Texas series. There is such a rich, fun cast of characters in this town that I couldn't bear to abandon it just yet. So look for at least three more books featuring folks from Turnabout coming soon. For more information, please visit my website at www.winniegriggs.com or follow me on facebook at www.facebook.com/WinnieGriggs.Author.

And as always, I love to hear from readers. Feel free to contact me at winnie@winniegriggs.com with your thoughts on this or any other of my books. Wishing you a life abounding with love and blessings.

Winnie Griggs

Questions for Discussion

1. Eileen has been trying to hide the true state of her finances from her neighbors. Do you think she was really successful? Have you ever tried to do something similar?

2. What did you think of Eileen's determination to implement routines in the children's lives? Were they successful? Why or why not?

3. After his sister died, Simon turned the day-to-day care of his niece and nephew over to Miss Fredrick. Did that make him seem less heroic in your eyes? Why or why not?

4. How do you think Simon handled his new responsibilities in the beginning? How would you handle being thrown into such a situation?

5. What role do you think Dovie played in the household?

6. At what point in the story did you begin to feel Eileen would make a good mother to these children? Why?

7. Did you believe Eileen's about-face to allow a dog in the house was true to her character? Why or why not?

8. How do you feel about Simon's decision not to allow the children to see Miss Fredrick before she passed away? Do you think he regretted that decision later? What would you have done?

9. Why do you think Fern was so angry at Eileen all the time?

10. What did you think of the Thanksgiving Festival they created for themselves?

11. Do you think Eileen handled Fern's theft of her shawl appropriately? Would you have done anything differently?

REQUEST YOUR FREE BOOKS!

2 FREE INSPIRATIONAL NOVELS
PLUS 2
FREE
MYSTERY GIFTS

Love Inspired.
HISTORICAL
INSPIRATIONAL HISTORICAL ROMANCE

YES! Please send me 2 FREE Love Inspired® Historical novels and my 2 FREE mystery gifts (gifts are worth about $10). After receiving them, if I don't wish to receive any more books, I can return the shipping statement marked "cancel." If I don't cancel, I will receive 4 brand-new novels every month and be billed just $4.74 per book in the U.S. or $5.24 per book in Canada. That's a saving of at least 21% off the cover price. It's quite a bargain! Shipping and handling is just 50¢ per book in the U.S. and 75¢ per book in Canada.* I understand that accepting the 2 free books and gifts places me under no obligation to buy anything. I can always return a shipment and cancel at any time. Even if I never buy another book, the two free books and gifts are mine to keep forever.

102/302 IDN F5CN

Name _____ (PLEASE PRINT) _____

Address _____ Apt. # _____

City _____ State/Prov. _____ Zip/Postal Code _____

Signature (if under 18, a parent or guardian must sign)

Mail to the Harlequin® Reader Service:
IN U.S.A.: P.O. Box 1867, Buffalo, NY 14240-1867
IN CANADA: P.O. Box 609, Fort Erie, Ontario L2A 5X3

Want to try two free books from another series?
Call 1-800-873-8635 or visit www.ReaderService.com.

* Terms and prices subject to change without notice. Prices do not include applicable taxes. Sales tax applicable in N.Y. Canadian residents will be charged applicable taxes. Offer not valid in Quebec. This offer is limited to one order per household. Not valid for current subscribers to Love Inspired Historical books. All orders subject to credit approval. Credit or debit balances in a customer's account(s) may be offset by any other outstanding balance owed by or to the customer. Please allow 4 to 6 weeks for delivery. Offer available while quantities last.

Your Privacy—The Harlequin® Reader Service is committed to protecting your privacy. Our Privacy Policy is available online at www.ReaderService.com or upon request from the Harlequin Reader Service.

We make a portion of our mailing list available to reputable third parties that offer products we believe may interest you. If you prefer that we not exchange your name with third parties, or if you wish to clarify or modify your communication preferences, please visit us at www.ReaderService.com/consumerschoice or write to us at Harlequin Reader Service Preference Service, P.O. Box 9062, Buffalo, NY 14269. Include your complete name and address.

LIH13R

SPECIAL EXCERPT FROM

Love Inspired

Don't miss the conclusion of the
BIG SKY CENTENNIAL *miniseries!*
Here's a sneak peek at HER MONTANA CHRISTMAS
by Arlene James:

"Robin," Ethan said, just before his face appeared in the church belfry's open trapdoor, "come on up. It's perfectly safe."

He reached down a gloved hand as she put a foot on the bottom rung of the wrought-iron ladder.

"How does this thing work?"

"It's very simple. There's a tall pole with a hook on one end. I used it to slide open the trap and then pull down the ladder. When I'm done, I'll use it to push the ladder back up and lift it over the locking mechanism, then slide the trap closed."

"I see."

"Oh, you haven't seen anything yet," he told her, grasping her hand and all but lifting her up the last few rungs to stand next to him on a narrow metal platform. In their bulky coats, they had to stand pressed shoulder to shoulder. "Take a look at this." He swung his arm wide, encompassing the town, the valley beyond and the snow-capped mountains surrounding it all.

"Wow."

"Exactly," he said. "There's a part of Psalms 98 that says, 'Let the rivers clap their hands, let the mountains sing together for joy…' Seeing the view like this, you can almost feel it, can't you? The rivers and mountains praising their Creator."

"I never thought of rivers and mountains praising God," she admitted.

"Scripture speaks many times of nature praising God and testifying to His wonders."

"I can see why," she said reverently.

"So can I," he told her, smiling down at her with those warm brown eyes.

Her breath caught in her throat. But surely she was reading too much into that look. That wasn't appreciation she saw in his gaze. That was just her loneliness seeking connection. Wasn't it? Though she had never felt this sudden, electrical link before, as if something vital and masculine in him reached out and touched something fundamental and feminine in her. She had to be mistaken.

He was a man of God, after all.

Even if she couldn't help thinking of him as just a man.

*Will Robin and Ethan find love for Christmas,
or will her secrets stand in their way?
Find out in HER MONTANA CHRISTMAS
by Arlene James, available December 2014 wherever
Love Inspired® books and ebooks are sold.*

"Just tell me what happened to my daughter."

"We don't know. You were alone when we found you."

"I need to go home." Scout jumped up, head spinning,
the room spinning. The knot in her stomach growing until
it was all she could feel. "Maybe she's there."

She knew it was unreasonable, knew it couldn't be
true, but she had to look, had to be sure.

"The police have already been to your house," Boone
said gently. "She's not there."

"She could be hiding. She doesn't like strangers." Her
voice trembled. Her body trembled, every fear she'd ever
had, every nightmare, suddenly real and happening and
completely outside her control.

"Scout." He touched her shoulder, his fingers warm
through thin cotton. She didn't want warmth, though. She
wanted her child.

"Please," she begged. "I have to go home. I have to see
for myself. I have to."

He eyed her for a moment, silent. Solemn. Something
in his eyes that looked like the grief she was feeling, the
horror she was living.

Finally, Boone nodded. "Okay. I'll take you."

Just like that. Simple and easy, as if the request didn't

go against logic. As if she weren't hooked to an IV, shaking from fear and sorrow and pain.

He grabbed a blanket from the foot of the bed and wrapped it around her shoulders then took out his phone and texted someone. She didn't ask who. She was too busy trying to keep the darkness from taking her again. Too busy trying to remember the last moment she'd seen Lucy. Had she been scared? Crying?

Three days.

That was what he had said.

Three days that Lucy had been missing and Scout had been lying in a hospital bed.

Please, God, let her be okay.

She was all Scout had. The only thing that really mattered to her. She had to be okay.

A tear slipped down her cheek. She didn't have the energy to wipe it away. Didn't have the strength to even open her eyes when Boone touched her cheek.

"It's going to be okay," he said quietly, and she wanted to believe him almost as much as she wanted to open her eyes and see her daughter.

"How can it be?"

"Because you ran into the right person the night your daughter was taken," he responded, and he sounded so confident, so certain of the outcome, she looked into his face, his eyes. Saw those things she'd seen before, but something else, too—faith, passion, belief.

Will Boone help Scout find her missing
daughter in time for Christmas?
Pick up HER CHRISTMAS GUARDIAN to find out!
Available December 2014
wherever Love Inspired® books and ebooks are sold.

Love Inspired HISTORICAL

Big Sky Daddy
by
LINDA FORD

FOR HIS SON'S SAKE

Caleb Craig will do anything for his son, even ask his
boss's enemy for help. Not only does Lilly Bell tend to his
son's injured puppy, but she offers to rehabilitate little
Teddy's leg. Caleb knows that getting Teddy to walk again is
all that really matters, yet he wonders if maybe Lilly can heal
his brooding heart, as well.

Precocious little Teddy—and his devoted father—steal
Lilly's heart and make her long for a child and husband of her
own. But Lilly learned long ago that trusting a man means
risking heartbreak. Happiness lies within reach—if she seizes
the chance for love and motherhood she never expected…

Montana
Marriages

**Three sisters discover a legacy of love beneath
the Western sky**

*Available December 2014
wherever Love Inspired books
and ebooks are sold.*

Find us on Facebook at
www.Facebook.com/LoveInspiredBooks

LIH28290